T0267805

Don't Be A Drag

Skye
Quinlan

PAGE STREET YA

For anyone who is not okay.

To Rain — you are perfect the way you are.

Copyright © 2024 Skye Quinlan

First published in 2024 by
Page Street Publishing Co.
27 Congress Street, Suite 1511
Salem, MA 01970
www.pagestreetpublishing.com

Distributed by Macmillan, sales in Canada by The Canadian Manda Group.

28   27   26   25   24   1   2   3   4   5

ISBN-13: 979-8-89003-950- 7

Library of Congress Control Number: 2023945226

Cover and book design by Rosie Stewart for Page Street Publishing Co.
Cover image © Bex Glendining

Printed and bound in China

author's note

Before reading *Don't Be A Drag*, please check the trigger warnings below, as this book contains graphic descriptions of mental illness.

Trigger warnings: alcohol, anxiety, blood, body dysmorphia, cancer (past, off-page), cursing, death due to AIDS (past, off-page), depression, drag bans, homophobia (past, off-page), intrusive thoughts, mental illness, mention of queer characters' deaths (past, off-page), nonconsensual touching (hair and arms), panic disorder, panic attacks, planned suicide attempt (past, off-page), suicidal ideation, suicidal thoughts, suicide (past, off-page), transphobia, and vomiting.

If you are currently struggling with suicidal thoughts or ideation, please don't be afraid to ask for help. You are loved, you are worthy, and the world is more beautiful with you in it.

one

*I*f I somehow make it off of this flying metal death trap alive, I promise to never take solid ground for granted again.

My ears pop as the plane starts to descend, the finer details of patchwork farmland and slate-gray cityscape coming into a rapid focus. Pastures bursting with speckled cattle bleed into the cracked pavement of looping, bumper-to-bumper freeways, and I'm almost positive that above the sound of my pulse thumping in my ears, I can hear drivers laying on their car horns to show their displeasure of the traffic.

My stomach twists into a knot of guts and acid.

I grip the edges of my seat, hard enough that my knuckles crack, and try not to think about all the ways this plane could still crash before landing. Maybe the landing gear won't disengage and we'll nose-dive right into the runway, or a bird will fly into an engine, or a wing will snap against the towering skyscrapers rising up from the ground, each one taunting me like fistfuls of scrap metal ready to impale me like a shish kebab.

I've never seen anything so terrifying, the mixed palette of steel, grime, and smoggy skyline stretching along the waters of the Hudson. Manhattan sprawls out adjacent to the river, my temporary home for the next three months before school starts again in the fall.

The window shade snaps down beside me, blocking my view of the city. I must be making some kind of face again, the one where my brow is furrowed with anxiety and I'm biting my lip hard enough to break the skin, because the snobby, middle-aged woman who's been keeping an eye on me throughout the flight gives me a pat on the shoulder. "We're almost there now," she says, settling back down into her seat from where she's leaned over my lap to pull the shade down. She straps herself in for landing, and I try to remember her name from the dozens of times she's told me: Claudia, I think.

"Now, remind me again, sweetheart. Who's picking you up from the airport? I can't just let you wander off alone, you're a baby! It'd be irresponsible of me."

"I turn eighteen next week," I say flatly, sucking in a breath as the plane lurches from the sky. My knee starts to bounce and the palms of my hands become sweaty. "And Beau is picking me up. My brother."

Claudia smiles and crosses her ankles, smoothing out her bright pink pencil skirt. "Oh, well, happy early birthday then, Briar!

You're nearly an adult now. How does it feel?"

"Fantastic."

"Now, Beau…" she continues, testing out his name on her tongue. There's judgment against my parents in her tone—why on earth would they name their son something so silly as *Beau*? Didn't they care if he got teased? But being named "Beau" was hardly what my brother was ever teased for. "Do you have a photo of him? What does he look like? I'll help you find him when we land."

The plane dips low and glides through the air in a wide, angled spiral, and I pray that we're aiming toward an open stretch of runway to land on. My heart starts to hammer beneath my rib cage, lodging itself deep in the back of my throat until I force myself to swallow it back down. Beau will kill me if he wasted his tip money on a first-class seat I had a heart attack in.

"I don't know," I tell Claudia tightly, sucking down air through the gap between my teeth. "He's probably in drag, and I don't know if he's wearing a wig. Beau's got lots of them, and you never know what you're going to get with him."

Claudia doesn't try to hide her shock.

"I see," she says, pursing her mouth in disapproval. I curl my fingers into fists, telling myself that it's because I'm nervous and they're shaking. "That's an…odd lifestyle."

"It's a perfectly fine lifestyle," I snap at her.

I wait for the insult that I know is on the tip of her tongue, and I hope that my expression is one that conveys how ready I am for a challenge: to either put her in her place or shove her out the nearest window. Beau had left our small, conservative Texas town as soon as he'd graduated from high school, mostly to escape from the cruelty of people like Claudia, and I would sooner face the consequences for defending my brother than let her talk badly about Beau.

She blinks before lifting her chin, her dark eyes dancing with authority. "There's no need for that tone."

The plane hits the runway in a series of brain-jarring thuds, cutting off a retort that would surely draw attention to my small, first-class cubicle, the one that Beau had nearly gone bankrupt to put me in. A shriek slips out of me instead, a tiny yelp that reminds me of the time Beau accidentally stepped on our dog's tail with the point of a stiletto heel. Our little sister Avery hadn't spoken to him for a week, too young to understand it'd been an accident and that Beau hadn't hurt the dog on purpose.

Had I not sniped at her about Beau, I'm sure Claudia would have tried to comfort me, especially since I'm trembling and my shoulders are hunched around my ears again. But she's busied herself with fixing her messy French twist instead, refusing to acknowledge that I exist now.

I tug my phone free from the safety of my jacket pocket, gripping the Sailor Uranus PopSocket on the back of it with shaky fingers. I switch it off airplane mode, and suddenly I'm reconnected with the world again, a flurry of notifications lighting up my screen as the plane rolls into the terminal. The flight attendant buckled into the seat across from me removes her seatbelt and traipses down the center aisle, thanking us all for flying with Southwest Airlines. "And don't forget your carry-ons, ladies and gentlemen. Welcome to New York!"

I slide my thumb across an old picture of me, Beau, and Avery to unlock my phone and catch up on the half a dozen messages my family sent throughout my flight.

Beau Vincent: omgggggg I cant believe youll be here soon!!!!!

Avery Vincent: i still cant believe u get to see beau without me ughhhh tell him i said hi

Beau Vincent: one more hour B!!!!!!!

Mom's Cell: Please call me when you land so I know you got there ok. I love you, sweetie.

Beau Vincent: 10 MINUTES TIL YOURE SUPPOSED TO LAND

Beau Vincent: LOOK FOR THE SPARKLY SIGN LIL B

I think he might be joking about the sign until I actually see him in the airport. He's waving around a white poster board that's shedding glitter all over the light blonde wig he's wearing, one that's long and straight and falls to the middle of his back. His pearly white grin is near-blinding as I approach, and he's jumping up and down like it's somehow possible to miss him. Beau isn't in full drag with his blue-jean capris and tattered, oversized Beatles T-shirt, but his eyeliner is on point and I'm jealous of how long his false lashes are. I smile at him despite the poster, then send off a text to let my parents know I've made it here in one piece.

Briar Vincent: I'm here. Your son made me a poster. It's embarrassing. Love you too.

"Briar!" Beau cries, holding his sign in his left hand and waving frantically with the other. I drag my carry-on toward him, my only piece of luggage because I'd stuffed enough books and clothes into it to last me the entire summer. "Over here, walk faster! Move those short little legs and come hug me!"

I can't help the smile that tugs at the corners of my mouth. In glittery, capital rainbow letters, Beau's sign reads, "Missing: Briar Vincent! Return to the drag queen if found!" A picture of me from when Beau and I had gone to Dallas Pride three years ago is glued to the center of the poster board, outlined in what I think might be gold pipe cleaners. I had just come out on social media, which was more than enough reason for Beau to deck me out in bi colors and parade me around the city.

I'd missed him so much.

Beau discards his sign onto the bench behind him, then flings his arms around my middle the second I'm within his reach. I abandon my suitcase and hug him, and Beau picks me up off the ground to spin me around in a circle. "Briar!" he says, squeezing me as tight as he can. "I can't believe you're really here. I was totally convinced that you wouldn't get on the plane. Fuck, dude,

I've missed you!"

"I've missed you too," I say, pressing my palms against the center of his chest so that Beau will set me back down. He obliges after a final spin, but he doesn't let me go, rocking us both from side to side until motion sickness sets in and I stifle a gag into his shoulder. "Texas isn't the same without you."

Our family isn't made of money, and Beau had spent the last several months saving up his drag tips to pay for my flight. I haven't seen him in nearly a year beyond Zoom calls, not since last summer when he'd scraped together enough cash to fly home for an old friend's funeral after he'd passed from a battle with cancer. Beau hadn't even wanted to come back, likely wouldn't have at all if the "old friend" hadn't actually been his first real boyfriend.

Connor had been good for Beau, and our parents and I had really liked him. But Connor's parents and most of his family had absolutely hated my brother, mostly for all of the reasons Connor loved him. Eventually, though, his parents' disappointment was too much for Connor, and he'd broken Beau's heart on the same premise—that he was simply just too much. Too queer, too femme, and too proud to be both.

Coming back for his funeral had been hard on him, and it'd been gut-wrenching to see him shut down, to bottle himself up and strip away the parts of himself that Connor's family hadn't liked. "They already hate me," he'd cried, curled into a ball at the foot of my bed the night before Connor's funeral. "I can't just show up in drag like I know Connor would have wanted. They'll kick me out of the funeral home and I won't get to say goodbye."

Our parents, Avery, and I had all gone with him the next day, Avery holding his hand as she sniffled. Connor had always taken her out for ice cream, and his family hadn't said a word about us being there.

I squeeze Beau a little tighter, trying to forget about the circumstances surrounding our last visit.

"Texas?" he says, planting a kiss on the top of my head before finally letting me go. He stuffs my homemade welcome sign into a nearby trash can, glitter cascading off the poster board as he crinkles it up, then takes my suitcase and hooks his arm through mine. "Fuck Texas. New York is where it's *at*, B. You're gonna love it here, I promise."

"You act like I plan on staying," I say, letting him guide me through the airport. I'm practically walking on Beau's feet, trying to stay close lest I lose him in the crowd or be stuffed into a duffle bag and kidnapped. "I'm only here for the summer."

"Summer, schmummer. You're almost eighteen and only have a year left of school." Beau veers around a tight corner and heads for an escalator packed full of people. "There's nothing tying you to Texas, Briar. And besides, if you think I paid all that money to fly you here just for a vacation, well…I guess you don't really know me, and I'm wounded."

My chest grows tight as I duck my head and squeeze onto the

escalator next to Beau. "Yeah," I say quietly, the real reason I've come all the way here weighing heavily on my shoulders. "You're staging an intervention."

Beau sounds exhausted as he lets out a sigh and hugs me close to his side. "I don't want to do this here," he tells me. "Because this *isn't* an intervention. We're just worried about you, and we thought getting away for a while might be good for you. Mom says you've barely been eating."

"I thought you didn't want to do this here."

"I'm not," he says, carefully tugging me off the escalator. Beau grips my arm as we duck and dodge and weave through the masses gathered near the airport's main entrance. I hold my breath and try not to think about the number of people we're surrounded by. "I'm just...scared, B. You missed an entire month of school because your anxiety kept you bedridden, and you *literally* told Mom that you wanted to——"

"I know what I told Mom," I say stiffly. "And I do not want to talk about it."

Outside, where a cool breeze whips through my faded blue hair, there are dozens of taxis lined up along a cracked yellow and gray curb. Beau hails one down that's empty, then drags me toward it before someone else can climb inside and steal our ride back to his apartment.

"Well, we're going to talk about it," Beau decides, motioning for the cab driver to pop open the trunk. He hoists up my suitcase, grunting under the weight of a good portion of my manga collection. "Eventually. But this is *not* an intervention, I promise. Yeah, I'm worried, and that's part of the reason I brought you here, but fuck, Briar, I've missed you too, and I want you have some fun this summer."

Beau yanks open the taxi door with fake grandeur, bowing at the waist like he's opened up some magical monolith that leads to a palace's grand ballroom. I roll my eyes and Beau flashes me a grin. "Oh, come on. It's New York! Fuck depression, screw your anxiety, and to hell with literally *everything*! You can be whoever and do whatever you want here."

I wish I could share his enthusiasm. I wish I believed New York could fix me in the same way it seems to have healed Beau, but I don't. He's all smiles as we huddle together inside the taxi, his long legs and knobby knees knocking against mine as the taxi spears into motion, but all I can think about are all the ways the car can crash before ever reaching his apartment, dimming that smile and ruining the life he's built for himself.

two

Beau's small one bedroom apartment is an explosion of color from the moment we walk in the door. Beau kicks a roll of fabric covered in shiny silver sequins out of his way before either of us can trip on it. He abandons my suitcase near a wobbly coffee table covered in glue sticks and feathers, then turns to look at me from over his shoulder and grins.

"Sorry about the mess," he says, but he is absolutely not sorry. Beau thrives in chaos. "I was going to clean, but like, I'm swamped with commissions and it's not like you don't know that I'm a trash human."

"Right," I say, taking a quick glance around the room.

An assortment of houseplants with dense foliage hang off hooks from the ceiling, their vines draping down from macramé baskets that nearly reach the floor. Smaller plants like succulents, ferns, and little bamboos in ceramic vases are spread across every bit of counter space, cluttering the kitchen that opens up from the living room. Beau has placed them all strategically; they're soaking up the only bit of sunlight filtering in through a dirty window above the sink, and if nothing more, at least they all look happy and healthy.

The rest of the living room is a different kind of disorganized, and I don't know for certain what the exact color of the floor is. What I think might be old, orange shag carpet is covered in colorfully tangled wigs, rolls of fabric that put any craft store to shame, and dangerously spiked stilettos that I don't know how Beau can even walk in. There are bottles of beads and containers of flashy sequins, a knocked-over mannequin half-pinned with a half-finished garment that Beau has sent me pictures of on Instagram, and elaborate jewelry that catches the sunlight not being gobbled up by plants.

It's almost like a pride parade threw up in here, but far more concerning is the actual human body that's sprawled across the caved-in yellow couch.

"Um…"

Beau follows my gaze with a frown. "Oh." He steps over the mannequin on the floor, then bends at the waist and rests a hand on the motionless body's bare shoulder. "Don't mind him. He closes down the bar and since my place is closer than his, he crashes here after work sometimes." Beau gives him a gentle shake. "Come on, Enzo. Time to wake up. You've slept all day and Nathalie will kill me if you're late again."

Enzo stirs, groaning softly as Beau shakes him into consciousness. "What time is it?" he slurs, lolling his head toward my brother. His dark, hooded eyes flutter open, and he smiles at Beau with dimpled cheeks and a crooked quirk to his mouth. "Hey, handsome. You look good."

Handsome isn't a word I would use to describe my brother, but Enzo? He's the literal definition of the word.

Beau glances at me from the corners of his eyes and noisily clears his throat. "Hey," he says, withdrawing his hand from Enzo's shoulder as he stretches. He curls his toes and lifts his arms above his head, arching off the couch until his spine gives a sickening crack. "I, ah. You remember what I told you about my sister, right? That she was flying in from Texas today?"

"Mhm." Enzo drags a hand through his curly brown hair, wincing as his fingers snag on tangles. "You still want me to go with you to the airport?"

"Um…no." Beau smiles down at him, sheepish. "I already picked her up."

Enzo stills for just a moment before cursing in Spanish. He bolts upright, his head nearly knocking against Beau's, and frantically pats both around and between the couch cushions. Eventually, he finds a black crew neck he quickly yanks on to cover himself. "Fuck, Beau, why didn't you wake me up sooner? You hate taking taxis alone." He drags a hand through his hair again, then looks up at me and balks a bit. "Shit, hi. You must be Briar."

I wave and give him a smile, one that's close-lipped and awkward and nearly identical to Beau's. "Yep, that's me. Enzo, right?"

He nods and rises to his feet. Enzo's tall, broad, and long-limbed, his arms packed with light chords of muscle that Beau pokes at with an index finger. "Enzo, Lorenzo, hunky bartender with a smile to fucking *die* for...he'll answer to just about anything."

Enzo rolls his eyes and swats Beau away like a fly. Indeed, Enzo is handsome with his high cheekbones and a sharp jaw that's covered in thick black stubble. His skin is a golden brown that complements his dark hair and eyes, and I can see why my brother might like him. Enzo's smile is easy, his energy calm, and Beau looks up at him like he's hung all the stars in the sky.

There's no way in hell that Enzo just crashes here after work.

"It's nice to meet you, Briar. Beau's told me so much about you."

I look up at Beau and raise an eyebrow. "Funny," I say. "Because he's never told me anything about you." Both boys wince as I cross my arms over my chest, glancing between them suspiciously. "Are you guys, like, together?"

Enzo's eyes widen, and he stifles a cough into the palm of his hand before looking up at Beau like the answer is somehow complicated. Knowing my brother, it is. "I—I mean, we're not— we're *kind* of—"

"It's not like that," Beau says, thumping Enzo on the back.

Something dims in Enzo's eyes, and it's not because Beau is trying to prevent him from choking. "We're friends. Co-workers. He's a bartender at The Gallery, where I work."

Enzo glances at the silver watch around his wrist. "It's after five," he announces, his voice softer than when he'd greeted me. "The bar needs to be restocked before doors open, so I need to head home and shower."

Beau frowns and jabs his thumb towards the narrow hallway branching off from the kitchen. "You can take one here, if you want."

"No thanks. I need to change clothes, too." Enzo's smile is lackluster as he snatches up a lanyard full of keys from the coffee table. "It was nice to meet you, Briar. I'll catch you guys later at the show."

Enzo slips out the front door with little fanfare, his head down and shoulders caved in around him, and once he's gone I turn to Beau with a grimace. "What was that about?" I ask. Beau's brow furrows like he doesn't understand what I'm saying. "You, Enzo, the fact that he sleeps over but apparently is *just* your co-worker? Come on, Beau, that was uncomfortable."

"Oh." Beau picks at a hangnail. "I mean, we *are* co-workers, but if, sometimes, we happen to have sex after a shift, well..." He shrugs. "What's the big deal?"

"What's the big deal? Oh my *God*, Beau!" I wade through the valley of wigs between us and flick my brother between the eyes.

He yelps and swats me away. "You're not just co-workers if you're sleeping together. Besides, didn't you see the look on Enzo's face when you called him that? It was like you'd broken his heart."

And he should know all about broken hearts.

Beau scoffs, but the guilt on his face is clear as day as he starts to straighten up the couch. "This folds out into a bed," he deflects, ignoring my comment entirely. "You can sleep on it however you want, but I will say that the couch is comfier than the mattress." I guess that explains why Enzo hadn't bothered to pull out the bed, then. "The bathroom is at the end of the hallway, and to the left is my bedroom. It is…a mess, so you should probably stay out of there."

"How can you even afford this place, anyway?" I ask, taking a seat on the couch. The cushions are lumpy but soft. "Doesn't it cost like a bajillion dollars to rent an apartment with a bedroom here?"

"Oh, yeah. Definitely." Beau sits down next to me and starts to fiddle with a glue gun that's seen better days. He picks up a half-finished headpiece that's covered in bright feathers and starts to glue more onto it, yelping as he burns his fingers. "But I hustle for my money and make good tips at The Gallery. It's right across the street if you look out the kitchen window, and the owners, Nathalie and Dominique, helped me find this place."

"That was nice of them."

"For sure." Beau burns his finger again and curses. "Pageant season is coming up soon, too, so I've got orders out the ass for commissions." He holds up the mask as an example. "Do you know how much I got paid to design and make this garment? A thousand bucks. A thousand frickin' bucks, B. You and Dad were right. My sewing machine really is gonna take me places."

I snort as I examine the mask, its neon feathers and deep purple rhinestones. "How much did it pain you to say that?" I've never even thought about having a thousand dollars in my pocket.

Beau huffs at me and sets down the mask again. "I want you to come to my show tonight," he says flippantly, refusing to admit that he hates it when someone else is right about him. But it's not about Dad and I being right—it's about my parents and I having more faith in him than Beau has in himself. "It's my first time headlining on a Friday, and it's kind of a big deal."

"But I'm a minor," I say, blinking away my surprise. "I can't just walk into a bar."

"You can if you're with me," he says, reaching across the coffee table to procure a black sharpie. "Just draw an *X* on the back of your hand so that the bartenders know you're underage. Enzo will be there, obviously, but the other assholes behind the bar suck at checking IDs if they think you might tip them."

I tug at my hair as Beau resumes his work on the headpiece. He presses a yellow feather to the mask. "Will there be a lot of people there?"

"Sure," he says, waving his hand as he burns the pad of

his finger again. "But everyone's there to have a good time, and I think you'll enjoy yourself, too. It's lots of dancing, some fist-pumping, and tonight is our annual Art-N-Glow."

"Art-N-Glow?"

Beau grins wickedly before leaning over the edge of the couch. He picks up a white T-shirt and tosses it into my lap. "Art-N-Glow. As in don't be surprised if someone in the crowd shoots you with a squirt gun full of glow paint. I've got some glow stick bracelets for you. It'll be fun."

I rub at my thighs with the palms of my hands to rid them of the sweat starting to gather against my skin. "I've never been to a bar before," I say, though it's not like it comes as a surprise to him. "What am I supposed to do while you're performing? What if I—what if I need you?"

Beau sets down his glue gun and looks at me, his brow unfurrowing from where it's been pinched in concentration. "You can hang out with me backstage, if you want. Meet some of the kings and queens. Enzo usually takes his break after I'm done performing, but you can always hang out with him, too. He won't mind." Beau places a reassuring hand on my shoulder, giving it a gentle squeeze. "If you ever need me, just shout. Literally. I'll jump off the stage and come find you, even mid-lip-sync if I have to."

"Promise?"

He sticks out his pinky finger and loops it around mine when I offer it to him. "I promise. I know you get anxious around people."

"I get anxious leaving the house."

Beau winces but is kind enough not to comment. "How about I doll you up tonight? I could do your hair, your makeup. How's that sound?"

"You contour like Trixie Mattel and Bianca Del Rio had a love child."

"Aw," Beau says. He holds a hand over his heart. "Thank you."

I roll my eyes and bite back the smile that's tugging at the corners of my mouth. Maybe coming here really is what I've needed. "Let's do it."

three

*B*eau is still gluing down his large, elaborately styled wig as I sneak a glance in the mirror attached to his vanity, admiring the sharp, pointed wings he's drawn around my eyes in black. "I still can't believe you managed to make me look so...*decent*," I say, failing to hide how impressed I am. He's smoothed away my acne scars with foundation, highlighted the angles of my rounder face and filled in my lips with a bloodred lipstick and gloss. My blue eyes pop from the dark brown makeup he's packed into the creases of my eyelids, the corners bright with a shimmery rose-gold glitter. "If drag doesn't work out for you, you've always got a future with Sephora."

Beau scoffs and taps down his lace-front hairline. "I will *never* go back to Sephora," he says. Beau whips his head from side to side, curled hair flying, to test that his wig is secure. "You have no idea how many people came through that hellhole and wanted to look like a Kardashian. I'm good with a brush, but like,

I ain't a miracle worker, you know?"

Beau rises, his arms and legs flailing with pent-up excitement, from his chaotically organized vanity. He's dressed in a skin-tight latex dress that's bridal white and splattered with neon splotches of pink, orange, and yellow, and he's gone out of his way to pad his hips and ass, making him look hourglass-shaped. "Fuck," he says, rolling his shoulders and noisily cracking his neck. "I can't believe I'm headlining tonight."

"You're gonna be great," I say, plucking at the collar of my plain white T-shirt.

Beau looks down at me and nods, a wide, toothy grin plastered across his face. His eyes are practically sparkling, an ocean blue beneath the warm light from his vanity, and I can see it there, in the brightness of his gaze, what headlining tonight truly means to him. "Fuck yeah, I will be!" He bounces on the toes of his stilettos, and Beau's excitement would nearly be palpable if I wasn't such a mess of frayed nerves and spiraling anxious energy. "I'll give the best damn show of my career tonight, and you, little sister, will be there to bear witness to me slaying the fucking house down."

I'd kill for an ounce of his confidence.

Beau looks in the mirror one last time, fixing one of his thick false lashes, then snatches up his phone from the vanity. "Let's go, B! The Gallery awaits."

Beau and I enter The Gallery through a narrow door in the back, squeezing past a tall, burly bouncer who shamelessly slaps him on the ass. Beau jumps onto the tips of his silver stilettos with a yelp, and there is absolutely nothing that can stop me from whipping myself around, a snarl on the tip of my usually quiet tongue.

"How fucking dare you," I hiss, curling my fingers into trembling fists at my sides. The bouncer looks down at me and raises a pierced eyebrow, his mouth quirking with amusement. "That is my brother, you——"

Beau grabs hold of my hand, gripping it tight as he hauls me back to his side. "It's all right. This is Micah, and he's a friend of mine." He smiles apologetically at Micah, who's shaking his head and trying his hardest not to laugh.

"I don't care who he is," I say. "He shouldn't be touching you like that."

"If you want, I can apologize." Micah looks at Beau for an answer. "You said you didn't mind."

"And I don't," Beau replies, slinging his arm over my shoulders. In his stilettos, he towers above me. "But Briar didn't know that, and that's okay. I appreciate you having my back, B." He grins and pinches my cheek. "Isn't she all cute when she's protective?"

Micah snorts with a nod. "Sure is. She looks underage, though."

Beau holds up our joined hands to show Micah the *X* on mine. "She is, but it's already been taken care of. Nathalie says she's good."

The bouncer nods again and waves us the rest of the way through the door. "Have a good show tonight, babe. Wish I could see it from back here."

My brother offers him a wink before turning to me. "Come on. Let's get you settled in the dressing room." He gives my hand a sharp tug to launch us both into motion. "I'm sorry," he says, waiting until Micah is out of earshot. "I didn't realize seeing that would upset you."

I shrug and wriggle my hand free. "And I didn't realize that you were okay with that. I'm sorry I almost mauled him."

He presses a kiss to my temple. "I'm okay with it when it's a friend," he explains. "But only when it's a friend. Thank you for being willing to go to bat for me, even though I'm supposed to be looking out for you."

I bump his hip with my elbow. "Yeah, yeah, you drama queen. Where's this dressing room you're always taking selfies in?"

Beau ushers me down the hallway. "I'll show you."

Music is pumping into the small area backstage, the heavy bass of an unfamiliar pop song reverberating off the washed-out brick walls. I can feel it in the soles of my feet, in the marrow of my bones like the beat is all-consuming, and I've already succumbed to soaking every bit of it up. My foot starts to tap in sync with the drums when Beau lets out a deafening squeal.

"Bitch!" he screams, flapping his arms as another queen whips around from where she's seated behind a rickety-looking vanity, her makeup brush raised and ready to throw at him. "Jacklynn, you're here! When did you get back from tour?"

Jacklynn grins at Beau, her face beautifully painted with blue eyeshadow and gold highlights as she touches up her lipstick in the mirror. "Last night," she tells Beau. "Did you really think I'd miss my youngest daughter's first time headlining The Gallery?"

Beau shuffles across the room, prancing on the tips of his toes to stay balanced on the uneven floor. "Aw, thanks, Mama. You're the best." He dramatically kisses the air above Jacklynn's cheek, careful not to smudge anyone's makeup. "B, come over here. Meet the woman who helped me get my shit together."

All eyes on me, I stumble a step forward and give her an awkward wave, trying my hardest not to sneeze; the entire room reeks of hairspray, sweat, and cheap perfume, and it doesn't bode well for my sinuses. "Hi."

"Jac," Beau says, crooking his finger to lure me farther into the room. "This is my sister, Briar. The one I was telling you about." He loops his arm around my neck when I'm close enough. "B, this is my drag mother, Jacklynn Hyde. She took me in when I first moved here and helped me get my first gig."

"Oh, hush," Jacklynn says fondly. "You got that gig all on your own. I just arranged a meeting with the club owner." Her smile is warm as she looks down at me, her dark eyes gleaming under the flickering fluorescent lights, and it feels as if Jacklynn is actually seeing me, and not necessarily for the first time. Like she's known me for my whole life. "It's nice to finally meet you, Miss Briar. Your brother has told me so much about you."

I try not to look as terrified as I feel; I've never been good at making friends or meeting new people, but Jacklynn is someone that my brother clearly trusts. Someone who's helped him since moving across the country. If he's introducing us, then I have no reason to be afraid. "All good things, I hope."

Jacklynn winks before turning to face the mirror again, fixing a false eyelash. "Only the best."

Beau rocks onto his heels, glancing around the room like he's looking for something. "Is Spencer around?" he asks. "I wanted to introduce him to Briar."

"He took the night off to watch your show, so he's wandering around somewhere out of drag," Jacklynn says with relief. "And it's a good thing, too, because he's a menace. I hate sharing the mirror with him and all that facial hair. He gets it everywhere and doesn't clean it up."

My stomach does a backflip because now there's someone else I have to meet. "Who's Spencer?"

Beau ignores me and raises a perfectly manicured eyebrow; he's drawn it on with flamingo-pink eyeliner. "You're not even performing tonight," Beau points out. "What'd you get all dolled up for?"

Jacklynn cranes her neck around to look up at him, her blue mouth pursed as if my brother should know better. "Instagram," she says, like it's obvious. "You think we're not taking any pictures tonight? Please. I should have told Spencer to bring his camera, but my phone will do just fine. You're headlining tonight, baby. And we have to document the occasion."

"Who's Spencer?" I ask again, trying not to sound desperate for an answer.

Beau has brightened with the news of an impromptu photo-shoot. "Spencer Read is sort of like my drag son, I guess. He's a king who performs here on the weekends. His moms own The Gallery."

"Spencer Reid? Like the guy from *Criminal Minds*?"

Jacklynn snorts as she adjusts the necklace at her throat, twisting it until the clasp is hidden beneath her hair. "Spencer *Read*. R-E-A-D. Spencer because he does like the show, and Read because he can read a bitch for filth and not feel bad about it. Don't be too disappointed, though. I'm sure he'll make his way back here at some point."

"Oh, good!" Beau claps his hands together, careful not to let the tips of his press-on nails touch. "So maybe you'll get to meet him after all. I really think you'll like him, B. He's fun."

"Fun?" Jacklynn says. "If you consider having an attitude

from hell and thinking that he's Gay God's gift to the queer community 'fun,' then sure. Spencer is a goddamn delight." Jacklynn turns in her chair to face me fully. "You steer clear of him, Miss Briar. You're too cute for him to go fucking with your heart."

Beau rolls his eyes and plops into the metal folding chair next to the vanity. "You know who else is cute? Spencer Read. You'll like him, B. Just you watch."

"Cute in drag or out of drag?" I ask. There's no harm in being curious, even if Jacklynn does sigh at me.

"Both." Beau grins. "The perfect person for your little bisexual heart. Spence is even cuter without the facial hair."

"Huh." I drum my fingers against the tops of my thighs to give my hands something to do. I hadn't even known that drag kings were a thing until Beau had told me over Zoom, but he'd never mentioned anything about Spencer. "So a drag king is just the opposite of a queen, then?"

Beau shrugs, propping up his elbow on the vanity. "Pretty much. Spencer is a cis woman who dresses up in masculine-presenting drag, but trans people, nonbinary people, agender people, gender-fluid people, or literally someone who says fuck gender altogether—*anyone* who wants to do drag, can, either as a king, queen, or whatever they want to be." He drops his chin into the palm of his hand and watches Jacklynn put her makeup on. "The Gallery's made waves in New York's drag community for being so inclusive and blurring the lines of who can and can't do drag. We don't tolerate that 'only cis gay men can do drag' bullshit here. Right, Jac?"

"Right. Which is why we deal with Spencer every weekend."

Beau's grin is lazy as he continues, "We've even got performers who are cishet and do drag for the fun of it. It's an art form, and who the hell are we to be gatekeepers?" He lets out a groan before clawing at his throat with the sharp tips of his nails. "I am parched. Briar, how much do you love me?"

It's almost as if I can feel the color as it drains from my cheeks, pooling somewhere inside of me where my gut is twisting with nausea. "Why?"

"Do you think you could grab me something to drink?" he asks. Beau's smile is as sweet as syrup, like he hasn't just asked me to completely step out of my comfort zone. "No alcohol, just water or some tea. You can get yourself something too, if you want. Just ask Enzo and he'll add the cost to my bar tab. I'll love you forever and a day!"

I suck in a breath of stale air and wrap my arms around my middle. "Only Avery gets to say that when she wants me to help her do a backbend. Why can't you go and get something to drink?"

Beau isn't looking at me as he says, "Because I'm the headliner, darling. The crowd doesn't get to see me until the moment I step onto the stage, which is soon. That's why we came in through the back."

"Beau..."

"Bow Regard," he corrects me with a wink. "And use she/her pronouns when I'm in drag, please. But you're gonna be okay. I promise. Just go to the bar and find Enzo.

Finding Enzo is easier said than done.

The bar is horrendously long, and dozens of people are lined up against the carved wooden countertop, packed together on tall stools as they listen to the comedy queen on stage. Just from what I've heard since venturing out from the dressing room, her jokes aren't really that funny, especially the one about a vegan dressed as a bunny.

I can barely see the bartenders moving back and forth behind the bar, much less find Enzo among the masses; their bodies are blocked by the patrons covered in glow-paint, lined-up like glow-sticks with beer cans and shot glasses cradled tightly between their hands.

My nerves start to swell up inside of me, a molten fire spreading beneath my skin as I realize that finding Enzo is impossible. Beads of sweat are gathering wetly against my hairline, hardly hidden by the hair that's escaped from my ponytail, and as I stuff my hands into the pockets of my jeans to hide the fact they're shaking, I'm positive that I'm going to pass out. Beau knows I can't handle crowds, that I intentionally avoid gatherings consisting of more than two people, even during the holidays when our family drives in from out of town.

This place, with its flashing lights and sticky floors and customers glowing neon is a setting straight from my nightmares.

And with this second realization comes the very worst of my fears: Even if I do manage to find him and ask Enzo for a drink for me and Beau, someone could easily spike it if I'm not careful. Or they could snatch me off the dance floor and drag me away into a van that's waiting outside. Better yet, maybe the building will catch on fire and come crumbling down all around me, trapping everyone inside until our bodies merge with the flames. Beau could escape with Jacklynn in the back, but the guilt would kill him even faster than the fire would me, and he'd never be able to forgive himself.

My chest grows tight as I back away from the bar, ping-ponging off college students too drunk to even notice I've run into them. I turn, a too-warm breath caught in the back of my throat—

A tall, prettily curved body barrels hard into my chest, cutting through the haze of my anxiety, and spills their drink down the front of my blindingly white T-shirt. "Fuck!" I yelp, leaping back until I'm pressed against a wall that's covered in old flyers and missing animal photos. Small chunks of crushed ice clatter to the floor in little *snap snap snap*s of sound, scattering between my feet and the culprit's, and it's as I'm staring down at myself that I realize, for a final time, this embarrassment isn't over yet: A massive brown stain flecked with pink and orange glow-paint has bloomed across the front of my chest. "Ugh!" I groan, plucking at the fabric to investigate. "This isn't even my shirt!"

The aforementioned culprit takes a step back and looks down at me, an impish smile curling around her teeth. "Oh, shit," she says with a laugh, guzzling what's left of her drink. "My bad, sweetheart. Are you okay—wait, you look *really* familiar. Do I know you?"

I cross my arms over my chest, hiding the stain that's surely beginning to set in, and pray that Beau didn't spend a lot of money on this T-shirt. "No," I grumble uncomfortably, kicking at a piece of ice. "You don't."

"Calm down," the girl says. She bats her ridiculously long lashes at me, drawing my attention to her stupidly beautiful green eyes. They're dark, the color of moss after it rains, and are a stark contrast to the pink and orange paint that's splattered all over her face. "It was just Pepsi, it'll wash out. And yeah, no, I'm almost positive I know you. I never forget a pretty face."

"You can't know me," I grumble, blinking to avoid meeting her gaze. "I just flew in this afternoon."

She snaps her fingers and grins at me. "That's it! Shit, you guys really do look alike. You're Briar, right? Beau's sister? She said you were flying in today, but I didn't think she'd bring you to the bar on your first night here."

"Me neither," I say, glancing pointedly at my shirt. It's completely soaked through from her Pepsi, and my light blue bra with little white flowers on it is completely visible underneath. My cheeks flush hot in what must be a noticeable blush, even beneath the flashing lights and heavy contour. "Like I said, this isn't even my shirt. It's Beau's."

At least she has the decency to wince. "I really am sorry. Here." She shrugs out of the oversized jean jacket hanging off her shoulders and hands it to me. "Beau can give it back to me tomorrow. It's not a big deal. I'm Selene, by the way. A friend of your brother's."

Eyeing the jacket carefully, I consider whether or not there's a knife or a needle stuffed somewhere inside of it that could hurt me. But all I find are iron-on patches in various shapes and colors: a pink triangle up around the collar, a lesbian pride flag wrapped around the arm. A camera, a crow, a patch that says trans rights are human rights. It seems harmless.

I deem the jacket safe before slipping my arms into the sleeves. "Nice to meet you."

Selene snorts. "You don't have to lie, angel face. But hey, let me make it up to you. I'll buy you a drink."

"I'm underage," I say, raising an eyebrow. Surely Beau must have told her that?

"Me too," Selene says, lifting her hand to show me the *X* on the back of it. "But the bar serves soft drinks, too, and I could go for another Pepsi."

"Good luck," I tell her, pinching the jacket shut over my chest before gesturing aimlessly at the bar. "I've been trying to squeeze in there for twenty minutes. Miss Bow Regard is parched and wants—"

"Iced tea?" Enzo, thank the goddamn universe, magically appears at the very end of the bar, where there aren't any stools to be sat on. Sweaty and haggard, Enzo props his elbows against the countertop, taking a moment to breathe as if this place is overwhelming for him, too. In through his nose, out through his mouth, and then he's slinging a white washcloth over his shoulder. "You'd better not be bothering her," Enzo warns, flexing his fingers to rid them of an anxious tremor. At least I'm not alone in this nightmare.

Selene responds with a devilish grin. "Too late."

Enzo murmurs something that sounds like an insult in Spanish, and I watch as he fiddles with the gold chain and cross at his throat. "It's almost time for Bow's set," he announces to the two of us, sparing me a look of what vaguely resembles pity. "And the bar is too busy for me to keep my eye on either one of you." Great, so he's abandoning me with Selene. "I wouldn't bother taking a drink back to Bow. If she has anything now, she'll spill it down the front of her dress. She gets jittery before going on stage."

I tilt my head in surprise, glancing behind me at the stage. "Really?" I've never known Beau to be nervous.

Enzo nods with a grimace. "Find yourself a spot in the crowd, just not too close unless you want her to pull you onto the runway with her."

"I'll tell you what, Enzo." Selene sidles up next to me, her long lashes fluttering as she runs her hand through her cropped, apple-red hair. It's shaved short on the sides with little zigzags cut around her ears, and if she hadn't spilled her drink on me when we'd met, I'd probably think it's cute. That it matches the rose-tinted flush of her cheeks. But my shirt is still wet and there's a piece of ice melting in my bra, so there's nothing about her that's cute right now, except maybe her sunstone gauges. "Grab me another Pepsi and whatever Briar wants to drink, and then I'll gladly do myself the honor of keeping an eye on my new friend tonight."

"We barely know each other," I point out glumly, wrapping my arms around my middle. Her jacket is heavy from all the patches, but at least it's loose on me and hides the stain on my shirt.

Selene looks over at me and winks, a tiny smirk starting to tug at the corners of her mouth; her bottom lip is double pierced with snake bites, small silver barbells nestled against the plum color of her lipstick. I blink before she catches me staring. Since when was she standing so close to me? "I'll tell *you* what," Selene says. "We'll give it until midnight for you to decide if we're friends. And when you decide we are, you can buy *me* a drink."

four

I am going to die.

As it turns out, a New York City drag show is even worse than being trapped at a rock concert, death walls and circle pits opening up and closing again around you. But at least there, I'd had Beau to keep me safe, his wiry body a reluctant shield as we clung to the barricades and ducked beneath crowd surfers. I'd never have gone to see my favorite band if it weren't for my brother insisting that he accompany me to the show, and even though he'd hated every second of it, he'd never once left my side. Not even to get himself the cute soundtech's phone number.

It's the only reason I've let Selene drag me so deep into this crowd: because I love my brother and he deserves my unwavering support. But despite the fact that Selene is squeezing my hand, that she keeps craning her neck around to ask if I'm doing okay, I'm still all alone in a blistering sea of feathers, glitter, and glow sticks, of sweaty bodies pressing flush against mine as Selene pushes me up toward the stage. "Move it!" she calls over the music, the beat and the bass thumping so hard I can feel them in the center of my chest. I can't think here, can't breathe here, don't *want* to breathe here—can't do anything at all except grit my teeth and wish I were anywhere else: backstage, back home, or even back at Bow Regard's colorfully cluttered apartment. "Baby gay, coming through!"

"Don't call me that!" I complain to Selene, yanking on her hand to demand she turn around and look at me. Her grin from the bar has yet to leave her face, and it's here, beneath the rapidly flashing stage lights, that I notice the gold, glimmering highlighter smeared across the tops of her cheeks. It covers the smattering of freckles that extend across the bridge of her nose, dotting all the way up to her temples, and I blink before she realizes I'm staring at her. "I have been very bi and very open about it since before Beau moved here."

Selene snorts as we finally emerge from the crowd. My knees bang into a dark runway that's low to the ground and looks too unsteady to stand on, but I know from the pictures that Beau has sent me it's safe. "Oh, I know," Selene says. She sidles up behind me and gets comfortable, resting her hand on the curve of my hip and gripping my arm with the other, like she's ready to take off with me if she needs to. My spine stiffens as I stand up straighter against her—no one has ever put their hand on my hip before—and Selene takes advantage of the added inch of height and rests her chin on my shoulder. "Beau's told me all about you. But in my opinion, since you've never been to a drag show before, you're still a cute little baby gay."

"There isn't exactly a drag scene where I'm from."

"*Ugh.* Fucking shame. Here." Selene reaches around me to dig into the pockets of her jean jacket, then slaps something green into the palm of my hand. "Take this."

"What's it for?" I ask, eyeing the crumpled one-dollar bills I'm holding. "I don't want your money."

Selene tips her head back in laughter. "It's for Bow," she explains, returning her hand to my hip again. "It's proper etiquette to always tip a drag performer, so if you wave them at Bow during her set, she'll see you, come get the money, and then probably kiss your hand. That's her thing. If you were one of her regulars, though, she'd probably kiss your cheek."

I stare at the money and frown. So these are the tips that Beau had saved up in order to fly me to New York, a bunch of ones that people threw at him on stage? My stomach twists like it's trying to flip itself inside out, and I think I might faint onto the runway. I *know* that Bow's a good performer, that she's done so well for herself she's headlining her very own show tonight. But how many people *actually* give her money? Certainly not enough to keep her from going without just to bring me here.

I don't deserve it.

This.

To be here.

I don't deserve a brother like Beau.

He never should have wasted his money on me. I'm not worth a single dollar that's been waved at him, especially when Beau has worked so fucking hard to accomplish his goals here in New York. The money he'd spent on my flight could have gone towards his rent, his groceries, some material for a new outfit to perform in. He could have taken Enzo on a date, taken a trip on his own to a place he's never been to get away for a while.

Beau's money would have been better spent that way, on something he needed or actually wanted or—

"Hey," Selene murmurs from behind me, worry coloring her tone as she gives my hip a squeeze. "Is everything alright? You got quiet."

My heart feels like it's spasming with guilt, clenching in my chest as I gasp down a rancid breath of air. The bitter tang of what tastes like beer curls against the back of my tongue, and— and when did my lungs decide they were going to implode? Are they going to implode? Bow might kill me if I ruin her show by imploding, and I want to meet our maker on my terms, not because she strangled me with her tights.

"Briar, are you okay?" Selene asks again. "You look like you're going to pass out."

I *feel* like I'm going to pass out, but I don't dare tell Selene that. "I'm fine."

"Are you sure?" Selene asks, leaning over my shoulder to look at me. "Beau told me you have really bad anxiety. And that's totally okay, you know? We don't have to watch her perform from here, I just thought...well, it doesn't matter what I thought. If you want to leave, we can. Promise. The view is fine from backstage."

I bite down hard on the inside of my cheek as she talks. If Beau told Selene that I'm anxious, what else might he have said to her? I love everything about Beau aside from the fact that he tends to be loose-lipped around his friends, even if he always has good intentions. But the last thing I want is for them to pity me, or to spend the summer walking on eggshells whenever Beau brings me around because clearly I've come here with a warning label.

Jesus. They must feel sorry for him, too, and think that he's crazy for trying to fix something better left broken.

"I'm fine," I repeat to Selene, who doesn't have the time to assess if I'm lying because the crowd around us bursts into high-pitched screams.

Bow Regard has taken the stage, and the sight of my brother takes my breath away. Not because she looks fabulous in her neon-splattered dress, but because she's radiating a genuine sort of confidence, something I've seldom seen from her unless she's dolled up in drag. But this is different—it's elevated and cranked up to a thousand. Nothing and no one can touch her tonight.

She struts onto the stage with a red-lipped smirk and a gleam in her eye that's heightened even still by the stage lights. Even her microphone is immaculately bedazzled for the occasion, and I find myself grinning as she brings it to her mouth and says, "Damn, y'all look fucking fierce tonight."

Behind me, Selene is jumping up and down, waving her arms above my head like she's trying to get her attention. Bow zeros in on us immediately, and even now I can see the change in her expression. It's subtle, hidden beneath the intricate layers of her makeup, but it's there in the lines of her face, a drag queen's fear that her little sister is in trouble. Bow assesses me quickly from beneath her false lashes before deciding that I'm safe with Selene, then prances across the stage and stomps down the center of the runway. "Spencer Read, you fucking dog! I just *knew* you'd sniff out my sister the second I left her unattended!"

"I couldn't help it!" Selene calls out to her, and it takes me a moment to realize exactly what's happened here. Bow is talking to *Selene*, and the girl whose hand is squeezing my hip is answering her. "She's cuter than all those Snapchats you showed me. Filters don't do you any justice, Briar."

I wheel myself around to look up at her. "You're Spencer?" I ask, filing it away in the back of my mind that my brother has shown her all my selfies. "Bow's drag king friend?"

Selene winks at me. "The one and only."

Bow is within close enough reach that she ruffles my hair from the runway. "Tonight is a special night, y'all," she says into her microphone, then pulls it away to thank the people who are frantically waving dollar bills at her. Bow snatches them up and tucks them into the collar of her dress. "Not only am I the head-liner tonight"—she pauses to let people scream at her—"but my baby sister flew in all the way from Texas today just to watch me perform!"

Selene places her hands on each of my shoulders and gives me a little shake, encouraging me to do...something. Wave? Say hi? Acknowledge the crowd that's turned to look at us expectantly? I find myself stepping back into her, like Selene alone can shield me from the eyes that are drifting curiously in our direction.

Bow must notice that I don't like the attention because she doesn't miss a beat and continues, "Give her a warm New York welcome and buy her a non-alcoholic drink tonight—can y'all *believe* she's gonna be eighteen next week? Ugh, time flies when you have the best little sister. Now..." She motions to someone backstage just before the opening notes of Lady Gaga's "Born This Way" flood through The Gallery's sound system. "This one's for you, B!"

I absolutely cannot stop it, the bubbling laughter that spills from between my teeth; I clap my hand across my mouth to try and stifle the embarrassing snorts that accompany it. I can't believe that Bow would choose this song to perform to.

When I'd first come out to Beau, I'd done so in a slobbering mess of tears and snot at the foot of his bed back home. Beau was already out to most of our family and friends, and even though the people who'd mattered the most had accepted him—especially Avery, who'd painted a massive poster board to look like a rainbow so that Beau could have a "pride flag" in his bedroom—I was scared that I'd be the exception. That our parents wouldn't support me in the same way they did Beau. Of course, he'd promised me they would, but I hadn't believed him until Beau had walked me downstairs to the dining room table before dinner, blasted "Born This Way" on his phone, and announced to Mom, Dad, and Avery that there was something we needed to discuss.

I know it's a queer community anthem, but it's an anthem for Beau and I, too. Whenever I text him during a panic attack, he finds a new cover of the song and sends it to me to listen to. Whenever I call him crying because I'm depressed, he'll sing it to me, usually in a funny voice with exaggerated syllables and vowels. I do it for him, too, mostly when he's sad and missing home, but always, *always* when he's struggling, especially so he knows he's not alone.

"Don't cover your mouth," Selene calls out to me over the music, reaching over my shoulder to gently swat at my hand. I huff into my palm as her fingers brush lightly against mine. "I like your laugh, it's cute. Bow told me this song was important to you guys, that she'd picked it just for you. No one ever really does Lady Gaga anymore."

I let myself do as I'm told, though it's mostly because Bow is trotting across the stage and mouthing every word with the occasional glance over her shoulder, looking to see if I'm singing along with her. It's none of Selene's business why this song is important to my brother and me, so I give her a nod and let myself be immersed in the moment, like Bow herself is Lady Gaga on that stage.

She prances around the stage and twirls like a nimble ballerina, kicks out her legs in mid-air splits, and death-drops down onto her back. Bow snatches up money faster than the bar's patrons can dig it out of their pockets, and it's halfway through "Born This Way" when I hold up the dollar bills that Selene had lent to me before the show started. Bow flounces down the runway to take it, giving my hand a gentle squeeze and a dramatic kiss before stuffing the money into a hidden pocket on her dress.

Bow is fucking *amazing*, but it's not until she does a backflip on stage that I actually start screaming at her from the crowd, bouncing on my toes as she lands in a confident crouch. "Since when can she do a backflip?" I ask, not expecting an answer, but Selene is prepared with one anyway.

"She's been going to the gym with Enzo," Selene says, leaning over my shoulder so she can speak into my ear so I can hear her. Her warm, minty breath tickles the skin at the back of my neck as she continues, "Enzo used to do gymnastics—was on track to be an Olympian and all that jazz. But he quit after he fell off the bars and fucked his shoulder up. You should ask him about it sometime. But for now, he's a personal trainer throughout the week, and Bow is his favorite client. Make of that what you will."

Bow...in a *gym*? Whatever she's been doing with Enzo has clearly paid off—she can do a backflip, for God's sake, and in heels—but I never thought I'd see the day she willingly walked into a gym.

"Born This Way" has come to an end, and Bow is using her foot to slide money people have thrown onto the stage for her toward herself. Most of it is crumpled into little balls, and it suddenly makes sense why the one-dollar bills that Selene had given me were so wrinkled; it must have been her own tip money from whenever she performed as Spencer Read. Has she ever headlined her own show before? I remind myself to ask her later as Bow launches into the next song of her set.

She doesn't perform for long, but it's clear that she doesn't need to: Four songs later and she's sauntering off the stage with handfuls of wadded-up cash, enough that she can't even carry it all. Bow finds me in the crowd as she's blowing kisses at her fans, gesturing backstage with a flip of her wig to let me know where she's headed. I nod at her so she knows I understand, then watch as she disappears beneath a glowing doorway that must lead back into the dressing room. Once she's gone and the crowd has begun to disperse, scantily clad men in bedazzled speedos clamber onto the stage in Bow's place, sweeping up the tip money that she hadn't been able to carry off the stage with her. They stuff it all into a garbage bag with her name on it, and even the plastic seems to have somehow been Bow-ified: It shimmers silver beneath the stage lights.

"Isn't she amazing?" Selene asks, almost dreamily. She tugs at my hip until I've spun around to face her fully, caught off guard again by the way she's standing so close to me. Selene is still grinning as the crowd thins out around us, most of the bar's patrons are filing off the dance floor in a single surge toward the bar; I almost feel sorry for Enzo, but as I stand on my toes to try and find him behind the counter, I don't see him. He must have wandered off after Bow.

A select few college kids have remained behind to dance, and it seems Selene has opted to join them as she sways in time with the music. "Did you have fun tonight?"

"Yeah, lots of fun," I say, craning my neck around to stare at the doorway Bow has just disappeared through. Maybe if I stare at it hard enough, she'll sense my distress and come rescue me. She hasn't done anything wrong, but I don't know how to politely shake Selene, and I refuse to embarrass myself by trying to dance with her. "Shouldn't we get going? Bow'll be looking for me."

Selene snorts and clicks her tongue at me, reaching up to fix the collar of her jean jacket. She bites on the post of her lip ring as she flattens down the lapels against my shoulders, then smooths out a wrinkle near the sunflower patch that's ironed onto my chest. It's Selene's jacket, but something about her fussing over it feels oddly intimate since I'm the one who's wearing it. "Believe me, angel face. You are the furthest thing from Bow's mind right now. Enzo takes his break after Bow's set, and the only place you'll find those two is lip-locked in a bathroom stall somewhere." Selene scrunches her nose with disgust, like she doesn't want to imagine what the two of them might actually be doing. "We've got at least thirty minutes before either one of them is decent enough for us to look at."

Maybe it's because my first impression of Selene was her stumbling out of a crowd and spilling her drink down the front of my pure-white T-shirt. Or maybe it's because I'm an anxious piece of shit that finds her distractingly attractive. But the words slip out of me before I can think to stop them: "So I'm stuck out here with *you* for half an hour?"

Selene's perfectly manicured eyebrows, dyed red to match her hair, shoot up towards her hairline as she looks at me, an ugly sneer curling her upper lip. "I'm sorry?" She takes a step back to cleave apart the little space between us. "Well excuse me for trying to be nice to you. Jesus. Bow didn't tell me you were a dick." Selene sticks her nose in the air. "Good night, Briar."

Fuck.

Dammit.

I'm so *stupid*.

Great going, Briar.

"No, wait—" I scramble forward and grab Selene's hand as she turns to leave me on the dance floor, the thought of being alone out here like a kick to the chest with the heel of Bow's stiletto. Rightly so, she tears herself free from my grasp, but at least she decides to stay put, even if she is still glaring at me. "I'm sorry. I didn't mean that. I just—this place is—" I swallow hard and drag a hand through my ponytail, my fingers trembling as they snag on a couple of tangles. "It's overwhelming, okay? And I don't even know why Bow brought me here. I'm—I'm anxious, like you said, and it's loud and I hate noise and the lights are too bright and there's so many people and—"

"Hey, stop. I get it." Selene's expression smooths out again, the lines of her face softening into something I don't recognize. "If you want to go backstage, we can. I'm sorry. I promised we could leave if you needed to. I can send someone in to get Bow."

"You don't have to do that," I say quickly, offering Selene what I hope is a reassuring smile. "I'd hate to ruin their...*whatever* it is they're doing. I'll be fine if we head backstage. It's crowded out here, and I'm really not much of a dancer."

Selene snorts good-naturedly. "Yeah, I could tell. I've never met anyone who just stands there when Lil Nas X comes on."

I quirk my head at her. "Was I supposed to find the nearest pole and give you a show? Because it's not like I don't know 'Montero.'"

Selene's eyes light up brighter than the stage lights, like I've finally said what she's been waiting all night to hear. "There's that snark your brother told me about!" She loops her arm through my elbow, pulling me against her as she smiles. "Keep that up, and you and I will get along fine. And for the record, when you go to buy me that drink later, I'll take another Pepsi."

I bite against the inside of my cheek. "Yep. Pepsi. Got it."

five

*T*rue to Selene's word, Bow and Enzo are nowhere to be found backstage. There is, however, an empty bottle of water and an untouched plate of still-steaming French fries sitting on the vanity, evidence of Enzo's earlier arrival before he and my brother wandered off to do. . .whatever it is they do after Bow Regard has finished performing. Jacklynn sinks into the chair behind the mirror, having watched Bow perform from backstage, and scoffs at the food before sliding it to the edge of the vanity. I try not to let myself think about it, why it looks like the two of them had left in such a hurry.

Selene is unbothered as she makes her way over and snatches up the plate despite Jacklynn swatting her away. "Child, put down those goddamn fries. They are not for you, and you know that." Jacklynn looks over at me and frowns. She gestures widely at Selene, indicating her entire existence. "Remember what I told you, Miss Briar."

Selene pops a fry into her mouth anyway. "Aww, you didn't warn her about me, did you, Jac?"

Jacklynn leans heavily against the vanity. "You bet your annoying little ass, I did."

"My ass is anything but little." Selene turns sideways, plate still in hand, and admires herself in the mirror, purposefully posing so that her butt looks bigger than it actually is. Jacklynn swats her away again, this time with her discarded blue lipstick tube, but Selene ignores her and continues to gawk at her own appearance. "You've been sitting here all night like you own the place, Jac! You can at least scoot over and let me see how good I look. Right, Briar?"

I stifle a cough into the palm of my hand as the both of them turn around to look at me. Selene's wide, bowed mouth turns up at the corners with a smirk, and her dark green eyes are twinkling in the wake of catching me off guard again. "Um. What?"

"Spencer, darling. Didn't I warn you about putting my sister on the spot like this?"

Bow's neon reflection appears in the vanity mirror, and I whirl myself around in time to watch as Enzo stumbles into the dressing room behind her, looking disheveled as he fixes his shirt and pops the collar of his button-up. Bow, unsurprisingly, still looks perfect aside from her lipstick being smudged, which is likely due to the visible mark that's pressed to the center of Enzo's cheek. Selene points at her own with a French fry, and

Enzo groans before scrubbing at his skin with his fingers, trying to wipe the kiss-mark off.

A breath of relief whooshes out of me at the familiar sight of my brother, and it's as my anxiety is beginning to subside that her performance tonight comes flooding back to me with a shocking sort of clarity. I still can't believe that she did a backflip in heels. "You were fucking incredible."

Bow's smile is bright enough to light up The Gallery. "Thanks, B! I was incredible, wasn't I?"

"Yeah, you were!" Selene dances across the room to give Bow a high-five before holding out the plate of French fries. She takes one with a smile. "That backflip into a death-drop? Ugh, come on! You have got to teach me how to do that. And holy shit, this outfit? When are you gonna teach me how to work with latex? It's such a hard material to sew, and the seams always pull apart on me when I'm finished."

Bow ruffles Selene's red hair with a snort. "That's because you're not supposed to sew it. You glue it. And as soon as you buy the fabric, you little shit. Latex ain't cheap and I'll be damned if I have to buy it for you." Bow sidles up next to me and wraps her arm around my shoulders, hugging me against her side. "How are you feeling? Hopefully tonight wasn't too hard on you."

"I'm feeling. . . okay," I tell her, and it's not entirely a lie. Bow doesn't need to know about the meltdown I'd had with Selene, that she'd almost abandoned me in the middle of the dance floor because I'd been acting like an asshole. Of course, I'll tell her about it later, as well as the fact that I'd nearly had a panic attack trying to find Enzo at the bar. But right now Bow Regard is flying high on cloud nine, and I'm not going to take that away from her. She deserves to celebrate a successful show where she alone had headlined, not worry about her sister who doesn't even deserve to be here.

"Seriously, stop looking at me like that. I'm okay!" I insist, then promptly try and change the subject. "You should see all of the photos I sent to Mom and Dad. Avery's having a field day in the family group chat."

I can tell Bow wants to inquire about my half-truth by the way she moves her mouth, her painted lips pursed with the outline of a frown. She always crinkles the bridge of her nose when she's about to call someone out on their bullshit, but she's suddenly interrupted when someone comes scrambling into the dressing room, skidding over the tiles and knocking into the stack of rusted metal folding chairs piled too-high near the doorway. They crash to the ground like quick little snaps of gunfire.

"Jesus, Achilles, you scared us!" Selene cries, gripping Jacklynn's shoulders from where she's hidden behind her. The older queen is tense in her chair, her fingers curled atop the vanity like she might punch the next thing that moves, especially if that thing is Selene. "I saw my life flash before my eyes, you klutz!"

The culprit of the fanfare—Achilles, I'm assuming—

straightens themself out from the doubled-over fetal position they're standing in, their body folded inward like an accordion. "Shit. Um. I'm—I'm sorry. I didn't mean to—uh—fuck." Their eyes are wide as they rub at the back of their neck, their fingers trembling and tanned skin slick with sweat. "I'll, uh, pick everything up, I swear. Shit. Um. Hi, Bow. Great show tonight, yeah? You did good."

My brother smiles sympathetically, though she's yet to release the grip she has on my shoulder, anchoring me against her as if she'd been prepared to yank me off the ground and take off with me. "Thanks, Keel. Good to see you."

"What are you even doing back here, Achilles?" Enzo drags a ring-clad hand through his hair, smoothing down the dark, curling strands that are in disarray from his gay bar bathroom escapades. I'd forgotten that Enzo was here, standing behind Bow like he's been waiting for my brother to acknowledge him, and I wonder how hard it must be for him: to want something more than a casual hookup but having to settle for whatever Bow might give him. "Don't make me regret talking to Nathalie for you—"

Achilles' expression is panicked as they flap their arms, their fingers flexing around air. "I'm sorry, I—It was Nathalie who told me to come get you. Your break ended twenty minutes ago, and she needs you at the bar. I tried to cover for you, but, uh, I can't exactly serve alcohol. You know, 'cus I'm not twenty-one yet? Two more years, though, and I got you."

Enzo sucks in a breath and stands as still as a statue. He stares at Achilles like they're the tall, broad-shouldered physical manifestation of his worst nightmares come to life, and it's not until Bow tentatively calls his name that Enzo shouts loudly in Spanish, his body lurching into motion again. "I'm late. Shit. I am late. She told me not to be late again. Goddamn it, Bow, this is *your* fault!"

Bow looks taken aback, going so far as to hold a hand over her heart, like she's trying to contain it within her chest. "My fault? You're the one who dragged me into the bathroom and—"

"*Bow!*" Enzo laments.

"*Enzo!*" My brother shouts back at him.

Achilles bites their lip. "Um, do you want me to—"

Enzo barrels around them with a final curse on his pierced tongue. "Take your break, Keel. I owe you one! Bow Regard, we'll talk about this later."

He's rounding the corner before Achilles can thank him for the break, his footsteps thudding down the outside hallway until they disappear into the music. Jacklynn lets out a low whistle. "You have got to quit riling him up like this, Bow. Nathalie won't hesitate to fire him, and I've seen plenty of bartenders come and go for less."

Selene waves her hand in dismissal and Jacklynn's nostrils flare wide in annoyance. "I'll just tell Mom it was my fault he's late. She only gets pissed when it's Bow's, and it's only because she knows what they're doing."

Bow heaves a sigh and sinks into the chair next to the vanity, where Selene has returned the half-eaten plate of French fries. "I don't know what you're implying," Bow says dryly. "We were talking and lost track of time. You remember how that goes, don't you, Jac?"

Jacklynn presses her lips into a thin line as she pats down the edge of her wig. "Hush, child. I have tights older than you. My bathroom hookup days are long behind me."

"Talking my ass," Selene grumbles, then raises an eyebrow as she looks across the room to Achilles. They've yet to move away from the doorway, hovering near the stack of fallen chairs like they're waiting for one of us to invite them farther into the room. "Keel, have you met Briar yet?"

Achilles shakes their head and offers me a tight-lipped smile, their bottom lip double pierced with snake bites, like Selene. "You're Bow's little sister, right? I've heard a lot about you from Enzo. I'm Achilles. They/them pronouns, please."

"Cool name," I say. "Like the warrior?"

Achilles grins at me, revealing the dimples in their round, pink-flushed cheeks. "Yep, exactly! And thanks, I really love history." They stuff their hands into the pockets of their oversized hoodie, the black material fading a dingy gray. "I changed my name to Achilles last year, but I use Achilles Patrick as a stage name. You can call me Keel though, if you want to. Everyone else does."

"Briar," I offer politely. "She/her pronouns are fine. So are you a performer, too? Bow said that lots of people do drag here."

"I'm a drag king," Achilles tells me, their sandy blond hair cut into a mullet-style flopping in front of their eyes. They're quick to sweep it back and tuck the loose strands behind their heavily pierced ears. "But only on Mondays and Thursdays, and then I barback on the weekends for extra money. Trying to put myself through art school, you know? Enzo helped me get the gig here, though. He lives in my building."

Selene throws her arm around my shoulders, tugging me against her as if we've been friends all our lives. "Art school is their 'back-up plan,'" she says, using her fingers as quotation marks. Achilles' blue eyes shift immediately, from staring at us to the ground beneath their feet, and I pretend not to notice how their fingers have started to twitch at their sides, how their face has gone masterfully blank. "In case doing drag doesn't work out for them."

I shrug Selene's arm off my shoulders. "Why wouldn't drag work out for them?" I ask, angling myself between her and Achilles. They probably don't need me to actually defend their honor, but Selene is clearly trying to mock them. To drag me to her side in whatever feud the two might have between them. But I'll be damned if I let her bully someone in front of me. "They perform here, so it sounds like they're doing fine to me."

Selene rolls her eyes again and gestures vaguely at Achilles.

"Come on, Briar. Don't be serious. Most of their drag comes from Goodwill, if you can even really call it that. It's all just clothes that they've patched up and tried to glue studs on."

Achilles' head suddenly snaps up to stare at us again, a forced smile tugging at the corners of their mouth. "I don't perform on the weekends because I'm not ready yet, but I will be someday soon," they say cheerily, brushing off Selene's comments with a shrug. "And my grandparents didn't leave my family with a massive inheritance when they died. I do the best I can, and that best doesn't include custom outfits that cost a fortune."

Selene curls her fingers into fists, glaring at Achilles like they're her enemy. "My outfits don't cost a fortune, you ass——"

"Selene," Jacklynn snaps at her, and Selene whips around on the heels of her shiny leather combat boots. Her dark eyes widen as she stares at Jacklynn with a pout, her plum lips puckered as if already prepared for a lecture. "I know that the little girl who begged for me to put her in drag is not trying to dictate what drag is, especially to a king who's as equally talented as yourself."

Achilles blushes, but Selene lets out a little huff. "But Jac——"

"There ain't no 'buts' in this game, child. Only that fake padded ass of yours." Jacklynn fixes her with a glare, pinning Selene in her place, and even Bow is visibly holding her breath as she glances back and forth between the two of them. "Now: Either you apologize to your fellow performer, or you turn the fuck around and get the hell out of my dressing room. Your mamas may own this bar, baby girl, but I am who runs this show. And dare I say it, they'd both be disappointed to hear you talk like this."

Selene's face flushes a deep shade of scarlet, though I can't decide if I think she's pissed or embarrassed. She stomps her foot indignantly, like a toddler throwing a tantrum, and I cannot believe the girl who'd managed to convince me to hang out with her is suddenly acting so childish. "You can say what you want about drag," Selene says. "But do you really think *Keel* is going to take home the crown?"

I tilt my head at this new tidbit of information. Is Selene's hostility really just about a competition? But now isn't the time to ask, especially when it's not any of my business. "What crown?"

"The crown for Drag King of the Year," Selene supplies. "It's a contest that The Gallery holds at the end of every summer, and the winner gets five-thousand dollars and a headlining spot on the weekends. It's just like a pageant, but for kings. It's the only one in New York, but if anyone is going to win it this year, it's sure as hell *not* going to be Achilles."

"Spencer came in second place last year," Achilles says with a frown. "So he's basically the front-runner for this year. It really kind of sucks, if you ask me."

"No one did," Selene points out.

Achilles ignores her. "Personally, I don't think he should be allowed to compete. His mom is on the judging panel, and it's not fair."

Selene looks absolutely feral as she knocks me aside and points a finger in their face. "I earned my ranking in the competition just like everyone else! It's not so hard when you actually have talent." Achilles surprises me by standing their ground and smiling, like they're happy they've somehow struck a nerve. It sort of makes me happy, too, with the way Selene's been treating them. "Last year, you hardly qualified. It's not my fault that no one even remembered your name."

"If it's so easy," I muse, crossing my arms over the front of Selene's heavy jacket. "And if all it takes is talent, then why haven't you won already?"

Achilles' eyes widen as they try their hardest not to laugh.

Selene turns around so she can glare at me. "Stay out of this, baby gay. This is between me and Keel." Selene tries to dismiss me with a quick wave of her hand, but I swat her away as it flutters too close to my face, nearly whacking me in the nose. "Shit, Keel, even Briar has a better shot than you, and she doesn't even do drag."

"Says who?" I ask, earning myself a frown from Selene. She arches an apple-red eyebrow, curious to see where I'm going with this. "You literally don't know me, and my brother does drag. Maybe I want to be just like him." The words tumble out of me before I can think them through. I've always wanted to be like Beau, and I've always wished that I was just as brave and could get up on a stage and perform somewhere. But Christ, I've never even told Beau that. "I could have a stage name, for all you know. Especially if drag is so easy."

Selene throws her hands up in frustration, her black fingernails glinting beneath the dressing room's floodlight. "We all know that you don't have a stage name. We all know that you don't do drag. Come on, Bow, are you listening to this? Tell your sister to be quiet."

Bow is on the edge of her seat, her blue eyes darting back and forth between us. She'll probably deny it later, but there's a shit-eating grin that's tugging at the corners of her mouth, and it's almost like she enjoys watching Selene and I argue. "I don't know, Spence. I think Briar might be onto something." Bow winks at me. "What about you, Jac? Do you think Briar could do drag?"

Jacklynn looks me up and down with a neutral, calculating expression. "I don't see why not." It's a weird vindication that I've never known I needed, Bow Regard's approval and Jacklynn Hyde's agreement, and something like pride starts to swell up inside of my chest. Back home, the nearest gay bar is two hours away in Dallas, and I've never really allowed myself to consider doing drag because it's Bow's thing. She'd always made that two-hour drive on the weekends, desperate to immerse herself in a community I never thought I could be a part of. At least not without stepping on her toes.

But maybe it'll be different in New York, where queer culture is everywhere and literally across the street from Bow's apartment.

Maybe I *can* do something fun this summer and experiment with gender and stop watching TikToks of Bow's performances.

Maybe I can actually perform with her.

Someday.

Right now I just want to put Selene in her place.

Selene stamps her foot again to draw me away from the revelation. "This is fucking ridiculous!" she cries. "Briar can't just decide to be a drag king!"

"Why not?" Jacklynn asks. "You did."

"That was different!" Selene insists, huffing until she's red in the face again. "I've been doing this for years and because I want to make an actual career out of it. Briar's just doing it to spite me." She whirls around to look at Bow. "Bow, tell her she can't do this. Tell her this is *my* thing, not hers."

Bow shrugs her shoulders and pops a fry into her mouth. "If it's something that Briar wants to do, I can't stop her. And besides, I think she'd make a killer king."

Achilles inches closer to me and claps their tattooed hands together; their fingers are dotted with little suns and moons. "I think you should do it!" they say, smiling in earnest now. "Drag is lots of fun, and you could even enter the competition! There's nothing in the rulebook that says you can't apply."

Selene curls her fingers into trembling fists at her sides. "You'll never make it that far," she sneers through her teeth. "You'll crack under the pressure. Have you ever even been on a stage before?" She takes my silence as confirmation. "You don't know how to perform, you don't know how to lip-sync, and you probably can't even sew. It takes more than all of that to be a drag king."

"She can learn!" Achilles says. "I can help her. Because that's what real kings do, Selene. We *help* each other. And besides, sewing isn't the requirement that it used to be. Look at you! Most of your stuff is made for you."

Jacklynn, with a soft groan as she stands, finally emerges from behind the room's only vanity. She's surprisingly tall with a plump waist that's been cinched into a beautiful maroon dress, the sequins shining as she saunters across the room to stand in front of me. "What do you say, Miss Briar?" Jacklynn places a hand on my shoulder. "Care to give Spencer a run for his money?"

I don't have to think twice about it.

Maybe it's because I want to knock Selene off her pedestal, or maybe it's because the idea of doing drag and being just like my brother kicks my anxious little heart into overdrive.

"Where do I sign up?" I ask Jacklynn, grinning at the queen whose smile is equally as radiant.

six

Spencer Read's Instagram has nearly thirty-thousand follow-ers, and it's as I'm scrolling through his dozens of photos that I come to a grim realization: Everyone makes mistakes, but entering a knockoff of *RuPaul's Drag Race* when I don't even do drag was a colossal fuck-up on my part. God, what was I *think-ing*—challenging Selene in an element that is clearly her forte? With her cherry-red hair slicked back straight and a seemingly endless supply of perfectly tailored suit jackets, she looks so good in drag it's almost not even fair.

"Quit agonizing over how hot you think Spencer is and just *go* already," Beau complains, slapping his hands against the tiny cof-fee table that he, Enzo, and I are seated around. A Trouble game board is sitting on top of a caved-in plastic cake lid, and I've lost track of how long we've been moving our colorful pegged pieces around it. "But if you send me back to Home *one more time,*

B, I will send *your* ass back home to Texas. I don't care that it's your birthday!"

Enzo snorts with amusement, and from his seat on the couch behind Beau, affectionately ruffles his short, bubblegum-pink hair. My brother, seated crisscross on the floor between Enzo's knees, squawks like a bird as he throws back an elbow to gently knock him away. "You're just mad because Briar is as ruthless as you are." Enzo fixes his hair for him by combing his fingers through the stands. "Seriously, though. I *hate* playing games with him. He's competitive, and not in a fun way."

Avery Vincent: i cant believe im missing ur birthday party

Briar Vincent: You're not missing much, I promise. 🖤

Briar Vincent: We're playing Trouble. Lol.

"He's been like this for as long as I've been alive," I say, leaning forward to pop the dice on the game board. It lands on one and Beau squeals in delight, moving his yellow peg back into the starting hole on his corner of the board. "You should see him play video games."

"Oh, believe me. I have," Enzo laments. "My landlord threatened to evict me last month because Beau was screaming at my Switch."

"Sounds about right." I sneak another glance at my phone as Enzo takes his turn, popping the dice to roll a three and move his peg around the board. Avery hasn't responded yet, so I open up Instagram to keep scrolling through Selene's photos.

"Does she *actually* have a tattoo of a pumpkin on her arm?"

Beau lets out a groan before he leans across the table and plucks my phone out of my hands, then promptly tucks it under his ass. "That's it. You've officially lost your Instagram privileges. *Yes*, she has a tattoo of a pumpkin, and *no*, I can't tell you why. You're obsessed. Let it go."

"I'm talking to Avery, too, Beau. Give that back."

He sticks out his tongue and continues to hold my phone hostage. "Too bad."

I try not to panic over not having my phone to keep my hands busy. Tapping on the screen or scrolling through a timeline is usually enough to keep my everyday anxiety at bay, but taking it away feels like Beau has cut off a part of me. Enzo must notice that my hands have already started to shake, though; he reaches into his pocket and procures an actual fidget spinner, one I've seen him fiddling with whenever the room gets too quiet. He tosses it to me with an understanding smile.

"Thanks," I say. "And I'm not obsessed with Selene, I'm curious. There's a difference."

"Difference, schmifference," Beau says, taking his turn to pop the dice. It lands on one and he scoffs. "It's not Selene's fault that you decided to sign up for the contest."

"You encouraged me!" I cry, then pitch my voice into an octave high enough to make my head spin. "'*Oh, I don't know, Spence. I think Briar might be onto something. I think she would make a killer king.'*

Those were *your* words, Bow Regard. Not mine."

Beau reaches into the bowl of popcorn that's sitting on the table and launches one of the burnt pieces at my head. It misses, soaring behind me and into the streamers Beau had hung around the apartment this morning. "First of all, I do *not* sound like that," he says. "And secondly, I was just being a good brother. You said you wanted to do drag! How was I supposed to know that you were talking out of your ass?"

"I wasn't talking out of my ass! I was trying to put her in her place. Didn't you see the look on Achilles' face when Selene insulted their drag? God, Beau, I wanted to—"

"Kiss her?" he asks with a smirk. "Yeah, I saw your face, too."

My skin heats with an unwanted blush as I twist and turn Enzo's fidget spinner. I balance it on the tip of my finger, watching as the chrome blades blur. "I don't want to kiss Selene."

"But you *did*!" Beau accuses, grinning so wide that I can see the solitary silver cap on his back tooth. "Selene can be charming when she wants to be."

"She can also be a bit of a jerk," Enzo adds, wrapping his arms around Beau's shoulders and giving him a gentle squeeze. "She's on a constant mission to prove herself, and I think that sometimes her charm gets lost in translation."

Beau casually shrugs him off, lifting his shoulders to loosen Enzo's grip. He immediately lets him go, like he knows that Beau is purposely keeping him at arm's length.

He'd never been like this with Connor.

"She wouldn't be on a mission if Nathalie and Dominique weren't so hard on her," Beau says. "Who cares if she doesn't go to college?"

"Nathalie and Dominique," Enzo says dryly, like they've had this conversation before. "It's your turn, birthday girl."

I pop the dice and roll a five. My final blue peg is on its way to the finish line when it lands on one of Beau's yellow pieces. He shouts in outrage as I yank out his peg and replace it with mine on the board. "So," I begin quickly, before he can comment on the betrayal. "Is it true that Selene's mom is in charge of the competition, like Achilles said?"

Beau angrily slams his peg into a hole on his side of the board. "Nathalie is, yeah. She's on the judging panel." He glares at me from beneath his false lashes. "But that doesn't mean that Selene just gets a free pass, you know. Despite whatever Achilles might have told you. She had to find a sponsor and will compete just like everyone else."

"A sponsor?" I inquire, frowning.

Enzo answers carefully, "You can't compete without one. It has to be a queen or another king." He glances apprehensively at Beau. "Didn't anyone tell you before you signed up?"

It feels as if the air has been sucked from my lungs as I drop Enzo's fidget onto the carpet. "No one told me anything about a sponsor," I say, turning to look at Beau with an expression that

I hope conveys my disbelief. "Why would you not tell me that I needed one?"

Beau shrugs his shoulders and stares back at me, as if withholding this information was part of his revenge plan for kicking his ass in Trouble. But I know him. He'd been caught up in the drama of the moment, enjoying the banter as Selene and I argued back and forth, and telling me about a sponsor had simply slipped his mind.

"You didn't ask about the requirements."

"Because I didn't know there were any!" I push myself up onto my knees, looming over the game board as I glare at him. "You're a queen, so. . . can't I just say that you're my sponsor?"

He finds a sudden interest in his fingernails, chipping away at the shiny purple polish he'd painted them with earlier this morning. "I'm already Selene's sponsor for the competition. You'll have to find someone else."

The heat of my brother's betrayal prickles up the length of my spine. It coils under my skin before settling like a rock in my stomach, and it feels like I'm going to throw up, or scream, or cry.

I stare at Beau long enough that he's forced to eventually look up at me. "I'm your sister."

"And I love you," Beau says, without sympathy. "But quitting on Selene to sponsor you would be giving *you* a free pass, and I can't do that. Selene has put the work in, Briar, and if you want to compete in this contest, then you'll need to do that, too."

He must sense the tension growing between because Enzo interjects with, "I would offer to sponsor you myself, but my days as Ella Fate were short-lived."

Beau lets out a laugh that, albeit a bit forced at first, blossoms into a high-pitched cackle. "Oh, God. I forgot about Ella Fate! Shit, B, if you think Enzo's a pretty boy, you should have seen him as a queen. He was *gorgeous*."

Still is, I want to say, but keep the thought to myself.

"Until I fell off the stage," Enzo says. "And busted my lip wide open."

"You *literally* fell off the stage?" I ask. "Holy shit."

Enzo nods with a grimace. "And I haven't stepped foot on it since." I wonder if it reminded him too much of his gymnastics injury, but I don't dare ask him about it.

"Ugh," Beau groans. "It's a shame, too. Ella Fate was *such* a good drag name."

I watch my brother as he tips his head back into Enzo's lap. Beau reaches for a lock of his hair, twirling one of Enzo's dark curls around his index finger, and I *hate* the way that Beau keeps stringing him along.

I like Enzo—he's a stellar balance for Beau, a steadying calm in Beau's whirlwind storm of glittering sequins and chaos—and I know that Beau likes him, too. So I don't understand why he's keeping such a distance between them. Why he's bothering with him at all if he never plans on making a real move.

I don't think Enzo gets it, either. His smile falters as Beau springs up and out of his lap, the moment between them a fleeting one.

"Keel gave you their number last night, right? You should text them," Enzo suggests quietly, smoothing out a wrinkle in the shoulder of Beau's orange T-shirt. "They might know someone who can sponsor you."

"Why would they help me?" I ask, even though Achilles had offered to help me last night. "I'm their competition."

Enzo leans over Beau to pop the dice, rolling a four. "Keel is a klutz," he tells me. "But they have a heart of gold and introducing people to drag is their favorite thing to do. Trust me, Keel will want to help."

Beau removes my phone from under his ass and slides it across the table. "You'll like Keel. Just don't talk to them about Van Gogh. Or history—*especially* not history. I've learned more about *The Odyssey* since moving to New York than I ever did in high school."

Van Gogh and *The Odyssey* are a small price to pay for the information I need to put Selene in her place, so I unlock my phone and scroll to Achilles' number in my contacts. My thumb hovers over the keyboard, unsure of what to say because I'm not used to texting anyone other than Beau, Avery, or our parents.

Briar Vincent: Hi, Achilles. This is Briar. We met last night at the bar. I'm Bow's sister.

Achilles' response is immediate, like they've been waiting for me to reach out.

Achilles Patrick: hi Briar!!! r u ready to take Spencer down?!

I look up at Beau and grin. Maybe I hadn't liked Selene on his recommendation, but I think I've found an ally in Achilles.

"When you asked if I was ready to take down Spencer Read, this is *not* what I had in mind."

Achilles huffs as we huddle together in The Gallery's too-cramped dressing room. "You're the one who picked a fight with a drag king," they remind me, taking my measurements and logging the inches in their phone. "Can you put your arms up? I need to measure around your chest, if that's okay. Do you plan on wearing a binder?"

I do as I'm told, staring up at the ceiling while Achilles does their thing, their pale cheeks darkening with the hint of a blush like this is somehow more awkward for them than it is for me. "Am I supposed to?"

Across the room, Jacklynn snorts as she tucks her bra strap beneath the neckline of her skintight bodysuit.

"You don't have to, but most kings do something to hide their boobs." Achilles fiddles with their measuring tape, pulling it tighter around me. "I wear a binder, but Selene uses kinesiology tape to cover her nipples and pull them to the sides because she likes going topless on stage."

"Topless?" I say, though I know I shouldn't be surprised. Selene is the queen—king?—of confidence, especially on social media with her thousands of dedicated followers. But I hadn't realized that she's not wearing binders or skin-colored tank tops beneath all of her flannels and leather jackets. "Like naked topless?"

Achilles shrugs their shoulders, as if the thought of Selene naked doesn't phase them in the same way it does me, apparently; I don't think I know what to do with this new revelation. "When she first started, she used to wear bodysuits and binders, but only because she was so young. The second she turned eighteen, she started taping her tits."

"How old is she now?"

"Nineteen."

"*Jesus.*" I drag my fingers through my hair. "Beau and my parents would kill me."

Across the room, Jacklynn Hyde groans as she rises from the vanity, her spine cracking in several places. Achilles and I flinch as she turns to look at us, a fiery determination blazing in her golden-rimmed eyes. "Now you listen to me, Miss Briar. I quite like you, and not just because you're Bow's baby sister."

Achilles stiffles a giggle behind the sleeve of their tattered black jacket, a whole in the wrist from where they've cut out a place for their thumb. I nudge them in the ribs with an elbow.

"But if you're going to do drag in my bar," Jacklynn continues. "Then I am going to need something from you."

My brow furrows as I nod at her.

What could Jacklynn possibly want from me?

"Get out of the mindset that it's okay for you to judge other performers, because it's not." She gives Achilles a look, like Achilles should already know this. "We all have our schtick. That thing that each of us are known for. But make no mistakes, baby girl. Our drag is our art and it ain't for the fans or the fame. It's for ourselves."

Jacklynn places a hand on her hip, her shiny nails and golden bangles shimmering beneath the room's singular floodlight. "I discovered my womanhood through drag, and I've never stopped performing, even now, because I love what drag represents. Because I believe in this movement and community."

Achilles loops their arm through my elbow, giving it a gentle squeeze. "She's not upset with you," they murmur, and it's only then that I realize I'm picking at my fingernails.

Jacklynn confirms this with a smile, "I just want you to know what I know, because believe me: The fans and the fame that might come with the gig sound nice, but most of us don't end up on *RuPaul's Drag Race*. Most people don't know who we are. Which is why we all love what we do, because otherwise, we probably wouldn't be here."

Jacklynn struts over on a pair of short-heeled wedges that

sparkle gold beneath the floodlight. "I know you're mostly doing this to rattle Selene," she says, placing her hand on my shoulder. "And that's fine. I've met kings and queens who've ventured into drag for less. But if you're planning to parade around my club and put that little shit in her place, then you're going to be held to the exact same standards I hold your brother, Keel, Selene, and everyone else who calls The Gallery their home too."

There's nothing that I can do to stop myself from bouncing on the heels of my battered black boots. I can't decide if I think I'm being scolded or simply spoken to, and even though Jacklynn hasn't raised her voice at me, I feel as if I've already disappointed her. "I'm sorry."

Achilles drags their fingers through their messy, dirty blond mullet. "You really don't need to apologize," they tell me. "I think what Jacklynn is trying to say is that Selene taping her boobs and going topless. . .she doesn't do that for the fans, the fame, or a solitary chance at the spotlight. And it's not as taboo as I think you might think it is." They offer me an encouraging smile and loop their arm through my elbow again. "I know you're from Texas, and the environment down there—what is and isn't accepted, tolerated, or is outright being banned—is different from the environment up here."

Jacklynn nods her agreement.

"You'll understand soon," Achilles continues. "But being on stage, dressing in drag, and performing. . .that's where and when a lot of us feel the most at home, and it's not any different for Spencer."

"Even if she's an asshole?" I ask.

"Especially if she's an asshole," Jacklynn answers. "You can dislike Selene all you'd like, Miss Briar, but you still have to respect her drag. It's her art, and it's not fair for anyone—you, me, Bow, or Keel—to judge her for doing what she loves, even if you can be damn sure she's going to judge the hell out of you."

"So what you're saying is to be the bigger person."

"Yes, ma'am. Exactly that." Jacklynn pats me on the shoulder before she suddenly drops down into the splits, laughing as I yelp and jump away from her. "I'm a performer, darling. Don't let my age fool you. Keel, be a dear, and go fetch my daughter from the bar. I need her to help me stretch."

"Sure thing," Achilles says, then bolts from the dressing room to do as they've been told.

"Are you performing tonight?" I ask Jacklynn, toeing at the floor beneath my boots in a half-assed attempt to ground myself. I don't know how often she still does shows, but I'm curious to see her perform.

Jacklynn bends over her thigh to stretch out the muscles in her back. "I'm the headliner," she says, her voice muffled as she groans into the fabric of her rhinestoned tights and reaches for the tips of her toes. "And I might be old, Miss Briar, but I can still outdance any baby gay that comes into this club. Just wait until you see me do a duck walk. It brings the house down every time."

"Damn right it does," says Bow, flouncing into the dressing room on sparkling six-inch stilettos. I don't know where she'd gotten it from, but there's a feathered boa wrapped three times around her neck, long enough for her trip over despite her height and heels. She catches herself against the doorframe before she can hit the ground. "I heard you needed some help."

Jacklynn sighs with thinly veiled despair. "How much have you had to drink?"

Bow holds up her hand, pinching her thumb and index finger together as if to indicate that she hasn't had anything, but Jacklynn and I both know better, and I can see the flush of her cheeks beneath her contour. "Just a *wee* dash of Fireball."

She's had more than just a dash, but apart from tripping over the boa that's shedding purple feathers, she doesn't seem so drunk that she can't perform her set tonight. Jacklynn must realize this, too, because she waves her over with a hurried hand and nails sharp enough to cut a bitch. "Help me up out of these splits."

Bow does a twirl on her way across the room, her sequined leotard gleaming ice-blue and gold. "Anything for you, Mama."

As she's clumsily helping Jacklynn up off the floor, Achilles reappears at my side, nudging me with an elbow. They hand me a neon pink solo cup with a dark, bubbling liquid inside that I swirl and observe with suspicion. Because it's not that I don't trust Achilles, but I also don't know them, either. "Bow said you like Dr. Pepper."

"Thanks," I say, cautiously sipping from the rim. Soda fizzles against the back of my tongue, not a trace of alcohol or something worse to be found, and my shoulders sink in relief. The last thing I need is for my drink to be spiked and to become so intoxicated that I stumble from the bar in an unknown city and get kidnapped, or jumped, or *killed*, or—

Achilles touches my arm, their fingers gentle as they tug on the sleeve of my hoodie. "It's safe," they reassure me, nodding at my solo cup like they can hear my thoughts starting to spiral. "I got it myself. Perks of being a barback, and all. I can help myself behind the counter."

"Thanks," I say again, offering them a tight-lipped smile. "So, who's all performing tonight? Is it just my brother and Jacklynn?"

Achilles takes a sip from their solo cup. "Jac's headlining, and Bow is one of her openers," they tell me. I glance across the room where Jacklynn is bent over the vanity, Bow massaging her neck. "Spencer is about to go on, I think. He's supposed to be doing Panic! At The Disco tonight."

I shouldn't—I *know* I shouldn't—but I glance at the wall that doubles as the back of the stage with a budding sense of curiosity. I haven't seen Selene all night, haven't so much as glimpsed her fiery hair sweeping past the doorway of the dressing room. Bow had mentioned that she lives upstairs in the apartment above

The Gallery with her moms, so had she opted to get ready up there tonight, away from the chaos of the bar?

Away from me, who had outright challenged her?

I wonder what she plans on wearing tonight: a bedazzled leather jacket with her name studded onto the back? A sequined blazer that had to have cost a small fortune? I've seen both as a part of her aesthetic, and on Instagram, Selene's drag has earned her praise from every corner of the internet.

In the videos I've found of her on TikTok, her natural hair is often slicked back out of her face, but sometimes, she's wearing a wig instead, black or blonde or a midnight blue that compliments her sun-kissed skin. Will she wear her shiny leather combat boots tonight? Or will she go with the platforms that snap all the way up to her knees, the ones with shiny silver buckles that clink together when she dances in front of a mirror and records herself.

Achilles nudges me with an elbow. "I know that look."

"What look?" I ask innocently, staring into my solo cup.

"Spencer is intimidating," they say, furrowing their brow as they study whatever expression is on my face. "He's good, Briar. Really good. You'll count yourself out before you even start if you go watch him."

"If he's really that good," I start to say. "Then I think I should scope him out. You know, to see what I'm up against."

Achilles takes a swig from their solo cup, grumbling something about wishing they were twenty-one. "The last time I watched Spencer perform, I couldn't get on stage for a week. He was incredible, and it honestly scared the shit out of me." They find a sudden interest in the thumb hole through their hoodie sleeve. "He had the crowd just—just eating from the palm of his hand, and they screamed for an encore after he left the stage."

Damn. Even Bow hadn't gotten an encore, just a shitload of tips that she'd used to buy me a birthday cake. "But I can't go out there alone," I tell Achilles, swirling the soda in my solo cup. "I nearly had a panic attack after Bow sent me out there on my own."

"See if she'll go with you," Achilles says. "She loves to watch him perform."

I purse my lips with a small, indignant little pout. Asking my brother to watch Spencer perform with me sounds like another scene from my worst nightmare. "Please, Keel?" I beg. "I don't want to listen to her fangirl about Spencer when I want to do this, too."

Achilles stares at me for a long, long while, like the weight of the world is resting on their shoulders and I've asked them to carry another planet. But eventually they heave out a sigh, one that they chase with the rest of whatever they're drinking. "You're really lucky I like you," they say.

I toss my cup in the overflowing garbage by the door, then loop my arm through Achilles' waiting elbow. I wouldn't normally feel so comfortable around someone I don't really know, but Achilles' sincerity and their love for drag is infectious. "You're the best," I say, noting the way that their eyes light up. They give my arm a squeeze, and I call over to Bow, "Keel and I are heading into the crowd!"

Bow doesn't bother looking up at me as she responds with a distracted, "Have fun."

seven

The way that Spencer interacts with the crowd is *phenomenal*. It's like he's been doing this all his life, like he was put on this earth for the sole purpose of doing drag, and my mouth gapes open like a goddamn fish out of water. At my shock, Achilles whisper-shouts a smug "I told you so" in my ear, their arm wrapped tightly in a protective embrace around my hips: a buffer between me and the patrons closing in on the stage, pushing to press closer to Spencer Read.

He swaggers down the runway with a seductive grace that makes *me* want to press closer, too, and I would if it weren't for Achilles, who's holding me back so that I don't get crushed by the masses. Panic! At The Disco's "Don't Threaten Me with a Good Time" is blaring through The Gallery's sound system, and Spencer is snatching up dollar bills faster than the beats of the music, then stuffing them into the pockets of his black skinny jeans.

He's wearing his knee-high leather boots tonight, the silver buckles glinting bright beneath the stage lights. His white button-down dress shirt is open in the front and tucked into the waistband of his pants, and part of his performance consists of him fiddling with the black suspenders that are loosely stretched over his shoulders. His ring-clad thumbs are hooked through the elastic like he might pull them down or take them off, and the crowd goes wild whenever he gives them a tug.

Spencer smirks teasingly from beneath a false goatee, and it is absolutely unfair how attractive he is, especially since Selene is a raging asshole beneath all the makeup and contour.

He drops to his knees at the end of the stage's runway, taking the hand of a girl who's been screaming since the moment he stepped onto the stage. A die-hard fan, no doubt, and one who looks like she's ready to faint beneath the weight of Spencer's attention. He smiles and kisses her fingers, a schtick of sorts that he's clearly adopted from his drag mother. And Jesus, the girl practically *swoons*, but so would I if Spencer were looking at me like that.

Achilles pokes me in the rib. "I told you Spencer was good."

I try to sound unimpressed. "He's all right."

"You're drooling."

"I am *not*."

Achilles grins and stabs their finger into my ribs again. "You like him, don't you?"

"Fuck, no." I wriggle out of Achilles' embrace. "Spencer is an asshole."

"So?" Achilles must realize I'm uncomfortable with all of their poking because they grant me the mercy of taking a small step back. "The mildly attractive and spectacularly talented ones *always* are—that's a given. But it doesn't mean that you don't have a crush on Spencer, and I'd bet my whole paycheck that you do."

I huff and turn toward the stage again, refusing to give Achilles the satisfaction of an answer. It's so fricking *obvious* that I don't like Selene, and there's nothing about her worth crushing on, though I will admit that she makes a damn good drag king, especially when she—

—Is currently *walking toward me.*

I let out a yelp and cross over the space that Achilles has placed between us.

Because apparently, Spencer Read has decided to come down off the stage, and he's carving out a path through his screaming fans that'll eventually lead him to me. Right to where Achilles and I are standing.

With a curse on the tip of their tongue, Achilles dives behind me to avoid any oncoming conflict, fully prepared to sacrifice me to our enemy, who is smirking from the realization that Achilles and I have come here specifically for him. To watch him perform and take some notes.

The song has changed to Panic! At The Disco's "Hallelujah,"

and Spencer is sauntering toward us with swaying hips and an easy, confident swagger. He rolls up the sleeves of his dress shirt, and if I thought that Spencer was a stunning king on Instagram, it's nothing compared to actually seeing him in person. His heart-shaped face has been heavily contoured to sharpen the angles of both his cheeks and jawline, and he's wearing a short black wig tonight, the strands slicked back and away from his face with a copious amount of glittery hair gel.

"Why does he look so *good*?"

Achilles peaks over my shoulder. "Do *not* let him hear you say that."

Spencer raises a pierced eyebrow as he moves to stand in front of us—in front of *me*. He's mouthing the words to "Hallelujah," something about sinners and showing praise, and I know that I've heard this song before, that it's somewhere on one of my playlists. But all I can focus on are the way his lips form perfectly around every word, like it's actually him singing and not an audio being pumped into The Gallery.

"Is this necessary?" I shout over the music, squirming uncomfortably as the crowd begins to close in around us, lured here by the king who is snatching up tips and shoving them down the front of his jeans now. His pockets look like they're ready to burst, and maybe Spencer enjoys this all-consuming attention—the kind that leaves you breathless because there's something or someone coming at you from all sides—but I don't.

It makes my skin crawl. I *hate* it. "People are staring."

Spencer gives me a wink. "You'll get used to it."

Before I can snap out some witty retort, Spencer turns abruptly on the heels of his knee-high boots, a silent way of telling me I'm no longer worth his time; I pretend not to notice the way my heart sinks from the dismissal. He's already redirected his attention, focusing on the girl who's been hopping around next to me instead, screaming her head off because she's clearly another die-hard fan. Spencer smirks as he lip-syncs the rest of "Hallelujah" to her, and he doesn't mind the way she launches herself at him when he's finished, taking the time to pose for a photo before he takes her hand and presses a kiss to the back of it. The half-drunk college girl practically melts under his affection, dissolving into a fit of high-pitched giggles as Spencer takes a bow and makes his way back toward the stage.

Achilles lets out a breath the moment that Spencer is gone, dancing across the stage to another song as he snatches up money from the crowd. "What was that about?" they ask, their eyes wide as they glance back and forth between me and Spencer. "I mean, he always comes down off the stage. He likes to interact with the crowd, but. . .you were right here and he couldn't give you any more attention?"

"I don't want his attention," I say, gritting my teeth as I reach for Achilles' hand. "But what I *do* want is to be out of this crowd and to go somewhere else where I can breathe."

Achilles takes one look at me—one long, hard, and seriously calculating look, their heavy brow furrowing with concern—and whatever it is that they see on my face, it prompts them to squeeze my fingers. "I have an idea," they shout over the music. "Do you trust me?"

I shouldn't, because I hardly know them, but it's either I go along with Achilles' plan or I stay stranded in the middle of this crowd. "I do."

They offer me a gentle smile. "Follow me, then."

Following Achilles is how we've suddenly ended up inside The Gallery's massive *freezer*, surrounded by packages of frozen hamburgers and french fries. I can already picture it now, us getting locked in here and freezing to death, our corpses purple with frostbite—my fingers are already numb, and as Achilles rummages through what looks to be a bag of ice, I shiver so hard that my teeth chatter.

"What are we doing in here?" I ask, my breath coming out in little gray puffs that hang in the air as my chest grows tight with unease. It's too cramped in here, too tight, and I can still feel the crowd pressing in on me, arms and legs and twisting shoulders and screaming girls and— "We're going to get trapped in here, Keel! What are you looking for?"

"We won't get stuck in here. I promise. The door doesn't even lock." Achilles procures what looks to be a handful of ice cubes, then nods towards the freezer door. "Out and to the right."

They don't have to tell me twice. I dive toward the door and launch the entirety of my weight at it, throwing it open and stumbling back into the heated kitchen where an assembly line of cooks are flipping burgers on a grill. Achilles steers me toward an open space in the back, where a muddy shag rug is laid out in front of a door that opens up into an alley.

"*Keel—*"

"Hold out your hands," they command softly, placing an ice cube in each of my palms the second I do as I'm told. They're no less frigid than the freezer as they melt against the heat of my skin, but Achilles closes my fingers around them anyway. "I know the ice is cold, but that's the point."

"What point?" I complain. "I can barely feel my hands."

Achilles snorts but covers my hands with their own, trying to squeeze some kind of warmth back into them. "The cold is supposed to help ground you," they explain. "It shocks your system into a reboot, so. . .focus on the ice and your breathing. You can close your eyes, if you need to."

This is the first time that Achilles has ever sounded confident in what they're saying, as if they've done this themselves and probably more than once. It's because of that confidence that I do as Achilles has instructed, closing my eyes as I focus on the ice and the way it's stinging my skin. The cold has already begun to settle in and seep down into my bones, aided by our time in The Gallery's freezer, and I can't stop the shiver that rattles its way up my spine.

I can feel it spreading throughout the rest of me, the glacial chill creeping its way up past my wrists, my arms, and my shoulders, and maybe I'm focusing just a smidge too hard because I can feel it in my chest now, too. It's like tiny little ice crystals have invaded my body and are filling up the parts of me that have decided they're going to implode, snuffing out the need for a full-on meltdown and making it a little easier to breathe.

"Where did you learn how to do this?"

Achilles lets out a breath of their own. They let my hands go, and I open my eyes to see them dragging their fingers through their hair. "I'm autistic," they tell me. "And it's really, really easy for me to feel overstimulated. Sometimes the music is too loud or the lights are too bright, and then everything all at once is too much." Achilles bites on the posts of their lip rings, as if talking about this makes them feel uncomfortable. "It's like my brain just. . .kicks into some weird overdrive and I can't shut it off, so sometimes I panic and start pacing. Or I'll cry and start pulling out my hair."

Guilt sinks deep into my chest, faster than the ice is melting in the palms of my hands. "Is that why you didn't want to go into the crowd?" I ask. "Fuck, Keel, I'm so sorry. I didn't—"

"You didn't know," they point out gently, even if that doesn't make it okay. "Enzo didn't realize either until he found me pacing in the alley. He's who taught me the trick with the ice, and it helps. Usually. I—"

"Am I interrupting something?"

Achilles and I both whirl around, the ice cubes in my hands clattering to the ground where they shatter into dozens of little pieces.

Spencer Read raises an eyebrow.

He looks so out of place in the kitchen, his wig in one hand while he fixes his real hair with the other, and it looks as if he's just run a marathon; his chest is heaving as he tries to catch his breath.

"What are you doing back here?" Achilles asks, tilting their head before smiling as if they're happy to see him. "I've never seen you in the kitchen before."

"What are *you* doing back here?" Spencer counters. "Bow's been looking everywhere for you, Briar. Why didn't you tell her you were running off to spy on me with Achilles?"

I try to shake some warmth into my hands again. "We weren't spying on you, and I did tell her. She just wasn't listening."

"Well, Bow's on next, so. . .you'd probably better go and find her. I think she's still interrogating one of the bouncers." Spencer stalks a little closer to us, enough to kick away one of the larger chunks of ice that's broken off on the floor next to my foot. "But before you go, you didn't answer my question. What are the two of you doing all cozied up back here?"

"Nothing," says Achilles, positioning themself between me and the reason we'd come back here in the first place. "Briar had a panic attack."

Something softens in Spencer's gaze, like whatever mood he'd stormed into the kitchen with has vanished. If I didn't know any better, I'd think that he might be concerned. "Are you okay?" he asks, coming closer. Achilles holds their arm up to keep enough space pressed between us. "Fuck, Bow is gonna kill me. She told me not to push your buttons, but I can't help it. It's fun." Spencer's eyes are bright with a plea as he continues, "Please don't tell Bow. She'll be so mad at me, she'll have me taken off the lineup for next weekend."

His request has me staggering back a step, and Achilles turns to face him completely. "That's all you care about?" they ask. Spencer has the nerve to look affronted. "Briar had a panic attack because of you! God, I always knew you were full of yourself, but I can't believe that you're so—so selfish now!"

Spencer blinks before his mood has visibly shifted again, his dark green eyes narrowing into a mossy glare. "Selfish? You'll take anyone's side who isn't mine, and she shouldn't have been in the crowd in the first place!" He crosses his arms over his bare, taped-up chest. "And she shouldn't be trying to do drag, either. Do you even have a stage name, Briar? Or a sponsor for the competition you signed up for?" Spencer's anger is palpable as he spits, "Do you even know how to lip-sync?"

"Well, I wouldn't want to take lessons from you," I snap at him, and I don't know why I'm even saying it. Why I'm purposely adding fuel to the fire. If Bow is going to kill anyone, it'll be me for pissing off her new bestie.

Spencer's jaw hangs open at the joints, and Achilles has slapped a hand over their own mouth. Either in horror or amusement, I'm not sure. "What is that supposed to mean?" Spencer demands. "I am a damn good lip-syncer."

"Are you, though?" I ask, and goddamn it, I know. I know I should shut my mouth, that I should stop trying to goad him into an even bigger fight. But maybe pushing his buttons is fun for me, too, even if it tempts my brother's wrath. "Also, your beard is smudged."

Spencer's hand flies to his face, as if he can feel exactly where the makeup has been smeared across the skin of his cheek. "Where?"

"Right here," I say, reaching up to poke him.

His tanned skin flushes a soft pink beneath his contour. "I really, *really* don't like you."

"Believe me, the feeling is mutual."

Before Spencer can open his mouth to retaliate—and *oh*, I can see it in his eyes, the unspoken words on the tip of his tongue that I'm sure would sting if he said them—an exhausted, unhinged Enzo appears from over his shoulder. "For fuck's sake, what are you three doing back here?" Enzo is looking at me specifically. "Your brother is worried sick, Briar. She thinks you got kidnapped and is refusing to go on stage!"

Shit.

I should have checked in with Bow, or never even left her in the first place. Scoping out Spencer and watching him perform hadn't gotten Achilles and me anywhere, and now my brother was probably feral and regretting bringing me to The Gallery.

"Calm down," Spencer intervenes. "It's my fault. Don't yell at Briar."

Achilles and I both turn to look at him, at his raised hands and easy eyes as he smiles sheepishly at Enzo. He spares a glance in our direction, taking note of the guilt on my face and continues, "I asked Keel to show her around tonight."

Enzo looks more than a little skeptical—he absolutely does not believe Spencer—but shouting erupts from somewhere beyond the kitchen and he doesn't have the time to call our bluff. "All of you—get out. Right now. Spencer, work on damage control. Briar, find your brother and calm her down before she burns this place to the ground." He pinches the bridge of his nose, and in Enzo's free hand is his fidget spinner, the blades spinning like a little fan as he grips it between his fingers. "Achilles, no more tours tonight. Your break was over twenty minutes ago."

Achilles' eyes are wide as they nod. "No more tours. Got it. Back to work. Goodnight, Briar. Text me."

I barely have the chance to raise my hand and say goodnight before Achilles is bolting from the kitchen, running as quickly as their long, thick legs will carry them, as if there's something or someone chasing them back out into the bar.

Enzo heaves a sigh as the kitchen's double doors swing shut

behind them with a bang. "I can't believe I ever wanted kids. You three are going to give me an aneurysm."

"Hey, I'm the innocent one here," Spencer says, defensive. "I was coming to find them, like Bow told me."

Enzo snorts and ushers us both from the kitchen. "You are the definition of guilty. Now shut up and tell the crowd that Bow will be on soon."

Before he heads off in search of a microphone to spout about technical difficulties, Spencer spares me a final glare behind Enzo's back. "This isn't over, baby gay. I can't wait to watch you get up on stage and *choke*."

I feel like I'm going to be sick, because I don't know how I'm ever going to make it on stage at all.

eight

*W*ho the *fuck* invented contour?

I've been sitting at Beau's vanity for the last three hours, his neon ring light blinding me as I scroll through makeup tutorials on TikTok. These other drag kings make doing this look so *easy*, but here I am with my brother's old contour stick from Sephora, smearing it across my face until I look like a freaking *road map*, not a king with a killer jawline.

"That's it," I declare, capping the stick and tossing it somewhere onto the vanity. Beau winces in the mirror from where he's laying behind me on his bed, flipping through some gardening magazine for plants that he wants to buy someday. Apparently, he's a big fan of coneflowers. "I quit. I should have kept my mouth shut to begin with. I shouldn't have tried to get involved."

Beau grunts an acknowledgement.

"Besides, why do I even *need* this?" I pick out a stained pink beauty blender from the array of makeup spread across the table in front of me. "Not all jawlines are sharp and boxy. Seriously, *why* can't I do this? It cannot be this damn hard."

He doesn't bother to respond, just shrugs and flips the page in his magazine.

I dab at my face with the beauty blender, trying to smooth out the harsh brown lines that are cutting across my skin. "I don't think my face is the right shape for this."

My brother finally cracks. "Christ, B. Stop complaining. You've literally never done this before and it takes practice." He slams his magazine shut. "Either quit or keep going, but seriously, you have to stop whining. Can't you see that I'm sulking over here?"

Beau rarely ever snaps at me, and all I want is to sink into this chair and disappear into the torn leather upholstery. I guess I have been complaining too much, and it's no wonder that Beau is annoyed with me. "Why are you sulking?"

"You mean apart from the fact that Enzo is ignoring my texts but isn't too busy to send you makeup tutorials on TikTok?"

The fact that Enzo is ignoring my brother doesn't come as a surprise, not when I'd heard them bickering late last night, just before Enzo had stormed out of the apartment and slammed the door shut behind him, forgetting I was asleep on the couch. He'd texted me this morning to apologize.

"What'd you do?"

Beau has the nerve to look offended. "Nothing!" he cries,

launching forward to sit on the edge of his bed. "Why do you just *assume* that I did something?"

"I don't know," I deadpan. "Because he's ignoring you?"

"But I didn't *do* anything!" Beau insists, his shoulders caving in around him. I turn in my chair so that I'm sitting with my chest against the back of it. "He thought I was flirting with one of my regulars at the bar last night, but I wasn't. Not really. They gave me a big tip and I thanked them for it."

I raise an eyebrow. "Thanked them how?"

"With a kiss," he says, then quickly continues when I open my mouth, "But I swear to God it didn't mean anything! It was a peck on the lips, and that was it. Innocent and consensual and Jesus, Briar, they gave me a hundred dollars."

I rest my chin on the chair. "And that was worth kissing someone who isn't Enzo?"

"When I'm short on rent this month, yes." Beau looks down at his lap. "I've already had to ask Jac for a loan. Otherwise we wouldn't even have groceries. That fucking tip meant *everything*."

My heart feels like it's going to explode from the middle of my chest and bleed out onto the floor. Beau never told me he was struggling to make his rent, and he'd never mentioned having to ask for a loan before. It doesn't make kissing some random stranger okay—not when he and Enzo have some kind of *thing* going on—but if Beau hadn't bothered with flying me all the way here, he'd probably have enough for his rent this month.

"I'm so sorry," I say. "This is all my fault."

Beau looks up at me and blinks. "What are you talking about? Of course this isn't your fault, B. Why would you say that?"

I shrug and stare at the floor, where Beau has discarded a thousand outfits and wigs. "If you hadn't wasted your money on bringing me here——"

Beau stands up faster than I've ever seen him move before, bouncing to his feet before he closes his arms around my shoulders, squeezing me tight against his chest. "Stop it," he says. "I *chose* to fly you out here. That's on me. And it wasn't a waste of my money, not when I knew you needed me." Beau presses a kiss to the top of head. "You'd have done the same for me."

"I don't have bills to pay," I remind him.

He snorts and lets me go. "I can't afford my bills because Enzo and I order out too much, not because I brought you to New York." Beau looks pointedly at the take-out containers sitting on his nightstand. "Do you know how expensive good lo mein is?"

I roll my eyes and playfully flick him in the nose. "I don't have adult money to spend on lo mein and takeout, so no, I don't know how expensive it is."

Beau snorts another laugh. "Enjoy it while it lasts, little B." I think he's going to lament more about Enzo or how much it sucks to be an adult, but he surprises me by saying, "We need to talk about it, you know. About that night." My heart skips a beat, because we most certainly do not need to talk about that.

Especially not right now, when I'm doing my best to forget it ever happened. "Do you think you could just tell me why—"

"I don't know," I say, shaking my head. It's spinning with ways to escape, and I curse Beau's apartment for its lack of easy exits.

So I do the only thing I know how to do, and get Beau talking about literally anything else.

"I'm in the middle of practicing my makeup," I remind him. "How can I fix. . .whatever it is that I did?"

Beau studies me for a moment, and I'm worried that he won't take the bait. But he takes my chin between his fingers with a sigh, and he doesn't push it any further. Not yet. "You could start by sharpening your cheekbones with the contour."

"What do you think I was trying to do?"

He winces and sits back down, folding his legs underneath him. "Maybe you should ask Jacklynn for help? She's who first put Selene in drag and helped her learn how to contour."

"Then why isn't *she* Selene's drag mother?" I ask, trying not to sound like I'm jealous that she'd gotten to Beau first—that she's my brother's drag son, and not me.

Beau waves his manicured hand in dismissal. "It's a long story. Why'd you try doing a beard with eyeshadow, anyway?"

"You were literally a makeup artist for Sephora," I complain, choosing to file away his deflection. "Why can't you help me?"

"Because I'm a drag queen. My literal job is making myself look like a woman, so I don't know how to make you look masculine." Beau points up at the ceiling. "Jac lives on the next floor up. Apartment 307. Head right down the outside hall and take the stairs on your left, turn left again when you get to the next floor, and Jac's a few doors down on the right."

Everything inside of me runs cold, like Beau has cranked the box fan across the room all the way up to its highest setting. "You're not coming with me?"

He shakes his head and flops back onto his bed, landing amongst a million decorative pillows, most of which are shaped like succulents and his favorite flowers. "I'm gonna try to call Enzo. You'll be okay, B. I promise."

"Beau, I *can't*."

Beau lifts his head up to look at me, his mouth tilted with a frown. "Yes you can—I *know* you can. There's a lot of things that you didn't think you could do before coming here."

I scoff and start gathering up Beau's makeup, stuffing it into the old leather traveling case he'd gifted me along with his expired eyeshadow palettes and contour kits. "Like what?"

"Like making friends with Achilles," he says, a stark reminder that the only friends I have are the people I've met on Ao3 from writing *Yuri!!! On Ice* fanfic. "And wandering around The Gallery without me, even though I swear to God you did not tell me you were leaving."

"I literally did, but you weren't listening."

Beau pretends not to hear me, sparing me from another lecture on how not to give him a heart attack in a gay bar. "You're entering a drag show. A *drag show*!" His grin is lopsided as he squirms around on his bed, rolling until he's lying on his stomach. "And a competitive drag show at that, just to spite a king you don't like. That takes guts, baby sister, and you never would have done it back home."

"I'm not just doing it to spite Selene," I tell him, zipping the traveling case shut. "I want to do drag, like you. Knocking her off her pedestal is just a bonus."

He snorts and grabs his gardening magazine, flipping through the pages where he's circled different plants with a pink sharpie. "I don't think you'll knock her off her pedestal," Beau says. "She's good at what she does. I don't know why the two of you can't just get along. You could really learn a lot about drag from her."

"She treats everyone around her like shit," I remind him. "And all she does is insult people."

"You have no idea what she's been through, B. Cut her some slack and get to know her."

"Whatever she's been through is not an excuse, and what I do know about her, I don't like." I stand from behind the vanity and sling the traveling case over my shoulder. "Thanks for the encouragement, though. I appreciate it."

He rolls his eyes and waves a hand at me in dismissal. "Tell Jac I said hi and I'll pay her back this weekend."

"You are the fucking *worst*."

"I know. I love you too."

nine

Jacklynn Hyde's real name is Jacqueline Roseborough, and no, I may not use her government name.

Her apartment is both bigger and significantly cleaner than Beau's. Apart from the pile of unopened mail that's sitting in a basket on her coffee table, it's almost entirely spotless. Jacklynn had given me a quick tour when I arrived, proudly showing off the guest bedroom that she's converted into a closet for her drag, her dresses and wigs impressively organized by style, length, and color.

There's an extra half-bath in the hallway, and a small dining area off to the left of her kitchen, where we're currently seated at a table beneath an open window. Jacklynn doesn't have plants sprawled across every inch of counter space—although she does have a small succulent that was likely a gift from my brother sitting in the windowsill—but there are dozens of books with cracked spines and countless dog-eared pages.

"So..." I say awkwardly, swinging my feet because they

don't touch the ground from the tall stool I'm sitting on. "You like to read?"

Jacklynn hums an acknowledgement as she weaves a braid into my dull, faded-blue hair, pulling the strands tight so it'll fit beneath the wig cap that's sitting on the table between us. "When I can find the time, I sure do."

"What genre do you read?"

"Romance, mostly. If it's gay enough." Jacklynn ties off my hair with a clear rubber band and then pats my shoulder to let me know she's finished. "Do you like to read, Miss Briar?"

I nod and turn around to face her, touching the braid with gentle fingers, afraid it might come loose if I'm not careful. "We have a library down the street from our house. Beau used to make fun of me because I'd come home with a basket full of books and then have them all read by the weekend." Jacklynn motions for me to keep talking as she stretches out the wig cap. "I like fantasy books, mostly. And graphic novels. Manga, historical, sometimes contemporary, too…Have you ever read *The Song of Achilles* by Madeline Miller? It's one of my favorites."

"Once or twice." Jacklynn gestures to the tall bookshelf behind me. "I have every special edition that's been released so far, and my original copy is beat. Now come here, and let me get this thing on you. I think it might be too small. Damn thing was meant for your brother's tiny-ass head."

I scoot to the edge of my chair and lean toward Jacklynn.

She forcefully yanks the wig cap down over my head, and it is small, but she manages to tuck the tail of my braid beneath the fabric. "Hey, Jac?" I say, wincing as she sets to work on uncovering my ears and adjusting it. She hums again. "Can I ask you something?"

Jacklynn snorts as she takes my chin, turning my head from side to side to ensure that all of my hair is covered. "Sure," she answers, stuffing a few loose strands beneath the cap. "Your brother should take a note from your book. He has no manners and likes to pry into my personal life."

I smile crookedly because it's true. "When did you start doing drag?"

It must not be the question that Jacklynn is expecting; it gives her pause as she settles into the back of her refurbished barstool. "I was young," she says, her tone soft as she admires her handiwork. "Maybe your age. Hand me your makeup case."

I do as I'm told and watch as Jacklynn rifles through Beau's expired makeup, grunting with disgust. "Did you know for a long time that it was something you wanted to do?"

She blows out a breath through her nose, and I pretend not to notice the way she glances at the picture frame that's propped in the center of the table. An unlit candle sits beside it, and the frame looks old and like it hasn't been dusted for a long, long while. Like Jacklynn is afraid to disturb it. The photograph is of a younger Jacklynn Hyde, her smile wide and cheeks dimpled as she flings her arms around the waist of another queen. A tall, sparkling crown sits on her head, neatly tucked into the center of her thickly braided wig, and Jacklynn is looking up at her like she's a woman deserving of worship.

"I think so," Jacklynn tells me, drawing my attention from the photograph. She opens up a bottle of liquid foundation, tapping it upside-down on the table to get the contents to roll toward the top. "I've been doing drag for nearly thirty years now. It's all I've ever really known, and it's hard to remember what life was like before I put on my first pair of heels." Jacklynn pours some of the foundation onto the back of her hand, then uses her fingers to start dabbing blobs of it onto my face. "But I'll tell you what I do remember, Miss Briar."

I close my eyes as she procures a beauty blender from somewhere deep in Beau's makeup case. Jacklynn uses it to even out the foundation, wetting it first with a half-empty water bottle before smearing it across the top of my cheeks, chin, and nose. "What?"

"I remember knowing that I was different." I crack open an eye to look up at her. Jacklynn's brow is furrowed deep with concentration, and I have to wonder which of the two is more difficult: telling someone she hardly knows part of her story, or trying to make me look like a boy. "When I was a child, I used to put on my mother's heels and pretend that our living room was a stage. I'd perform for her and my sisters—for anyone who would watch me, really. And then, when I got older, I would steal her makeup and experiment with it." Jacklynn sets down the beauty blender when she's finished with it; I open my eyes to find her staring at the photo. "She used to get so angry, always wondering who kept stealing her lipstick. But I think she knew who it was. Who I was. And I think that I did, too. Deep down."

Jacklynn clears her throat and turns away from the photo.

"Did she...accept you?" I ask, hoping the question isn't too personal.

She shrugs her shoulders, wiping what I think might be a tear from her eye before she begins to dig through Beau's makeup again. "She came around, in the end. We didn't speak for a few years, though." Jacklynn finds the contour stick I'd wrestled with earlier and scoffs as she checks the expiration date. "I think my being a woman was the hardest thing for her to grapple with. She couldn't let go of her son." She can't hide her sniffle as she continues, "She came to some of my shows before she passed."

I sit up straighter in my chair. "I'm so sorry, Jac. I shouldn't have asked—"

"It's all right, baby girl." Jacklynn smiles and taps me on the nose with the contour stick. It must be an intentional dab of the darker shade because she smears it thick down both sides of my nose, like she's trying to make the bridge of it appear wider. "I think you and I both know how cruel this world can be, and sometimes, it has a way of giving us a taste of what we want before the universe rips it all away again. And at that point, all we can do is keep on surviving and learn how to roll with the punches." Her expression softens into something fond and familiar. "I know my mother loved me. As best as she could and in her own way. That's what matters the most."

I tap my toes against the bronze legs of the barstool. "My parents accepted Beau right away," I tell Jacklynn. She nods as she fusses over my nose, and I wonder if Beau has ever told her about our parents. About me or Avery or how much he knows we love him. "I think they always knew what he was, too. That he was gay—that he was destined for a stage somewhere." I smile to myself, remembering the summer that our parents had scraped together enough money to send Beau away to a week-long theater camp in Dallas. "They want to come and see him perform someday, but I always show them his videos on TikTok. All his backflips and splits and handstands…they think he missed his calling as a cheerleader."

"He certainly is a flexible little bitch," Jacklynn comments, using her thumb to smooth away a bit of misplaced contour. "And what about you, Miss Briar?"

"Oh," I say. "I can't even do a cartwheel."

Jacklynn tilts her head at me, her dark eyes roving over my splotchy face from where I'd scrubbed it clean before coming here. "That isn't what I meant," she tells me. "You talk an awful

lot about your brother, but I want to know more about you. Were
your parents as accepting when you came out?"

"Oh," I say again, because no one ever really asks about me.
I've always just been Beau's little sister, or Avery's big sister, or
that girl who sits quietly in the back of the classroom and writes
fanfic instead of taking notes. I'm lucky if people remember
I even have a name. "I came out as bisexual a few years ago,
and my parents were…" I drum my fingers against my thigh,
remembering the night when we'd sat around the dinner table
and discussed what being bisexual meant for me. "Fine with it,
I guess. I don't know if they saw it coming, not like they did
with Beau. Avery was really excited, though. Our little sister. She
hugged me and asked if I was dating anyone."

"Were you?" Jacklynn asks, smearing contour around my temples.

I fight the urge to shake my head and answer, "No. I've never
dated anyone."

"That surprises me," Jacklynn says, poking me in the forehead as I raise an eyebrow. "No scrunching. This makeup is shit
and I don't want lines in your foundation. But you're a cute little
thing, Miss Briar. I would have thought you'd have boys, girls,
and everyone else beating down your door for a date." I laugh,
because it sounds so outlandish. The only boy who'd ever asked
me out had done so on a dare and then didn't show up to the
movie theater. Girls don't even look in my direction. "Beau says
you like to write."

"I do," I admit. "But it's only fanfic, and I'm not any good at it."

Pinching my chin between her fingers, Jacklynn tilts my head up as she says, "Everyone has to start somewhere, and I'll bet that you're better than you think you are. What do you write about? I think I'd like to read it sometime."

"Oh, um..." I press my lips together as Jacklynn uses the contour stick to sharpen my jawline, smudging it around the rounder lines of my face. "Nothing interesting. I've written fanfic about Loki and Tony Stark before, and I've been working on this story about *Yuri!!! On Ice*, but I haven't really touched it in a while. I've got writer's block."

"*Yuri!!! On Ice*," Jacklynn snorts. "Is that that gay anime about figure skaters that Keel keeps prattling on about?" She smooths out the contour with Beau's beauty blender, dabbing it against my skin to help blend it in with my foundation. "They keep on telling me I should watch it, but—ugh. You and your brother and these goddamn cheekbones. I know queens who've paid thousands to have a face that looks like yours."

My 'goddamn cheekbones' grow hot with a blush as she smears the contour beneath them. "You won't hurt my feelings by admitting that Beau is the prettier one. He looks just like our mom and it's hilarious, because he sounds like her, too. Same voice, same optimism, same everything."

"I wouldn't sell yourself so short," Jacklynn chides. "Because if I didn't know any better, I'd think that the two of you were twins. Like those queens who prance around on TikTok. Herb and Seasoning, or whatever their names are. They were on Drag Race."

"Sugar and Spice," I say with a grin. Beau and I know exactly who they are. We send each other their videos all the time. "Beau's still prettier than me, though."

Jacklynn frowns as she finally puts the cap on the contour stick. "Like I said before: You're a pretty little thing, Miss Briar. Why else do you think that Selene has been so flustered?"

"Because drag is her thing?" I suggest, paraphrasing her reasons for not liking me. "And I'm stupid enough to try and compete with her."

It happens so quickly that it catches me entirely off guard— Jacklynn's palm connects with the back of my head as she slaps her hand against my braided hair and wig cap. It isn't a hard hit by any means, more of a tap that I know is meant to knock some kind of sense into me, but that doesn't stop me from yelping dramatically, anyway.

"What was that for?" I complain, rubbing my fingers over the mesh fabric of the wig cap.

"Knock it off with that self-deprecating bullshit, little miss. You don't have any reason to be so goddamn hard on yourself." Jacklynn retrieves Beau's beauty blender from the mess of makeup on the table. She pats it against my cheek, my chin, my temples, smoothing the darker brown contour into sharp, masculine angles. I don't know what I'll look like when she's finished, if

I'll look like a drag king or a version of myself I don't recognize, but the spark of excitement that ignites in my chest is enough to soothe the sting of Jacklynn's scolding. "Your brother was the same way when he first got here too, you know. Always talking so bad about himself. Christ, I couldn't stand it. But you'll learn, just like he did, that I won't just sit here and let my babies insult themselves. I'd be a shitty drag mother if I did."

I grumble something about insults and speaking the truth, caught up in the flurry of Jacklynn's fussing, before I realize what it is she's just said. "Your babies?" I say, tilting my head as she rifles through Beau's makeup for eyeliner. "Are you talking about Beau and Selene?"

I know my brother's confidence can be shaky, but it's hard to imagine that the girl who parades around as Spencer Read has anything negative to say about herself. She's cocky, and arrogant, and she's full of herself, but Beau keeps insisting that I don't know her, that Selene wasn't always like this. So maybe it's just her trying to overcompensate for something.

Or maybe she's not, and Selene is truly this annoying.

Jacklynn snorts as she sharpens the stick of eyeliner she'd found stashed in the bottom of Beau's makeup case. "Selene ain't my baby. She's Beau's problem. I'm talking about you and your brother. Tilt your head up for me."

"Me?" I say, lifting my chin. "I know that Beau is your drag daughter, but I'm—I'm no one. Just his sister."

"Which makes you a part of my drag family." Jacklynn uses the eyeliner to draw thin, wispy strands of dark stubble across my chin and jawline. I squirm in my chair as she pinches my face between her fingers, holding me still, but it's hard to sit still when she's just said that I'm a part of her drag family. "Normally, I wouldn't use eyeliner for this, and I'm sure Keel could give you better advice on how to do a beard, but I just want you to see the whole picture."

I'm still reeling over being a part of her drag family; Beau hasn't even referred to me as his drag family. Not that I expect him to, of course, because he's already said he won't be doing me any special favors, but… "Hey Jac?"

She raises an eyebrow as she draws a little line above my lip. "Yes, Miss Briar?"

I curl my fingers into the dark gray fabric of my sweatpants. My palms are sweaty. Jacklynn is staring at me as if she knows what I'm about to ask, her dark eyes crinkling with encouragement as she places the eyeliner on the table. "Um…" My tongue won't form around the words. My teeth won't unclench to just speak. Jacklynn doesn't even know me. Why would I even think that I'm within my rights to ask her for any kind of favors? "A-Are you—um—do you think that—maybe—"

"It's all right, baby. Take your time." Jacklynn's smile is patient, and she reminds me so much of my mother in this moment that it makes me wish she were here, too. "I can wait here all night, if I need to. Find that confidence, Miss Briar. I know it's in there somewhere." Jacklynn pokes me in the chest, indicating the heart inside. "You just have to know where to look."

I take a breath. Loosen my shoulders. Jacklynn Hyde isn't scary, and the worst that she can say is no, get out, I hate you and your brother and I never want to see you again, how dare you—"Are you sponsoring anyone for Drag King of the Year?"

"I sure ain't," Jacklynn says, still smiling. "Why do you ask?"

"Um..." I force myself to take another breath. Let go of the death grip I have on my sweatpants. The worst she can say is no, nothing more, and nothing like my brain is defaulting to. "Do you think that—that maybe you could—um—do you think that maybe you could sponsor me?"

Jacklynn begins to pack up Beau's makeup, grinning to herself like she alone has been entrusted with the world's greatest secret. "Before you leave," she says. "Go in that drawer over there and grab the paper on top. I've already signed it. Take it with you and bring it to The Gallery on Friday. Achilles can show you where to put it."

My heart nearly stalls in my chest. "What paper? Is that—are you—are you agreeing?"

Jacklynn raises an eyebrow as she zips Beau's makeup case shut. "Of course I am. You need a sponsor, and I'm your queen. I was just waiting for you to ask."

"But—but why?" I ask, trying to ignore the salty tears burning in the corners of my eyes. "You don't even know me, and—and I shouldn't have even asked, because who the hell am I to you except Beau's stupid little sister? And—and I'm sure you don't actually have the time, and—"

"I'm agreeing to sponsor you," Jacklynn says gently, reaching for the box of tissues that are sitting in the center of her dining table. She hands them to me so I can wipe away my tears with something soft instead of the back of my hoodie sleeve. "Because I can see how much you want this, if only just to prove to yourself you can do it. Beau might have introduced you to drag, and Selene might have lit a fire under your ass, but I can feel it, Miss Briar. How special you are."

I shake my head as I dab at the corners of my eyes. "I'm not."

Jacklynn takes my hand. "You are. And you want this. And if you're willing to put in the work—to do what we need to do to get you ready for this competition—then I'm going to help you get there. I'm going to put in the work, too." Jacklynn's smile is blinding. "There's a smidge less fuel to fan your flames than I would like, but we can fix that, Miss Briar. You and me. I take being a drag mother very seriously."

There are words on the tip of my tongue. Words that are plastered to the back of my teeth because there's nothing I can say to her that will adequately describe how I'm feeling. What it's like to have someone who believes in me—someone who's not Beau or Avery or our parents. Someone who's not obligated to help me take on the world.

I'm grateful. So immeasurably grateful because Jacklynn is offering to do what Beau can't and be my sponsor.

I'm excited. So freaking excited that there's a hum starting to spread beneath my skin. A vibration that's full of adrenaline and an eagerness to get up on a stage and perform somewhere.

But then my throat tightens to the point of pain as my lungs refuse to expand, and fear is going to smother me because now this is suddenly real. I'm not just "talking out of my ass" anymore. With Jacklynn Hyde as my sponsor, I can officially compete in the competition. I can go toe-to-toe with Spencer Read and openly challenge him at something that's entirely his element, failing as I try to beat him at his own game. And I don't think that I know what's worse: losing to Selene and proving that she's the better drag king, or seeing the disappointment on Jacklynn's face when I've lost and let her down.

Jacklynn is watching me carefully, and suddenly I remember that Beau had brought me to New York City with a warning label: anxious and catastrophic when provoked. "I can see you spiraling, Miss Briar. Tell me what's on your mind."

I hook my boot beneath the barstool's footrest to stop my knee from bouncing. "I don't want to disappoint you if I lose."

She snorts, picking up an eyeshadow palette that she'd forgotten to put back in Beau's makeup case. "Lesson number one, baby girl: Do not sell yourself short. Because if you stay focused and truly put in the work, I think you have a real shot here."

Jacklynn examines the palette, with its darker reds and various shades of matte black and silver. "And don't you bother worrying about disappointing me. I just want to see you have fun and live authentically." She opens the palette to reveal a smudged little mirror. "So, what do you say? Would you like to be my son and learn how to put on a show?"

I don't have to think twice about it. Jacklynn Hyde is the perfect mentor for me. For whoever I'll become when I learn how to do drag on my own. "Maybe I should learn how to do this first," I suggest. Jacklynn shows off her teeth again. "How do I make my jawline look like it was carved out of granite?"

Jacklynn hands me the eyeshadow palette, and as she points to all of the places where I'm meant to start contouring my chin, I can't help but to stare at my reflection. At the face of the stranger staring back at me. They haven't entirely taken form yet—are still a little rough around the edges—but the stranger is unmistakably still Briar. Still me.

And maybe my brother was right: Maybe New York really is the place for me to be, because I've never been so excited in my life.

ten

The store Achilles has dragged me all the way across town for is called Fabrics Save-A-Thon. On the outside, it doesn't look like much, just a tall brick building with apartments on top and the store's name written in white on the windows. But on the inside, it's an explosion of color that reminds me of Beau's apartment. There are rolls of brightly-dyed fabric *everywhere*, either tossed haphazardly onto the rickety aisle shelves or knocked onto the floor by careless customers. Achilles picks them up as we move throughout the store.

"So," they say cheerily, fiddling with a roll of sheer, icy-blue fabric. "What kind of looks are you going for?"

My fingers are aching from how tightly I've got a grip on our shopping cart. "What are my options?" I ask. "What kind of king are *you?*"

Achilles wrinkles their nose, grumbling something about non-stretch fabric being too difficult to work with. "My drag doesn't fit neatly into any one category," they tell me, shoving the fabric roll back onto the shelf with a huff. "I like a lot of things, a lot of styles, and honestly? I get bored doing the same thing over and over again. So sometimes, my drag is super masculine, like what society says men are supposed to look like. And then sometimes, it's feminine but still male-presenting, like when Billy Porter wears a skirt with a tux on the red carpet." Achilles smiles over the cart at me. "Gender is a construct, you know? And what I love about drag is that I get to be whatever I want, and almost always without judgment. Does that make sense?"

"Sure," I say. "But who's Billy Porter?"

It's almost as if my words have physically struck them with the way Achilles gasps. "You don't know who Billy Porter is? Haven't you ever watched *Pose*?"

I bite at my bottom lip, hoping that I've not somehow offended them. Especially since Achilles is my only way home to Beau's apartment. "I've never heard of it."

"Oh, you poor unfortunate soul." Achilles wraps their arm around my shoulders, consoling me as if I'm devastated over not knowing who this celebrity is. "Listen. I'm off this weekend because Enzo is training a new barback, and a couple of my roommates are going out of town for some festival. You should totally come over to my place and we can binge-watch *Pose*. You'll love it."

The last time I'd been invited to spend the night at someone's house had been all the way back in the fourth grade, when Adelaide Bennett's mother had invited me to Adelaide's birthday party. It was mostly out of pity, I know now, because when I'd stopped fitting in with Adelaide's new friends from her fancy private school across town, she and I had called it quits on our friendship. But Adelaide lived next door to us, and her mother had once caught me staring from our front porch as Adelaide and her better-than-Briar friends went biking around the block together without me.

At her birthday party, Adelaide and her friends hadn't exactly been welcoming, and later in the night after she'd opened up all of her presents, we'd sat around the firepit in Adelaide's backyard eating s'mores and telling scary stories. They'd purposely tried to scare me away, and they'd succeeded after only a couple of hours. Apparently, there was a man who lived in the woods behind our houses, one who killed little blond girls that only looked like me, and Adelaide's mom had needed to call mine because I'd run into the house, screaming and terrified.

Mom had sent Beau to come and get me, citing the need for vengeance because Beau was still young enough to get back at them; he'd stuck our old gardening hose through the slats in our fence on her orders, spraying them down until they were soaked. This time, when Adelaide's mother had called mine, it was our dad who had answered the phone, assuring Mrs. Bennett that my brother would be punished for ruining Adelaide's party.

He'd taken us both out for ice cream, and Beau had been hailed a hero.

"I'll talk to Beau when I get home," I tell Achilles, who hums an acknowledgement while prodding at a roll of glittery purple fabric. They pinch it between their fingers, tug at the edges to see how well it stretches, and I wonder if they'll share with me how to weed out unfavorable fabrics. "He likes when I come to his shows. I think I'm an excuse for him to show off."

Achilles yanks the roll of fabric off the shelf and tosses it into the cart with a small, satisfied smile, as they've secretly found the gem that was hidden somewhere deep inside the sea of color we're surrounded by. "She *has* been a little extra on stage. Every time she does a backflip, Enzo literally grabs his chest like he's going to have a heart attack."

I push our cart into the next aisle, where the rolls of fabric are shades of black and teeming with cute designs. Naturally, I'm drawn to the one with little stacks of books on it. "Have you talked to him lately?" I ask, checking the price tag on the fabric. "Enzo, I mean. Is he doing okay? He and Beau aren't speaking right now, and to be honest, I sorta-kinda miss him."

Texting with Enzo hasn't felt right since he's still not responding to my brother, but I've really missed having someone to talk to who doesn't just talk about drag all the time. And talking about drag is fine—I don't resent Beau for letting it dominate our conversations, and I haven't minded Jacklynn and her endless lessons about drag. But at least with Enzo, he talks about more, like his favorite movies, his childhood in Puerto Rico, and alien conspiracy theories he finds interesting on TikTok. Still having Avery to talk to has been nice, and Mom and Dad have been chattier than usual during our twice-weekly phone calls where they're checking to make sure I'm still alive, but I really miss the no obligation, "can reply whenever I want and the world doesn't assume I'm dead" ease of texting Enzo.

I wish he and Beau would make up already.

"Enzo is hard not to miss." Achilles shoos me away from the fabric I'm looking at to examine it themself, then gives me a nod of approval. "He's like...madly in love with your brother, but Beau is *really* good at hurting him. I hate it."

I yank the fabric roll from off the shelf and stuff it down into the shopping cart. I don't know what I'm going to do with it yet, but Jacklynn had loaned me a hundred dollars to get enough fabric to fashion a couple of costumes. I'm sure there's *something* I can do with it. "Has this happened before?" I ask. "The whole 'Beau hurting Enzo' thing. Because I don't like it either, and I *know* that Beau likes him, too. I've seen it."

Achilles unravels a roll of shimmery fabric fashioned to look like a spiderweb. They wrap around their shoulders and try to pose with it, a hand to their forehead as they dramatically lean back and close their eyes. "All the time," they say, grinning as I retrieve my phone from the pocket of my hoodie to take a picture of them. In the notification bar is a text message from Dad, telling me to be careful while I'm out today. "It's like every time that Enzo thinks they're on the verge of a real relationship, Beau does something stupid to fuck it up. And it makes me so frickin' mad because Enzo is amazing and he doesn't deserve all this heartbreak."

They're right, of course. Enzo doesn't deserve the way Beau treats him, but that doesn't stop me from raising an eyebrow at Achilles. The way they talk about the bartender, the way their cheeks flush whenever he's around…I can't help but to smirk and poke them playfully in the arm. "You have a crush on Enzo, don't you?"

I half-expect them to deny it, to be flustered and red-faced as they answer me. But instead, Achilles stands up a little taller, their thicker frame towering over me as they lift their chin and say with a shaky sort of confidence, "Who doesn't have a crush on Enzo? He's sweet, and he's kind, and if he wasn't so in love with the guy who keeps on hurting him…maybe we would actually have a chance."

"Have you talked to Enzo?" I ask curiously. "Does he know you like him?"

Achilles nods a bit grimly. "I blurted it out at work after he tried to calm me down during a panic attack. He looked mortified, but he let me down easy." They bite on the back of their lip rings. "You're not upset, are you? That I like Enzo?"

I frown and shake my head. "Of course not. Beau doesn't own the right to liking Enzo. I just wish he would treat him better, or cut him loose instead of stringing him along if he's never going to commit to him."

"Ugh. Same." Achilles leans against the shopping cart. "I can respect that Enzo is in love with him, but like…that hasn't stopped me from being irritated with Beau." They pause to add, "No offense. I know he's your brother."

"None taken," I say, because I'm still irritated with him, too. But at least Enzo has Achilles, however close they might be, to help him nurse his broken heart and whatever pieces of it my brother has left intact. "You're…a really good friend, Keel. I don't know if anyone has ever told you that. But you are." And I don't deserve you. "I'm sorry if—if maybe you had other things to do today. I don't know what your work schedule looks like, or if you're taking summer classes, or if—"

Achilles places their hand on my shoulder, smiling gently. "I don't have anywhere else to be today. Only here. Don't worry." They give me a squeeze before popping off the edge of the cart. I watch as they twirl across the aisle, skimming through fabric rolls before pulling a silvery one off the shelf. It's covered in little stars and crescent moons. "Enough about first loves and heartbreak. Tell me what kind of king you want to be. The persona you want to embody while in drag."

It's as loaded a question as any, and the pressure for an answer both solid in its concept and equally as impressive is astronomical. It manifests like a pit inside my stomach. Given what I know about Achilles' drag—and Selene's, but I don't want to think about her—I have an idea as to who I want to be. Who the stranger was in that mirror when Jacklynn had held it up for me.

I've always been afraid to be that person. To step into their shoes and live as authentically as Beau does. Because sure, I want to do drag. I want to be somebody else. But the line between pretending and who I really am starts to blur whenever I think about that stranger. That face. That part of myself that I've never explored because drag was always Beau's thing and not mine.

"I want to be someone more...androgynous," I tell Achilles, drumming my fingers against the shopping cart. They nod their head encouragingly. "I don't necessarily want to look super masculine, but I also really want to confuse people. Does that make any sense?" I pluck at a nearby fabric roll. "I don't want anyone to know what my gender is just by looking at me."

Achilles tilts their head at me. "Do you want to use they/them pronouns in drag?"

I bite at the inside of my cheek. "Maybe someday."

Maybe out of drag.

Not today, though.

I'm not ready to explore that part of myself. Who 'Briar' might be if I could just stay in New York with my brother.

"All right," Achilles says, still smiling. "So your aesthetic is what we call 'genderfuck,' which is sort of like gender-nonconforming. We can work with that!" They accidentally knock over a roll of sheer fabric and scramble to pick it up. "What kind of vibe are you going for? Goth, punk, anime? I do a lot of cosplay myself, and I do a lot of different takes on popular characters. It runs in my drag family, too! My drag mother, Rita Book, has performed on stage as Pikachu and has lip-synced to the Pokémon theme song."

As someone who used to write fanfic about Ash and Brock, and as cool as I think that sounds, I cannot imagine myself dressing up as a Charizard and stomping around to "Gotta Catch 'Em All." But I don't dare tell Achilles that. "I'm a punk at heart," I say instead, gesturing to the front of the faded Blink-182 shirt I'm wearing. "There are plenty more where this came from, and I own a fuck-ton of beanies. I think I should stick with what I know."

"Sure, that's fine!" Achilles says. "Are you a fan of flannels and old jean jackets?"

I nod as we round the corner into another aisle, this one containing faux leather fabrics that Achilles scrunches up their nose at. "My entire wardrobe is made of up flannels, and I used to wear jean jackets all the time, but none of the ones I have still fit me."

"Okay, so, hear me out." Achilles shoos me around the next corner, and we suddenly find ourselves in a sea of colorful sequins.

"It's really hard to make clothes from scratch, especially if you're doing drag on a budget and don't have the material to waste. I still have all of your measurements, so technically we could print off patterns and trace them onto fabric in your size, but unless you know how to sew and tailor things to fit your body..." Achilles offers me a sheepish smile. "Obviously Jac and I can teach you, but really, when you're first starting out, it's easier to take something that's already been made and deconstruct it. It'll help you learn exactly how pieces fit together, and learning how to sew is a piece of cake when there are already marks in the fabric."

"What do you mean by deconstruct?" I ask, taking an interest in a fabric with sequins that change from red to black when you run your fingers against it.

Achilles turns to me and tugs on the sleeve of their hoodie. "I used to cut off the sleeves of all my jackets, then sew new ones on in a different fabric. It was a process, but I learned how to make sleeves. Then I'd cut the hoods off and make new ones. I know that Spencer likes to laugh about it, but I *do* get a lot of my drag from thrift stores because like...*why* would I want to pay a bunch of money for something that I'm gonna tear apart?"

"That...is actually kind of genius, Keel."

Their cheeks darken with a bashful blush as they pull a roll of green fabric off the shelf. "Thanks. I do my best. But what I'm trying to say is—if you don't want to decimate the clothes you brought with you from home, there's a massive thrift store right around the corner that we can go to. Anything you can imagine, they have it. *Oh!* I could teach you how to stud things. That always adds a bit of extra flair, especially if you're going for a punk look."

I watch as Achilles continues to browse through the fabric. "Keel, can I ask you a question?"

They turn to look up at me through wide, gray-blue eyes, blinking as if I've caught them off guard. "Yeah, sure. Go ahead."

"How come you're helping me?" I ask. Achilles furrows their brow. "As soon as I said that I was going to do drag, Selene was immediately my enemy. But not you."

They don't even have to consider their response. It's immediate.

"Not me," Achilles repeats. "Because I really, truly love drag. It helps with my gender dysphoria, and it's helped me learn how not to hate myself." They lean against the edge of the cart again, their hooded gaze dropping to stare at the colorful fabrics inside. "But I'm not going to lie to you, Briar. Everything in my life is shit. A giant pile of steaming shit that I haven't been able to figure my way out of yet." Achilles drags a hand over their wavy, blond hair. "I have seven roommates just so that I can afford my apartment, and it's always so loud in there that I can't even hear myself think. It's—it's so fucking triggering, you know? I'm constantly overstimulated. That's one of the reasons winning Drag King of the Year means so much to me. The cash prize and a headlining spot might mean I could move out on my own eventually."

I realize I've been holding my breath. "Jesus, Keel, I'm—"

They shake their head and continue in a softer tone, "Drag is my escape from that place. From that shit. Even if just for a little while." Achilles sighs heavily and looks up at me again, their mouth curved with a weak smile that doesn't reach their eyes. "Achilles Patrick has saved my life in more ways than one. More times than I can count."

Everything inside of me cracks open wide as my heart breaks in two for Achilles. It's enough to make me want to shatter things. To go to their apartment and scream at their roommates to be quiet. But it's that very same heartbreak that thuds to life inside of me, too, and I lower my chin until it's practically touching my chest. "Do you think drag could save me, too?"

Achilles rests a hand on my shoulder again, as gentle as if I were glass. "I do," they say. "Which is exactly why I'm helping you. Beau told me about what happened before you came here. How you'd locked yourself in the bathroom and told your parents that you wanted to—" They wince as they cut themself off, like they can't bring themselves to say the words. "That was a bad night at The Gallery."

I sniff, squeezing the shopping cart in a white-knuckled grip until my fingers hurt. "Beau missed a performance that night, didn't he? So that he could be on FaceTime with me."

They nod, carefully prying my hands off the cart, smoothing out my fingers and gently massaging my palm. "I've never seen anyone so worried before," Achilles tells me. "Spencer and Enzo had to both walk him home so he could call you, and Spencer filled in for him on stage that night. He even gave Beau all of his tip money."

"Seriously?" I ask, not trying to hide my surprise. "So Selene isn't always an asshole?"

"No," Achilles says, looking away again. "Not when she actually likes you."

We continue to make our way around the store, Achilles picking out enough fabric to clothe a small army of drag kings. Most of it is material for themselves since they know how to sew, and the rest of it was on clearance so that I can start from the beginning and learn how to make sleeves with something cheap. But it's as an employee is cutting all of the fabric into several yards that Achilles, fidgeting with their hands while we wait, leans in close to me and whispers softly, "Are you going to be okay?"

No, I want to tell Achilles, because there's a part of me that's angry that my brother has told everyone what happened on the night he'd missed that show. It was nobody's business but mine—no one else's story to share but mine—and yet Achilles still knows what I confessed to our parents from behind a locked bathroom door.

That I had told them I wanted to die.

That there was nothing they could do to try and stop me.

That I was going to kill myself because everyone would be better off without me.

But then our father had called Beau right before he'd gone on stage, and he'd answered. Eager to perform and happily half-drunk, he'd answered. And as soon as I opened the bathroom door, coaxed from the room by the tears in my brother's voice, Dad had shoved the phone into my hands. Had sobbed and begged Beau to stop me. To save his little sister because he and our mother just couldn't. Because they didn't know what else to do.

Beau had been crying then, too, his makeup smeared and running down his face because goddamn it, Briar, his eyeliner wasn't waterproof.

And then we'd made the plans for me to come here. To spend the summer in New York because maybe it would give me something to look forward to. Beau had made all of the arrangements. He'd booked the flights, bought pillows and a blanket for the futon, and he'd told all of his friends that I was coming. How long I'd be here. What the circumstances were.

Because maybe he'd needed them in the same way that I had needed him.

I let out a breath before looking at Achilles with a smile. "I'll be fine," I answer them just as quietly. "Do you think that we can carry all of this into the thrift store?"

Achilles blinks as if the thought hadn't actually occurred to them. "Where exactly have you been all my life? It's like I already need you to function." They heave a sigh and lean against the back of the shopping cart. "Looks like we're gonna need to hail a cab. I hate cabs. But I refuse to lug all of this fabric onto the subway. I wouldn't dare put my new bestie through that torture."

An actual smile tugs at the corners of my mouth. "Bestie?" I say. "I've never really had a bestie before."

"Me neither," Achilles says, hoisting a fabric roll up onto the counter to be cut. "At least, not for a long time. Turns out, they weren't much of a friend after all. But you're different, B. I know you are. And I'm glad to have you around."

"I'm glad to be around," I tell them, and I mean it.

eleven

"*C*ome the fuck *on* already!" Beau cries, slamming his phone onto the weird little chess table between us. I jump and nearly spill my iced coffee: a cupcake-flavored frappe with whipped cream and sprinkles that Beau had recommended from his favorite coffee shop. "It's been two weeks and I keep on telling him that I'm sorry—I cannot fucking believe he's still mad at me!"

"And *I* can't fucking believe we're still talking about this." I glare at Beau from where I'm sitting next to him at the table. We're meant to be exploring Central Park right now, but so far all we've done is sit here so that Beau can argue with Enzo. "You can't just kiss someone else and expect the guy you're seeing to be okay with it."

Beau purses his mauve-painted lips at me. "Why do you keep taking Enzo's side in this?"

Speaking of the thing that I can't believe we're still talking about, my phone vibrates with a text from Enzo.

Enzo Santiago: watch this video when you get a chance because I swear to god you're Korra

Enzo Santiago: KORRASAMI BEING BI ICONS FOR 5 MINUTES STRAIGHT

Briar Vincent: Text my brother back when YOU get a chance.

Briar Vincent: He's driving me insane because he misses you.

Briar Vincent: We're supposed to be having fun in Central Park right now.

Enzo Santiago: 😳 😳 😳

I place my phone face down on the table. Beau's shoulders are tense as he stares at me.

"I'm not taking anyone's *side* in this," I say, stirring my iced coffee to mix in some of the whipped cream. "But expecting him to forgive you is a dick move when you're the one who's in the wrong here. Enzo didn't do anything to hurt you, Beau."

"So you *are* on his side!" he accuses, leaning in closer to me to point his finger in my face. I slap it away with my cup. "I can kiss whoever I damn well please. Enzo and I aren't even in a relationship!"

"And whose fault is that?" I remind him, crossing my arms as I slouch into the back of my seat. "Enzo loves you, but you keep stringing him along and it's not fair. If you *don't* want to commit to him, that's fine. But at least cut him loose so that Enzo can move on and get over you."

There's something in the way his bottom lip trembles that tells me this thought has never occurred to him. He slouches over the width of the table, an air of defeat sitting heavily on his shoulders, and in a weirdly unlike-Beau silence, he stares, and stares, and *stares* at me, all without trying to defend himself. It's like a light has gone out somewhere inside him, a mental switch flipping off in his brain that's dulled him out around the edges, and I wonder if maybe I'd been too hard on him.

But then Beau blinks and there are tears in his eyes, and my stomach clenches with guilt. "You really don't get it, do you?" he asks, sniffing through the crack in his voice. "I am so fucking in love with him that it *hurts*, B. Is that what you were wanting to hear?"

He doesn't give me the chance to actually answer him, and God, I'm such a piece of shit.

"But the last time I loved someone, they left me," he says. "Then they died still thinking that I was too much and too gay to love back. And I *know* you don't know what that feels like. Loving Enzo scares the shit out of me."

I dive across the table for his hand—Beau offers it without me having to ask. "You are *not* too much of anything, Beau. And Enzo is not like Connor." I squeeze his fingers as he drops his chin to his chest, choking back a fresh round of tears. "Fuck him for ever making you feel like this. Have you told Enzo about him?"

He shakes his head and stares longingly at his phone, waiting for the screen to light up with a message from Enzo. "No, because I was afraid he would think the same thing."

"Obviously, I don't know him as well as you do," I say softly. "But I *know* that Enzo doesn't think that. He loves you and your drag and how eccentric you are, and he'd love that you love him, too."

A tear rolls down my brother's cheek, carving out a path through his makeup. "So what you're saying is that I should tell him about my trauma. Great. Because guys totally dig that."

I use a napkin to wipe away the tear from Beau's face. "I *think* you should probably start with 'I'm sorry and I'm so fucking in love with you,' then tell him about your trauma when he—"

"Holy shit! *Why are you crying?*"

I've already learned how to tune out the raspiness of her voice, so it takes me a moment to realize that Selene has joined us. That she's appeared from somewhere around the nearby fountain to wedge herself between me and Beau. "Are you okay? Do I need to kick someone's ass? Point me in their direction and I'll—"

"What are you doing here?" I ask tersely, scooting my chair away to make room for her to kneel next to Beau. She replaces my hand with her own ring-clad fingers, holding him tight as she chooses to pretend I don't exist. "Beau Christopher, what is Selene doing here?"

He sniffles and looks up at me with a grimace. "I invited her."

I sink into the back of my chair again. Of *course* he invited Selene, his knockoff little sister who is...not being harsh with him, like I was. How Avery wouldn't have been if she were here. Instead, Selene is looking at him with genuine concern shining in her dark green eyes, and I wonder if she meant it when she said she would kick someone's ass for him.

But right now, that ass would be mine, since I'm the one who made him cry.

"You brought me here for a tour and invited her along without telling me?" I ask, trying to speak gently so as not to upset him further. And to avoid provoking Selene's wrath. "I wouldn't have cared, if you'd just told me."

Selene looks over her shoulder at me, like she's prepared to call me on my bullshit. "He didn't tell me you'd be here either, you know. Otherwise, I probably wouldn't have come. I thought I was supposed to be taking new headshots for him." She picks up the camera that's dangling around her neck and shows it to me. "So don't get shitty with me because your brother played us both."

Beau sniffles as he stares between the two of us. "I'm sorry, I just—I thought that if two of you could meet on neutral ground, maybe you could actually get to know each other. And then maybe, you would stop being so hostile." He rubs at his eyes with the back of his hand and sighs. "I love both of you so much, but I hate that you guys don't like each other."

I open my mouth to tell him that this wasn't his place, that Selene and I don't have to be friendly, but as soon as Beau's phone buzzes on the chessboard table, he dives so fast for it that he knocks Selene out of his way.

She careens backward and into my knees with a shout, flailing her arms before she gets a grip on her camera. "Jesus Christ, Beau!" she cries, staggering to her feet before deciding that she's going perch on my knee, sitting there delicately atop my leg as she clutches her camera to her chest. "Do you know how expensive this is?" she asks, meanwhile I am trying my goddamn hardest not to think about the heat of her body. About her shoulder as it presses into mine. About her breath as it tickles my cheek, minty and warm as she assesses her camera for damages. "You could have broken it!"

"Enzo texted me," Beau breathed, like they haven't been arguing all morning.

"Good for you," I grumble, then poke Selene in the spine. She yelps. "*Get off of me.*"

Selene does as she's told but isn't happy about it. "Your knee is boney, anyway."

"Your ass is boney," I shoot back. Selene has the nerve to look affronted as she spins in a circle to try and observe her own backside. "What'd he say, Beau?"

He's typing out a response to Enzo, his thumbs moving so quickly across the screen that I wonder how many typos he's ignoring right now. "I have to go," he says suddenly, his voice pitched high in desperation. Beau jumps out of his chair and

snatches up the pair of shiny pink sunglasses he'd abandoned on
the table when we arrived, stuffing them into the front pocket
of his shorts. He stumbles around Selene and me to leave, nearly
knocking us both over on the way. "He wants to talk. Right now.
I have to go to him."

I leap out of my chair, too, reaching for Beau's arm to haul
him back from where he's already turned to abandon me. "Tell
him that you have to take me home first."

Beau shakes his head and wretches himself free from my
grip. "Enzo lives on the other side of town, and he wants to talk
right now. Here." He reaches into his back pocket and tosses me
a set of keys. "Have Selene take you home and you can let yourself in. Or, you know...maybe you could show her around Central
Park?" He leans around me to look at Selene with raised eyebrows. "Please? I promised her a day out."

It is clear on Selene's face that she wants to tell him no, that
she has other plans and things to do today. But my brother is
full-on pouting now, his bottom lip puffy and puckered. Selene
glances at me with a groan. "*Fine.* But only because I love you."

Beau sighs with relief before staring down at me for the final
say, satisfied already with Selene's answer. He's going to leave me
with her regardless, it's just a matter of how long I'll be stuck
with her. "Please, Briar?"

The smell of freshly cut grass tickles my nose as I draw in a
breath and hold it. I should tell him that Enzo has only texted

him because I asked him to. But I don't have the heart because I know how much this means to my brother. How badly he wants a second chance.

So I curl my fingers into fists, refusing to admit to him how terrified I am to be alone in a new city without my brother. I could get mugged, or murdered, or taken hostage. I could get hit by a car, or a tour bus, or get arrested for a crime I didn't commit. I could be in the wrong place at the wrong time, or have any number of horrible things happen to me because New York is so absolutely *terrifying*.

But if this is his chance to make things right with Enzo, after everything that Beau has done for me...I can tolerate Selene for a couple of hours, assuming she doesn't plan on taking me to the nearest skyscraper just to throw me off it.

"Come on, angel face. Don't look so pained," Selene says, and I feel my cheeks grow warm with a blush. "If you're going to experience New York, it should be with a true New Yorker. Beau only knows *some* of the cool places here."

"It's a park," I point out glumly. "How many cool places can there be?"

"I'm going to pretend you didn't say that," Selene says, turning to smile up at Beau. "I'll keep her safe, don't worry. Text me when you're headed home and I'll bring her back in one piece. Promise."

Beau stares at me with a hint of desperation. "B?"

"Yeah, all right." I try my best to smile at him, too. I know he sees right through it, but the relief in his eyes is well worth the pain of spending the afternoon with Selene. "Just tell him how you feel, okay? Tell him about Connor and what scares you. He'll understand."

Selene's face scrunches with confusion, and I wonder if this is something he's never told her. But then— "You're *finally* gonna tell Enzo that you're in love with him? Holy shit, dude. Congrats."

I try not to let it sting that she knew about Beau being in love with Enzo before I did.

Beau steels himself with an expression of weirdly fierce determination, though it's a little rough around the edges. He'll crack if Enzo doesn't forgive him. "I can do this."

We both give Beau a thumbs-up for encouragement. "You can do this."

Beau is gone within seconds, weaving through the masses of sightseeing tourists and back out the way we'd come in, all the while squinting at his phone. Just before he disappears completely, I see him hold it up to his ear, probably calling Enzo to let him know that he's on his way.

I hope they both get what they need from each other.

But without him, an awkward silence settles between me and Selene, and I have never been more determined about anything else in my life—I will *not* be the one who breaks the quiet. So instead of striking up a conversation, I stand there and sip from what's left of my iced coffee, watching as Selene fiddles with the neck strap on her camera. She's wearing a pair of checkered Converse that, strangely enough, perfectly match her camo-print skinny jeans and black crop top. Her hair, recently buzzed shorter on one side, has been curled with a curling iron to delicately frame her stupidly pretty face.

I try not to stare too hard at her, glancing back and forth between her heavy black eyeliner and the thin, intricately designed underboob tattoo that's peeking out from beneath her crop top. My cheeks flush with shame as I wonder what the rest of it looks like, but the last thing I need is for Selene to catch me staring and to think that I actually like her.

"So," Selene says eventually. I turn my head away as she looks at me. "How much of the park have you seen so far?"

"Not much. Just what we saw coming in." I drain the rest of my coffee and toss it into a nearby trash bin. "Beau was too pre-occupied with Enzo."

"Shocker," Selene scoffs. "All right, so...I can show you the Bethesda Terrace, if you want. There's a massive fountain that sits right next to a lake, and it's actually pretty gorgeous, if you ask me. Um. There's some hiking trails, a few gardens, the Belvedere Castle...Do you like animals? There's a zoo."

I chew on the inside of my cheek, trying not to think about the dozens of ways today can go horribly wrong. As fun as the places she's suggested sound, I can't help but to wonder how busy they are. How many people might be lurking around hidden corners. I'm not even from here and I know how dangerous this city is, especially for people like me.

"Is there anywhere...quieter?" I ask, tugging at my hair and twisting a lock of it around my index finger. "Somewhere a lot of people don't go?"

Selene nods with a surprisingly easy smile, and if she knows that I'm asking to go somewhere quiet because I'm an anxious piece of shit who's afraid of people, well...she certainly knows better than to open her mouth and say so. "Shakespeare Garden is pretty low-key, and you can see Belvedere Castle from the walkways. Most people don't even realize it's there, especially tourists. It's a bit of a trek, if you're up for it."

"Why is it called Shakespeare Garden?" I ask, falling in line next to her as Selene takes the lead and guides us to the nearest pathway. "He's not my favorite playwright in the world, but I've read a lot of his work."

Selene raises an eyebrow as she nudges me to take a left. "You read plays...for *fun*?"

"What's wrong with that?" I ask. "I like to read."

She holds up her hands as if to fend me off, her silver rings gaudy and glinting in the sunlight. "Nothing. I just don't know many people who read plays, that's all. Who is your favorite, if not Shakespeare?"

I shrug my shoulders as we round down a pathway that's

curved and leads to a bridge. It's beautifully quaint with dark wooden panels that stretch across glistening blue water, and Selene pauses to lean over the reinforced banister. She closes her eyes as she draws in a deep breath of air, sunlight shining on her highlighted cheeks, and all I can do is stand and stare at her.

"Plays aren't really my thing," I tell her, distracted by the way that her mouth has turned up with a smile. "I just wanted to see what made him so special. Which is nothing, by the way. He's overrated."

Selene snorts as she flicks on her camera. She squints through the viewfinder as she snaps a quick photo of the ducks swimming on the lake. "I don't like him, either. Hamlet was boring as shit."

I nod, but Selene isn't looking at me. Not like I'm looking at her. "I like the classics, like *Frankenstein*, but—"

"Mary Shelley, right?" Selene studies the picture on her camera screen. "Isn't she the one who had sex on her mother's grave?"

"Yeah, actually. She's the one."

Selene's smile is wry as she looks at me and turns off her camera again. "I like everything horror I can get my hands on, so I read *Frankenstein* when I was like…eight."

"That explains *so* much."

She playfully slaps her hand against my shoulder. "Don't be a dick. I'm only just starting not to hate you." Selene winks at me as she hooks her arm through my elbow, pulling me the rest of the way across the bridge. In a short-sleeved T-shirt instead of my usual hoodie, I try not to think about the warmth of Selene's skin against mine. About the pumpkin tattoo that's on her forearm, rich with color and with a date inked in black underneath it. "Beau did mention that you like to read, though. I told him he should take you to the library. It's frickin' massive—you would *love* it. We can go today, if you want? I have an old library card and some time to kill."

The random act of kindness comes as a surprise I'm not prepared for. "I...thank you," I say. "I still have some books I brought from home, but I read really fast, so I'm sure I'll need a library soon. How far is it from here?"

"Well, it depends on which one you want," Selene tells me. "The main library is literally a work of art, and sometimes I go there to stare at the walls and take pictures."

This doesn't come as a surprise, not with the camera hanging around her neck. But I wonder what kind of photography she might be into, if she likes shooting landscapes or taking portraits of people.

"I used to go there all the time with my ex-girlfriend, but—but I haven't been there in a while." Selene purses her lips as she purposely turns her head away from me, like she hadn't wanted to bring up her ex. "It's about fifteen minutes from here by subway, but I'm not sure you'd find what you're looking for. Not unless you like to do research." Her smile has returned, more discreetly, like she already knows that that's not what I'd be looking for in a library. "What do you like to read, anyway? You never actually told me."

My stomach does a backflip inside of me. It feels weird to tell Selene that I mostly read manga and graphic novels. She'll probably think I'm weird for still reading books with pictures, and that sometimes what I read needs to be read from back to front. "A little bit of everything," I deflect. Selene raises a red eyebrow at me. "Some fantasy, some sci-fi. You know. Anything that sounds good."

"Huh. Aren't you a super huge anime nerd?" Selene inquires. "I'm surprised that you don't read manga."

"Who told you that?" I demand, panic creeping into me for literally *no* fucking reason. My palms begin to sweat as I squeeze my hands into fists, and if there were ever a race for the human heart to lodge itself into someone's throat, mine would be the goddamn winner. "Was it Beau? I swear he can't keep anything to himself!"

Selene catches her bottom lip between her teeth, and I notice the marks from where she's chosen to not wear her lip rings today. "Don't be mad at Beau. It wasn't him. I…kind of…sorta… *maybe* looked at your Instagram." At my horror, she quickly continues, "I was curious! You literally came to New York and said 'fuck Spencer Read' and I *had* to know something more about you. Beau never really told me any of the good stuff."

I haven't posted on Instagram in so long that I don't even

remember what's on there. Some older photos of Beau and me, sure, and probably a few with Avery. But what did I post that would have told Selene I like anime? I guess the possibilities are endless, and short of whipping out my phone to go and look for myself, Selene could have found *anything* on there to laugh about.

"You posted a picture of Viktor and Yuri from *Yuri!!! On Ice*," Selene tells me. "And were complaining that there wasn't a second season. You…also posted the link to your fan fiction account, and since I've never actually watched the show before, I…I might have read some of your stories. Which are good, by the way. You should update them. That last cliffhanger was torture."

It's like I can feel myself melt into a puddle of embarrassment, sweat starting to gather against the nape of my neck from where I've left my hair down. "Oh, my God," I lament. I stop in the middle of the walkway, burying my face into the palms of my hands to try and hide my embarrassment. Selene crowds around me to protect me from the prying eyes of onlookers, murmuring to other visitors that she's sorry we've stopped right in front of them. "I cannot believe you read my fanfics!" I say, my voice rising an entire octave. "Ugh. Why would you do that? Now I have to go and delete my Ao3 account!"

"No!" Selene says, and if I didn't know any better, I'd say that it sounds as if she's on the verge of laughter. She tugs at my hands to pry them away from my face, her fingers slipping around my wrists in warm, gentle vises. "Please don't delete your account. I liked reading your stories. You're really, really good at it. Writing, I mean. You're good." She smiles as I peek at her between my fingers. "I think you should keep on writing. I want to know what happens next, especially in that AU you did where Yuri and Yurio own rival bakeries."

It's official—I'm gonna die. Right here. In the middle of Central Park with Selene as my witness, I am going to die of embarrassment. "You don't mean that," I wail dramatically, vaguely aware that Selene has wrapped her arms around me, that she's hugging me to her chest as she giggles gleefully into my ear. "Why did seventeen-year-old Briar have to be such a nerd?"

"Didn't you *just* turn eighteen?" Selene points out. "I think you're probably still a nerd. But that's okay! I like nerds. Especially cute ones who watch anime and write fanfics."

I wriggle out of her arms. "Just take me to the garden so that I can die there quietly in peace."

Selene snorts and loops her arm through my elbow again. "If you want, I can send you off Viking-style? There are places to rent boats around the lake, and I've actually shot a bow, once or twice. Never with a flaming arrow, but...I'm versatile. I could learn."

"No way," I tell her. "Because if you accidentally shoot a duck while trying to light my corpse on fire, I'd have to come back here and haunt you for it."

She gives me a wink and nudges me further down the walk-way. "I wouldn't mind."

At the end of our current path sits a beautifully tall castle that must be the one Selene mentioned earlier. There's a landing near the top where a crowd has gathered in their finery, and I realize as we walk by there's a wedding taking place; an officiant announces that the groom can kiss the groom, and cheering erupts from the castle.

"How much farther?" I ask.

Selene tugs me a little closer. "It's just over this bridge," she tells me, then pauses to bite her lip. "Actually, you know what… close your eyes. I want it to be a surprise."

I turn to her, my eyes doing the opposite as they widen. "*What?*"

"Oh, come on, angel face. I promise I won't let anything happen to you." Selene squeezes my arm. "It's one of my favorite places in the whole park, and it's beautiful. Please?"

"You're asking me to put my life in your hands," I point out, and I don't miss the irony that my life is probably *better* in Selene's hands than in my own.

She moves to stand behind me, reaching up slowly to cover my eyes with her hands. "If it's in my hands, then you can't die from embarrassment. Now keep walking forward until I tell you to stop."

I take a deep breath and close my eyes, my lashes fluttering against her palms. Maybe she'll actually take me to the garden, or maybe she'll shove me into the lake, where I'll drown because

I don't know how to swim. Either way, Selene ushers me forward, and it suddenly hits me with the weight of an entire skyscraper that this somehow feels like a date, where Selene has been flirting with me since the moment Beau left us alone together.

I'm gonna kill him, I think to myself, but let Selene guide me over the bridge.

twelve

Maybe I *won't* kill Beau after all.

The garden is absolutely beautiful, just as Selene said it would be, and I stifle a gasp against the back of my hand as she slowly uncovers my eyes. The view beyond her ridiculously soft palms is a lot to take in, but only in the best possible way: the intimately narrow pathways of different-sized cobblestones winding around patches of colorful wildflowers; the small bronze plaques that are sprinkled throughout the garden with quotes from Shakespearean literature.

There's a small, rustic wooden cottage that Selene informs me is actually a theater on the inside, one she visited frequently and where she used to watch puppet shows with both of her moms growing up. It's surrounded by yellow tulips and pink pansies, and much to Selene's overjoyed delight, there are several monarch butterflies fluttering between the flowers that she scrambles to capture with her camera.

I've never felt so content in my life, like nothing and no one can touch me in a place so beautiful, and I wonder if Beau might have been right. If all I'd needed was to see the world that existed outside of our hometown.

"*Oh!*" Selene says suddenly, grabbing me by the wrist as she gently pushes me toward the cottage. I'm careful not to step on any of the flowers. "Stand right here for me and pose. The lighting is *perfect.*"

I shake my head and wrap my arms around my middle. Had I known she was bringing me here to use me as a model, I wouldn't have agreed to come. "What was wrong with the butterflies?" I ask. "Can't you just take pictures of the flowers?"

From behind her camera, she says, "I prefer people."

"There are people over there," I point out. "Ask them if you can take their picture."

Selene looks up from where she's adjusting the settings on her camera. "I don't want to take pictures of them. I want to take a picture of *you.* I can tell you how to pose, if you need help. And besides, I came to the park today thinking I was gonna shoot with Beau. He lured me here with the need for new headshots."

"So, is this your hobby, then?" I ask, hoping not to sound too curious. Selene tilts her head at me in confusion. "Photography, I mean. Is it something you like to do for fun?"

She shrugs and takes a step back, then looks at me through the viewfinder on her camera. "Sort of. Photography was my

backup plan in case drag didn't work out for me." Selene shuffles
back a little farther, and it takes everything in me to *not* point
out that she'd shit-talked Achilles for having a backup plan. "All
right, so—stand up a little bit straighter, but not so stiff that it
looks like I've tied you to a pole. Good!" Selene adjusts something
on her camera. "Now: Roll your right shoulder back but not your
left, and drop your chin against your chest."

"Selene—"

"*Shhh*," she says, flapping her hand at me in annoyance. "On
the count of three, I want you to look up at me. You can smile if
you want, or don't. Are you ready?" I nod with grim resignation.
"All right, cool. One…two…three."

I feel silly as Selene snaps a picture, her lens whirring as
it focuses. "Please don't make me do that again," I complain.
"There have to be other people you can take pictures of."

"Nope," Selene says flatly, fiddling with her camera and squinting closely at the screen. "This may come as a surprise to you, but I
don't exactly have a lot of friends. The ones I do have don't like having their picture taken, and holy *shit*, you're gorgeous. Wanna see?"

For what must be the thousandth time today, the heat of a
blush creeps beneath my skin to redden my cheeks with embarrassment. "I really don't need any fake compliments," I say,
rocking onto the toes of my battered boots and back down again.
Selene looks up at me with a frown. "A butterfly would be a better model for you than I am."

"I wouldn't lie to you," Selene says, closing the distance between us. She flips her camera around to show me the image on the screen. "Look at how perfect you are in this picture. See the way the light hits your face? I couldn't have taken this in a studio."

The picture is...fine. I guess. If you like girls like me in oversized T-shirts and ripped gray skinny jeans who look like they're angry at the world. But I don't want to insult Selene's work, so I offer her a smile that I know looks as uncomfortable as I feel right now. "I like it."

Selene snorts as she turns the camera away from me, and as she's scrolling through the pictures she's taken today, I feel a quick *buzz* in my back pocket. I twist around to fish out my phone, though I can't say I'm surprised to discover new messages from my brother. "Beau texted me," I announce to Selene, sliding my thumb against the cracked screen to unlock it.

"What'd he say?" she asks, leaning against my shoulder to try and see for herself.

Beau Vincent: hope you're having fun lil B! 🖤

Beau Vincent: hey so I'm gonna be out late tonight...I'll txt you when I'm on my way home!

I let out a groan from somewhere deep in my throat, resisting the urge to chuck my phone into the nearest patch of wildflowers. "He said that he's going to be out late tonight," I say. Selene purses her lips with disapproval. "What are the chances that he actually comes home instead of spending the night with Enzo?"

"Slim," she admits with a grimace. "But he gave you his keys so that you can let yourself in. You'll be fine, just lock the door behind you."

It takes everything in me not to vomit all over Selene's fancy camera. She takes a step back like she's anticipating the reappearance of my iced coffee, and I wonder if Beau had forewarned her that I get nauseous when I'm anxious. "Being alone in New York is a person with anxiety's worst nightmare." I drag my fingers through my hair, tugging hard on the faded blue locks that are loose around my shoulders. "I was wrong. *So* wrong. I'm not going to die from embarrassment. I'm going to die because—"

"I have never heard anyone talk so casually about dying before," Selene says, and as annoyed as I think she wants to sound right now, her brow is still creased with concern. "It's just—I don't take that kind of shit lightly, you know? People talking about dying. It makes me all anxious and jittery." She's holding her camera in a white-knuckled grip as she stares at me, eyes assessing. "If you're really that scared to be alone, you can always come stay the night with me. My parents will be thrilled if they think that I actually made a friend today."

Spending the night with Selene sounds just as horrifying as spending the night alone in Beau's apartment. Because sure, she hasn't tried to insult me today, and yeah, she probably wouldn't murder me and then toss my body into the Hudson, but that's only because we haven't talked about drag yet. As soon as we do,

I know that everything will go back to normal. That we'll be at each other's throats because Selene doesn't think I can do drag, and I can't stand how freaking arrogant she is.

"You know, you *really* don't have to look that pained when you're thinking about me." Selene, for what it's worth, looks slightly less confident in the wake of whatever is on my face. "If you don't want to stay, that's fine. I can take you home and try to convince Beau to have makeup sex with Enzo some other time."

I bite at my lip, because no, I *really* don't want to spend the night with her. But it beats the alternative of spending the night alone in an apartment that creaks and where the lights flicker off on their own. "You haven't asked your parents if it's okay."

Selene pulls her phone out of her pocket. "They're not going to care," she tells me. "But if asking them for permission will make you feel better..." Her thumbs move clumsily over the screen as she types out a message to her moms, and the obnoxious *ding* of an immediate response has her smiling fondly into her palms. "See? They don't mind. But I hope you like gnocchi."

"What in the world is gnocchi?"

Selene's jaw falls open as she stares at me, and it's the first time that I've ever seen her truly offended. "Gnocchi. It's...*gnocchi*. Do they not have gnocchi in Texas?"

"Um...no? At least not where I'm from."

"*Ugh.* You Texans are so uncultured." Selene loops her arm

through my elbow again, giving me a gentle tug. "C'mon, baby gay. Let's introduce you to some proper Italian cuisine."

✦ ✦ ✦ ✦ ✦ ✦ ✦ ✦ ✦

I was absolutely wrong about airplanes; subways are the worst of all the terrifying modes of transportation. For the entire ride back to Selene's end of town, I'd kept my face buried in her lap, my only relief from the colorful smears of graffitied phrases that stretched between the smoggy windows. Watching it all bleed together inside the narrow tunnel had made me nauseous, and Selene had sported a look of alarm as I'd dry-heaved onto the floor at our feet.

Surprisingly, though, Selene hadn't laughed at me even once, speaking instead in a hushed tone as she rubbed my back and told me about her parents as a distraction. How they'd met at The Gallery before her birth mom, Nathalie, had bought the bar as an investment, using up a sum of the inheritance left behind by her grandparents. Proceeds from the bar and the way they'd rebranded it was how they had paid for IVF to have her, Selene had joked, even though I knew that it probably wasn't far from the truth. Parenthood for queer people is expensive if you don't already have money.

Just from what little she had told me, Nathalie is stricter than Selene's other mom, Dominique, who's an ASL interpreter by day, and a pastry chef turned graphic designer by night. Dominique had been born deaf, Selene explained, then patiently taught me a couple of signs that would help me introduce myself to her mom. On the flip side, for Nathalie's part, she mostly runs The Gallery on her own, but Dominique helps create all of the promo for social media, and occasionally she takes over the bookings.

Selene looks nervous as we squeeze down a narrow walkway that leads into the alley behind The Gallery. Her mouth is pinched at the corners, her palms sweaty as she wipes them off on her jeans. There's a rickety-looking fire escape that scales the brick wall of the building, eventually opening up onto an even ricketier balcony, and Selene turns to look at me without a lick of amusement. "Normally," she says, jabbing her thumb toward the ladder. "I'd just bring you in through the front." She fumbles a set of keys out of her pocket, nearly dropping them twice. "But it's so early in the day that Mom hasn't unlocked the actual bar yet, and I don't have a key for that door. So, angel face…it's up the fire escape we go."

Forget vomiting. I'm going to pass out on the rocks and broken glass crunching beneath my feet. "You are absolutely shitting me right now."

Selene stares at me with a deadpan expression for a moment too long for comfort—as if she is absolutely *not* shitting me right now—before she snorts and offers me a nod. Air whooshes out of my lungs. "Just trying to lighten the mood. You still look a little flushed from the subway."

I'm about to snap out some witty retort about how awful she is— or just throw her into the dumpster, honestly—when the reason for her distraction suddenly hits me. "Oh, my God," I say. Selene's face flashes with alarm. "You're *stalling*! You knew I'd have a meltdown about the fire escape and that dealing with me would buy you some time! Why are you so nervous to take me inside?"

"I'm not nervous!" Selene argues, her voice pitching higher than I've ever heard it. "Why would I be nervous? It's my house and my parents and—and *you're* the one who should be nervous!"

I raise an eyebrow and point at myself. "I'm *always* nervous. But you..." It's ridiculous how giddy I feel right now, knowing that I'm the root of her sudden waver in confidence. "Have you never brought a girl home before?"

Selene looks outright offended, but beneath the bravado, there's something sad there, too. It's in the way that she lowers gaze, the way her shoulders cave in fractionally around her. "I've brought plenty of girls home, thank you very much." She twirls her key ring around her index finger and steps aside, revealing a dented metal door. She uses her foot to kick away some of the debris and empty cardboard boxes that are piled up in front of it. "I just...*ugh*. You're so annoying. Come on."

She wrenches open the door with a groan, which opens up into a narrow stairwell with a flickering yellow light. Selene stomps up the steps in front of me, grumbling about Beau and how he owes her a favor, but I can tell from her tone that she isn't *actually* annoyed with me, just nervous and slightly inconvenienced.

I think.

The stairwell, higher up than it looks from the bottom, eventually curves open at the top. We emerge from the corridor and onto a small landing where a black door sits decorated with the lesbian pride flag. Selene sticks a key into the lock, then turns to look back at me with her bottom lip caught between her teeth. "Do you remember how to sign hello?" she asks, and I nod, demonstrating. Selene smiles. "Good. She's a hugger, by the way. Dominique, not Nathalie. Sorry. It's weird calling them by their names."

"What do you call them?" I ask curiously. Selene tilts her head at me in confusion. "Are they both 'Mom,' or do you call one of them something different?"

"Oh," Selene says, and the door unlocks with a click. "I call Nathalie 'Mom' and Dominique 'Mama.' It's been that way since I was little, and they picked what they wanted to be called before they had me. Are you ready to meet—"

The door flies open, and she yelps as the doorknob disappears from beneath her hand. A taller woman with purple hair and a freckled face that's identical to Selene's is suddenly standing in its place, glancing back and forth between the two of us, her eyebrow raised with suspicion. "I thought I heard someone out here," she says, her dark green eyes honing in on *me* with a terrifying laser focus. She must be Nathalie. "Has anyone ever told you that you look just like your brother?"

I swallow noisily and shift uncomfortably on my feet. "All the time. Has anyone ever told you that Selene could be your twin?"

Selene's mother smiles and steps aside to let us into the apartment. "All the time."

For having a bar underneath it, the inside of their apartment is beautifully modern with exposed brickwork and decorative wooden beams across the ceiling. The floor in the entryway is marbled black and white, melding into a plush beige carpet that's accented with plenty of patterned throw rugs, likely to reduce the noise from the bar below. There are two recliners and a large leather sofa in the living room, loosely wedged between a set of balcony doors and a round dining table that's meant for three but set for four with an extra plate and folding chair.

It's weird that I've already been accounted for, even though Selene had texted her mom and asked if she could bring me home for dinner tonight.

Nathalie tells us to take off our shoes and leave them in the front hall closet, then ushers us farther into the apartment, where a kitchen sits adjacent to the living room. There's another woman standing behind the stove, dressed in a lavender apron and covered in frosting and flour, and I know right away that this must be Selene's other mom, Dominique.

I watch as Nathalie steps into the kitchen and pats her hand along the wall, eventually finding a light switch. She turns the fluorescents on and off, and Dominique whirls around to look at us, grinning a toothy smile as she sets down a pastry bag of yellow icing on the counter. She immediately starts signing with her hands, and next to me, Selene begins to sign, too.

She moves toward her mom on socked feet before throwing her arms around her neck, hugging her so tightly that she lets out a small gasp of air. Dominique is shorter than both Nathalie and Selene, with wide curves and dark skin that's been dusted with flour from baking. Her hair has been twisted into colorful box braids that match the purple in Nathalie's hair, and as soon as Selene finally lets her go, Nathalie is quick to take her place. She wraps her arm around Dominique's waist and presses a kiss to her temple, and it's clear as day how absolutely sickeningly in love they are.

They almost remind me of my parents—how Dad will sidle up next to my mom in the kitchen, and how he'll hug her from behind as she cooks dinner. How she'll hang off his arm as he talks about his day at the office. I'm sure their dynamics are different, but the reminder of home is a welcomed one.

"So," Selene says to me, continuing to sign so that Dominique knows what she's saying. "These are my parents, Nathalie and Dominique, but I guess you already knew that. Did you still want to introduce yourself, or should I?"

"I think I can do it," I tell Selene, flexing my clammy fingers. She nods and translates for her mother, and Dominique smiles at me with encouragement. "My name is Briar," I say aloud, then slowly spell my name in ASL, trying to remember each letter. "And I'm..."

"She's Beau's little sister," Selene fills in for me, and I wonder how much, if anything, her parents might already know about me. If she's told them I'm doing drag just to spite her. "She's here visiting him from out of town."

Dominique looks at me and starts signing again, and this time, it's Nathalie who translates. "We're so excited to meet you," she says. Dominique nods as she leans into Nathalie's side, assessing Selene and I with soft, inquisitive eyes. "It's been a long time since our little Sel has brought someone home to meet us, and we've missed having company for dinner."

Nathalie reaches over to fluff Selene's hair. "Almost too long," she says, and she and Selene share a look. "Hopefully Briar is better than that last girl you tried to sneak in here through the fire escape. God, what was her name? Anna? Alanna? It doesn't matter. She wasn't half as cute as you are."

"*Mom!*" Selene cries, signing aggressively as her contoured skin flushes a bright shade of scarlet. Dominique presses lips together to keep from laughing. "Don't embarrass me!"

"I—she didn't bring me home," I say quickly, feeling myself begin to flush, too. Selene's eyes are wide as she stares at me.

"I mean, she brought me *home*, technically, but not because we're—I mean—I'm in your *house*, but Selene and I, we're not—Beau abandoned me in Central Park, and I—"

Selene grabs my hand and we make a break for it, staggering out of the kitchen as she yanks me toward the hallway that is meant to be our escape. "Holy shit, you're making it worse. Stop talking." She looks over her shoulder at her parents. "We'll be in my room until dinner is ready!"

Dominique and Nathalie are laughing as she shoves open a door, then shoves me inside what I assume is her bedroom and slams the door shut behind us. Selene sinks against it with a groan, murmuring something about parents and fire escapes and how they're never going to let her live this down. I try not to listen as she wallows in her embarrassment and instead take a look around her bedroom.

It's nothing at all like what I was expecting, but somehow still screams Selene D'Angelo.

Her small, low-framed bed has been pushed into the corner of the room, flush against an exposed brick wall that's been draped with false ivy and twinkling fairy lights. For someone who presents themselves as all about the glitz and glamor of drag, there's a surprising lack of color in her bedroom. The bedspread, pillows, and even the furry throw rug that we're currently standing on are all in shades of cream and blinding white.

It's not a large room by any means, but Selene has managed

to make the small space work for her, especially with her choice in decor. There are tall, black-and-white photographs hung up on the walls in expensive, glistening-gold frames, and the images are mostly of iconic New York scenery: the Statue of Liberty, the Brooklyn Bridge, and there's even a snapshot of The Gallery. But it's the larger canvas hanging above her bed that captures my attention and keeps it.

The photograph is of a fem-presenting teenager, hardly any older than me, and they're standing beneath an archway that's beautifully peaked and intricately carved out of stone. It's the only picture hanging on the wall that's in color, and the person in the photo is posed to lean against the doorway, their long hair a pop of orange in what looks like a library. Whoever it is, they're stunningly draped in expensive fabric and fur, and in the back of my mind, I wonder if Selene is responsible for taking the picture. If maybe it had been some kind of photoshoot, and this had been her favorite shot from a set.

An oversized bean bag chair sits unruffled near a meticulously organized vanity, as if Selene has never bothered to sit down on it. There's a massive tower of clear storage bins stacked in the corner of the room, each of them sporting a different white label with pristinely written letters: sheer fabric, sequined fabric, jackets, wigs, boots. I'd never imagined that Selene would be so organized.

But it's not the bins full of her drag that grab my attention next: It's the small white bookshelf that's pressed beneath the window and topped with a massive flatscreen. There aren't too many books on the shelves, mostly strange odds and ends and several different gaming consoles, but judging by what *is* there, Selene wasn't joking about being a fan of horror. Mary Shelley, Bram Stoker, Shirley Jackson…She has a small collection of special editions where the dust jackets are all different from the originals, shiny with foil and eloquently decorated to match the vibes of each book.

"Jesus, maybe I really *should* have just taken you to the library," Selene remarks, watching me curiously as I shuffle across the room to get a better look at her books. Her nervous energy has dwindled since escaping from her parents, but I can tell she's still on edge from the way that she's toeing at the carpet. "Should I be jealous that you don't look at *me* like that?"

I roll my eyes and drop to one knee in front of the bookshelf. "Get over here and show me which one's your favorite."

Selene sits down beside me, folding her legs up underneath her, and as she's reaching to trace her fingers over the pretty spines in her collection, my senses are assaulted by the cinnamon scented perfume she's wearing. I hadn't noticed it at the park or in Shakespeare Garden, and I definitely hadn't caught a whiff of it on the subway, but here in the quaintness of her small, too-clean bedroom, I'm overwhelmed by the fragrance.

"This one," Selene says, pulling one of the larger books off the shelf and handing it to me. "The Complete Collection of

Edgar Allan Poe. He's probably my favorite poet, and this is a limited edition that my parents got me for my birthday a few years ago. I think it was an anniversary exclusive."

"I like Poe," I say, studying the image of the golden-embossed raven on the front cover. "I read 'Annabel Lee' after Beau did a report on him in middle school. He'd practiced presenting it to me and our parents in the living room, but he'd misread 'Poe' as 'Foe' and got angry with me when I corrected him."

Selene snorts as she leans in closer to me, her shoulder bumping against mine. "That sounds like Beau," she says, prying open the cover to idly flip through the pages, and I can't help but to wonder when things had started sounding like "Beau" to her. "But I think that he might have been onto something—Foe sounds *so* much cooler, and it really fits the whole horror vibe."

I look at her and raise an eyebrow. "Edgar Allan *Foe?*"

Selene grins. "That's hella fierce. I like it."

Hella fierce.

An idea begins to form in the back of my brain as Selene takes the book and puts it back, placing it carefully between her two copies of *Frankenstein* and Bram Stoker's *Dracula*. "Edgar Allan Foe," I whisper quietly, more to myself than to Selene, but she turns around to look at me anyway, her head tilting curiously to one side. "Edgar Allan Foe! I mean technically, I'm your foe, right? Wouldn't it be *such* a good drag name?"

Selene stares at me for a moment too long before finding a sudden interest in her fingernails. "I do love a good pun," she says. "And a drag name can be whatever you want it to be. I picked Spencer Read because I love *Criminal Minds*, but I'm also just really good at reading people."

I raise an eyebrow. "Empathetically?" I ask. "Or insultingly?"

She heaves a sigh through her nose, like she doesn't want to have this conversation with me. And maybe she doesn't, because today was a step forward for us. "Both, I guess. Do you think you're going to use it as your drag name?"

Catching my bottom lip between teeth, I stare at Selene and shift uncomfortably on my knees. "Is it a good one?" I ask, hoping that she'll tell me the truth. "Do *you* think I should use it?" I don't know why her opinion even matters, but there's a part of me that wants her approval. "I guess I can come up with something else."

"I already told you that I liked it," she points out. "But I cannot believe that you're doing drag *and* choosing a name out of spite for me."

"It's not out of spite," I say defensively. "I really do want to do drag."

Selene is instantly heated, an insult budding on the tip of her tongue before Nathalie knocks on the door, telling us that it's time for dinner. She lets out a breath that's probably as hot as she's feeling right now. "Let's go," she grumbles, blinking away the ire that's shining bright in her eyes. "Because I also can't believe that you've literally never had gnocchi before."

Spared from her wrath by a weird Italian dinner dish, I can't help the excitement that's blossoming open in my chest. I've *finally* found a good drag name, even if it was my enemy who'd thought of it first.

thirteen

" *Y* *ou slept with the enemy!?* "

Achilles gawks at me from behind the bar, rinsing out a shot glass and wiping it down with an old rag. The Gallery is in full swing tonight, the bouncers turning people away at the door because the building is already at capacity, but thanks to Enzo shooing away a few of their regulars, I've managed to secure myself a seat at the bar where I can talk to Achilles as they work.

Not that Achilles wants to talk about anything except the night I'd spent with Selene.

"Keep your voice down," I hiss over the music, a soundtrack of early 2000s pop songs for a throwback night. "I didn't *sleep* with her, Keel. Jesus. I just…sort of slept in the same bed as her. It's not the same thing—stop laughing at me!"

Achilles' shit-eating grin is unnerving, showing off all of their pearly white teeth as they bounce on the heels of their feet.

They've been giddy since I got here, having swarmed me with a hug when I first arrived because I'd come to the bar in drag.

Sort of.

I'm dressed in a pair of dark gray jeans and a flannel with sleeves I'd cut off and replaced with black pleather. My hair is tied back into a bun, and I'd contoured my face in the way that Jacklynn had taught me, hollowing out my cheekbones and sharpening my jawline with foundation too dark for my skin tone.

It's not the greatest drag look in the world, the lines from where I'd drawn on a bit of black stubble too thick, but it feels so good to finally embody this new persona, even if he still needs a bit of work.

"I'm sorry," Achilles says, pinching their pierced lips together to keep from laughing. "It's just...I haven't seen Selene outside of the bar in years, and I have no idea what she's even like anymore." They rinse another shot glass as a bartender glances at them in warning. "What does her room look like? Is she still messy? Oh, I bet she's still messy."

I snort and take a sip from my half-empty glass of Dr. Pepper, which Achilles fills as soon as I set it back down. "Actually, there was no mess at all. She's really neat and organized." It feels weird to be talking about Selene like this, even though I know that Achilles' questions are all harmless. But it feels like betraying her trust, like she'd allowed me into her secret double life as the girl who loves photography and making her bed every morning.

Painstakingly so, at that.

I'd watched her smooth out her crisp beige sheets probably a thousand times.

"What did you guys *do*?" Achilles inquires, polishing another shot glass from the sink full of dishes they're standing behind. "Did you get to meet Nathalie and Dominique? Nat scares the absolute shit out of me."

"She was nice," I say. "Scary, I get it. But nice. She made gnocchi soup for dinner, and Dominique stuffed me full of sugar cookies. Have *you* ever had gnocchi soup before? Selene made me feel like I was crazy."

Achilles raises an eyebrow. "You're deflecting."

"I am *not*—"

"All right, listen." Enzo appears behind Achilles, tired but bright-eyed as he rests his hands on their shoulders, giving them a gentle squeeze. "If you're going to sit at the bar so that you can watch Bow perform tonight, fine. But please stop distracting my barback. They have a job to do, and I'm running out of shot glasses."

Achilles starts polishing the glass they're holding a little faster. "I'm so sorry," they tell Enzo, who claps them on the back and tends to the customer sitting next to me, one who Achilles wasn't able to serve because Keel is still underage. "But did you hear about Briar and Selene? She's filling me in on all the details!"

"*Keel!*"

Enzo whips his head around to look at me as he's emptying a bottle of Fireball into a shot glass. "I did *not* hear about Briar and Selene," he says, and compared to Achilles' fascination, Enzo's eyes are soft with a mild concern. If something happened and I don't want to talk about it, he won't make me, but if I'm inclined to share any details, well...I have his undivided attention. "Beau said you hung out together at Central Park on Monday."

"We did," I groan. "And because *someone* kept my brother out late that night, I had to spend the night at her house, where *nothing happened* except some popcorn and a horror movie marathon."

The tips of Enzo's ears turn red with a blush as he tugs at the collar of his turtleneck. "Sorry," he grumbles. "But a movie night with Selene, that's...wholesome. For her, anyway."

I frown and tilt my head at him, watching as Enzo suddenly busies himself with pouring another drink. "Wholesome?"

It's Achilles who answers me as they aggressively rinse out a glass. "Selene doesn't really do the whole 'dating' thing. Not anymore, at least. She's more of a casual hookup kind of girl."

"It wasn't a date," I say quickly, and both Enzo and Achilles look at each other and snort. "It wasn't! God, you two are the *worst.* I swear, it was really just a movie night. With popcorn and sugar cookies and gnocchi."

Achilles nudges Enzo with their elbow. "She met her parents."

Enzo's eyes nearly bulge out of his skull as he swipes a credit card off the counter. "Holy shit, hermanita. Selene doesn't introduce *anyone* to Nat and Dom. She usually sneaks her 'dates' in through the fire escape."

"It wasn't a fucking date!"

"What wasn't a date?" asks Selene, sidling up next to me in drag as Spencer Read.

I whip around to find him smirking down at me, only the affection is half-hearted because his mossy eyes are unusually dark and bloodshot. He's been crying, I realize, his contoured cheeks ashen beneath the brim of his biker hat.

"Are you okay?" I ask, but Spencer just waves me away, the several bracelets around his wrist jingling like little bells. I've never seen him wear them before. "You've been crying, Spencer. What happened?"

Enzo and Achilles make themselves scarce as Spencer dismisses me with a wave again. "I'm fine," he says flippantly, even though I can tell that he's not fine. That something has happened and it was enough to shake his resolve. "Well, well, well. Look at you." Spencer plucks at the pleather sleeve of my flannel, deflecting. He examines the fabric in the same way Achilles had before we bought it. "Did you make this? The stitchwork is pretty good for someone who's never sewn before."

My cheeks grow warm from the compliment, and all I can do is assess what he's wearing and compare it to what I'm not. A thin leather jacket is slung over his heavy shoulders, the one with his name monogrammed on the back of it in shiny silver studs, and he's wearing a pair of black knee-high platforms. The buckles jingle as he shuffles his feet, and it's a wonder that I hadn't heard him coming.

"Thanks," I say, shifting nervously on the barstool. "So, what are you doing here?"

"I am in desperate need of a distraction," he says, nodding at the empty stage. People have started to gather around at its edges, pushing each other out of the way to get to the front of the crowd, and I pray to whoever is willing to listen that he's not suggesting we join them. "Bow is getting ready to go on, and I thought that you might want to go watch. She's doing a Taylor Swift set tonight, which is weird, because like...I have never seen anyone lip-sync to 'You Belong With Me' before. But I guess it's a tribute to Enzo."

Enzo, close enough behind the bar to overhear, turns a bright red as he pretends to concentrate on taking a customer's order.

"I think you should go," Achilles says, biting their lip as I turn back around to glare at them. They're still polishing shot glasses at the sink. "You can see the stage from back here, but the view really isn't that great." They drop their voice to a softer whisper and continue, "He really does need a distraction tonight. I totally forgot what day it is."

"A distraction from what?" I whisper back, knowing damn well that Spencer is probably still listening. "What day is it?"

"It doesn't matter," Spencer says, offering me his hand without any further explanation. He's wearing a pair of fingerless gloves and a gaudy silver ring on his thumb. I've never seen the ring before, either. "If we're going to go, we need to go now, and I'm going with or without you, so…Offer going once, twice…"

Spencer wriggles his fingers at me.

I sigh and take his hand. "I really don't want to be crushed by the crowd."

Spencer's eyes darken as they help me down off the barstool. "I've got you, angel. Let's do this."

It is absolutely insane how dedicated my brother's fans are, how tightly they've all crammed themselves onto The Gallery's small, checkered dance floor because he'd tweeted about impersonating Taylor Swift tonight.

Gays are *such* freakin' Swifties.

"*Bow Re-gard! Bow Re-gard! Bow Re-gard!*"

I don't think I'll ever get used to it, the incessant chanting of Bow's name as we wait for her to come prancing onto the stage. She is definitely taking her time tonight—is likely still fussing over the short, out-of-the-bag wig that barely fits her head—but that's because she knows she *can*. Because she's earned this. Because Bow is the headliner and has all of the time in the world.

No one is going anywhere until they've seen her.

"Christ, they're so fucking pushy tonight!" Spencer complains, bracing his feet apart as the crowd surges forward from behind us. My knees knock painfully against the stage's rickety runway, and Spencer stops me from face-planting entirely by gritting his teeth and wrapping his arms around my middle. "And if the bitch standing behind me does *not* stop playing with my hair, I swear to God, I'm gonna kick them in the face!"

Spencer had managed to get us to the front of the stage, but mostly because he'd shouted about Bow Regard being his drag mother. Between her fans and his own, who'd recognized Spencer immediately, they'd practically fallen out of the way for him, carving out a path for us that opened up in front of the runway. He'd squeezed my hand with sweaty, trembling fingers, skillfully dodging all of half-drunk college kids brazen enough to reach and grab at him, and had refused to let go of me until the crowd filled in again around us.

Whether or not we'll remain in one piece tonight is unclear.

"I can trade you places," I offer, because at least my hair is tied back into a bun. Spencer's is down beneath his hat, apple red and unusually sticky with hair gel.

"I'm okay," he says tightly, but as I crane my head around to look back at him, Spencer is still gritting his teeth. His mouth is pressed into a thin line as he shoves his elbow behind him, setting a boundary between himself and whoever is touching him. "Don't worry about me. I'll be fine. I'm used to The Gallery's crowds. I just wish people would understand that drag is not consent, and that they wouldn't fucking touch me whenever they felt like it."

There isn't enough room for me to give him the space that I'm guessing Spencer needs right now, but that doesn't stop me from trying to shuffle forward anyway. "I'm so sorry," I say, crouching down until I'm halfway resting on the runway. Spencer takes a breath into the open air in front of him, his bloodshot eyes fluttering as he gathers his bearings. "I didn't think you minded it when random people touched you, otherwise I would have shoved you in front of me. You're always so reactive with the crowd whenever you're performing, but I guess that's not the same as being a spectator."

Spencer nods, hauling me back upright, probably afraid I'll be crushed. "It's different," he explains. "Because I'm in control during a show. I decide who gets to touch me and when. For how long. What is and isn't acceptable. And when I choose to come down from the stage, I'm consenting to have the crowd interact with me." His fingers curl into the fabric of my flannel as someone shoves him forward again. "When I'm not performing, that consent isn't there anymore. I just want to be another face in the crowd."

My heart hollows out in my chest, and I don't have to think twice about it—I grab him by the jacket and pull. "Trade places. Now."

Spencer stumbles as he slips around to stand in front of me, his own knees knocking into the runway. But I'd rather him be bruised than traumatized in any way, especially if I can help prevent it. "You didn't have to do that," he grumbles, staring down at me with concern flashing in his eyes. He'll trade right back, if I ask him to. "It was only my hair, and it's probably because they've seen me around before. I'm also feeling a little sensitive today—"

"That does not make it okay," I cut him off, firmly standing my ground on this. "You're a drag king, not an animal in a petting zoo. I'll be just fine right here."

Spencer's lip rings gleam beneath the stage lights as he smiles. "You're right."

I'm still smiling back at him when music comes flooding into The Gallery, the opening notes of Taylor Swift's "Bad Blood" ringing loud in my ears. The crowd goes absolutely feral as Bow Regard *finally* struts out onto the stage, dressed in a feathery black bodysuit with rhinestone embellishments and heels so tall that she's balancing precariously on her toes. She's swapped out her blonde wig for a red one, and Spencer gives me a quick little wink before he turns to watch the show, catcalling his drag mother as my heart does a backflip in my chest.

Since when does *Spencer* give me butterflies?

I don't have long to consider this new crisis because Bow is stomping down the runway, snatching up money that she stuffs into the hidden pockets on her bodysuit. She spots us immediately as she drops down into the splits, a look of surprise creasing her brow because I'd told her I would be watching her from the bar tonight. But I can't decide if she's surprised to see me in the crowd, or if she's surprised to see me standing here with Spencer, who's wriggling his hips and doing a weird little shimmy dance.

Bow twists around so she's sitting up on her knees, and I watch as she smiles at a woman wearing a white bride-to-be sash. She playfully caresses her face, then presses a kiss to the woman's hand before thanking her for coming to the show tonight. The woman squeals and thrusts out a handful of money, jumping up and down as Bow takes the cash and shoves it down the front of her bodysuit, her pockets already full.

"Bad Blood" comes to an end, but instead of returning to stage, Bow struts even farther down the runway, closer to where Spencer and I are standing at the very end. She steals his biker hat despite Spencer's yelp of protest, placing it on her own head as she gives us a wink and does a quick twirl to show off.

"I'm having a bad hair day!" Spencer complains, smoothing down his fiery red locks with both hands. His hair doesn't *actually* look bad, but the strands that are curling against the nape of his neck are a bit frizzy, like he'd stuck his head into a humidifier. "Give that back or I'll sacrifice Edgar to the drag Gods!"

It takes me a moment to realize that he's talking about *me*—that *I* am the sacrificial Edgar here.

Bow snorts and gives him the hat back, and I'm beginning to wonder if The Gallery is having issues with the music tonight because the sound techs haven't started the next song yet. Is she purposely trying to kill time? Because I've never seen her just stop in the middle of her set before, not without a microphone to interact with the crowd as opposed to just me and Spencer.

But then she holds out her hand, and I must be off my game tonight because it takes me too long to comprehend that Bow is reaching for *me*, not a tip that someone is holding out for her. I frown as she wriggles her fingers. "Come on, Edgar Allan Foe. You're going to perform this next song with me."

If not for the contour and the beard I'd drawn on with eyeliner, I am absolutely positive that my face would be as white as a ghost. "No the fuck I am *not*. I don't even like Taylor Swift!"

"No, but you like this next song!" Bow crouches down to reach for my trembling hand, the one that is tightly gripping the sleeve of Spencer's jacket, using him as an anchor to keep my feet planted firmly on the ground. "You've got to come up here at some point, B, and your first time might as well be with me. I promise, it's not that scary!"

She squeezes my fingers and then gives me an encouraging tug, trying her hardest to pull me up onto the stage with her. But I refuse to budge as I cling to Spencer and duck behind the safety of his shoulder. "No way!" I yell at Bow, pretending that I don't notice all of the people who are swiveling in our direction, curious as to why she is attempting to force me out of the crowd. "People are staring at us, Bow. *Please.* Bring Spencer up on stage with you, if you want, but—but I can't do it. Not yet."

"Yes you *can*—"

"You guys are causing a scene!" Spencer snaps, finding the room to step aside so that Bow is free to drag me up onto the stage. "Either get up there and perform or admit that you don't have what it takes, but standing here and arguing about it is ridiculous. You're wasting everyone's time!"

He should have just slapped me in the face, because suddenly, Spencer and I are enemies again, all the progress we'd made in our relationship wasted.

Bow fixes her drag son with a look of motherly disappointment, the same kind of look our own mom makes whenever we don't do something when we're told. It's not scathing, but Spencer should know better. "Take it easy, Spence. Not everyone takes to the stage as quickly as you did, and even you still get nervous sometimes. Don't be mean because you're having a rough day and he's scared."

Don't be mean because you're having a rough day and he's scared.

Something unusual thuds to life inside of me, and I am so fucking tired of being *scared*. Of Spencer always doubting me and insisting I don't belong in this community.

I am here, I'm queer, and I can *fucking* do drag if I want to.

It would be easy to push back against Bow right now. To stomp my foot and stand my ground and say, "No, I am *not* getting on stage tonight." Sure, Bow would be sad, and maybe even a little disappointed, but ultimately, I know she'd understand. That she would never actually force me to do anything I didn't want to do.

To hell with all of that, though.

Who cares if I embarrass myself because I don't actually know how to lip-sync? At one point, neither did Bow, and I'd watched her practice in front of a mirror for *hours* before she'd moved to New York.

Now, she's a headliner for The Gallery, and doing drag helps her pay her bills.

Barely.

But she's made it.

And goddamn it, I will, too.

I step around Spencer and reach for Bow Regard's hand; her painted-on eyebrows raise with surprise as she tightly grips my fingers. "Are you sure?" she asks, giving my hand an experimental tug before I let her pull me onto the stage. "You really don't have to do this. I'm sorry if I made you feel like you didn't have a choice."

"This *is* my choice," I say, planting my feet on the runway. It's sturdier than it looks. "Are you gonna introduce me as Edgar?"

Bow grins so wide that her bright red lipstick cracks. "Let me grab a microphone."

fourteen

The multicolored stage lights that are bathing the runway in flashing shades of purple and pink are blinding.

I feel nauseous as we stand underneath them, my skin prickling with beads of sweat because the lights are warm and I'm drowning from the heat of the crowd. My flannel feels heavy on my shoulders, the collar restricting as I try to breathe in through my nose, then exhale slowly through my mouth.

Maybe Spencer was right, and I *don't* have what it takes to do drag.

Bow is tampering with her microphone, slamming the bedazzled device against the palm of her hand because she can't get it to feed into the speakers. "Maybe we should just...get this over with?" I suggest, stealing a glance at my supposed enemy because the crowd is beginning to grow restless, and I'm worried he's going to get crushed.

But Spencer isn't standing where I left him.

He's vacated the dance floor entirely, and it takes me a moment of vigilant searching to find him near the back of the room, glaring down a sound tech who is frantically fiddling with a speaker. Did he ask them to cut the power to Bow's microphone? Is he determined to keep Bow from introducing me to the crowd? I'm tempted to tell Bow that Spencer is trying to sabotage our performance when I see him bend and retrieve an unplugged wire. He stuffs it somewhere into the sound system, and Bow's microphone thuds to life against her fingers.

"There we go!" Bow spins on her heels to face the crowd, smiling as they cheer at her and wave dollar bills in the air. "Sorry about that—we're having some technical issues tonight." She grabs the sleeve of my dampening flannel and pulls me closer to her side. I stumble, but Bow keeps smiling and gives me a wink of encouragement. "Anyway, there's someone special I wanted to introduce y'all to. Is that okay?"

The crowd goes absolutely wild. Bow grins.

"This, theydies and gentlethems, is my beloved baby sister, Briar!" She nudges my hip with her elbow, a silent plea to do something that won't embarrass her, but all I can manage is to stand up a little straighter and wave. "But apparently, drag runs in the family, so I want y'all to meet my brand spankin' new drag brother: Edgar Allan Foe!"

The Gallery descends into madness. I'm trapped in the thrall of it from the stage, and despite my best efforts, I find myself searching for Spencer again. It's harder to find him now, but I manage to spot him near the back of the bar where he's watching me with Enzo and Achilles. They both must have taken their breaks, because Enzo is sitting on the barstool where Spencer had found me, and Achilles is jumping beside him, waving frantically.

"Go, Edgar!" they shout across the room.

Enzo raises his empty left hand to give me a quick thumbs-up, a small reassurance as he sips from the rim of a green glow-in-the-dark solo cup. Spencer, whose mouth gapes open as if Enzo has committed the ultimate betrayal against him, reaches up to moodily slap his hand down.

Achilles doesn't seem to notice—or care. "You can do it, bestie!"

No one has ever called me their 'bestie' before and meant it.

I file this away to dwell on the sentiment later, smiling at Achilles and waving at all three of them despite the fact that Spencer is glaring at me. He crosses his arms over his naked, taped-up torso, a blatant refusal to return the gesture as he angrily bites at his lip rings. But I can't let him shake my already wavering confidence, so I turn to look up at my brother, ignoring Spencer entirely.

Or, at least, I try to.

It's hard not to notice him when I can practically feel him staring, like he's trying his hardest to manifest the stage collapsing out from under me. I don't know why Spencer is acting like this, why today is supposedly a bad day for him, but it doesn't excuse the sudden 180 in the way he's been treating me, which isn't unlike a piece of shit beneath his boots.

"Now, you'll have to excuse Edgar," Bow continues into her microphone, giving my sleeve a light pull to draw me back into the moment. "This will be his first ever lip-sync, so try not to be too hard on him. But it *won't* be his first time performing to this particular song, and fuck, I really hope you don't hate me after this."

My eyes snap up to Bow's face, painted prettily with amusement, and I realize that she's talking to *me*. "What particular song?" I ask nervously, shifting on my feet as Bow motions for someone to start the music. "Bow, I swear to God, don't embarrass—"

"ME!" by Taylor Swift and Brendon Urie comes flooding into The Gallery through the sound system, and I immediately want to shove her off the stage. When Bow and I were both still kids, "ME!" had been one of her favorite songs, and she'd conned me and Avery into creating an entire dance routine. We'd based it off their dance moves from the music video, but I'd never imagined performing it in front of anyone who wasn't in our immediate family.

Bow is already hitting every pose, shimmying into every choreographed move that we'd painstakingly rehearsed all those years ago. Naturally, she's taken Taylor's part in the song, but I had never minded sharing the role of Brendon with Avery, dancing behind closed doors and where no one could watch me stumble through every step.

"Stop thinking so hard!" Bow calls over the music, reaching across the empty space between us. She laces her fingers between mine, spinning me around until I'm giggling and sliding into step with her. "There you go!" she says, grinning as we clap our hands together. We hop from one foot to the other, and I'm sure the routine looks absolutely bizarre, but I'd barely been a teenager when she'd taught it to me, all without asking for my input. "You can do this, Edgar. Jump, wiggle, wiggle, and slide!"

It sounds as silly as I feel doing it, wiggling my body before sliding my feet across the uneven slats of the stage. Brendon's part is coming up soon, and my brain is scrambling to remember the words to the song. "I don't know how to lip-sync!" I say, my chest growing tight with panic. I stagger as Bow spins me around again.

"Sing, then!" Bow tells me. "But quietly. We'll work on your lip-syncing later."

She guides me down the small, nearly invisible step that connects the stage to the runway, and I try my best not to look quite so terrified as I skip halfway down the center of it, whisper-singing Brendon Urie's lyrics. I absolutely do *not* have his swagger, but the sound of Bow's fans all screaming up at me is enough to loosen the tension in my shoulders. They're far less judgmental than I anticipated, calling my name in a chant as they frantically wave dollar bills at me.

I don't feel right taking them—they're Bow's tips, not mine—but that doesn't stop her from snatching them up and then stuffing them right into my hands. "Use it to pay Jacklynn back for the fabric!" Bow tells me, her blue eyes wide and shining with what I think might be pride. "Anyone who waves any money at you, take it. You can have the tips from this song."

Guilt churns my stomach because I know Bow needs the money. She'd told me this morning that she wants to save up enough extra cash to take Enzo out on a real date, one where they sit down at a fancy dinner so she can prove to him that she's serious about their relationship. Enzo had insisted that a movie night, takeout, and referring to him as her boyfriend would be enough, but Bow thinks that Enzo deserves better after the way she's been treating him.

"Are you ready for the big finale?" Bow asks, dragging me back onto the stage with her.

Our "big finale" consists of Bow lifting me up into the air, mostly because I'm not strong enough to pick her up. She's tall and all limbs and when she's dressed up in drag, she's weighed down even heavier by a wig and three different corsets. When we were kids, we almost never pulled this off, Bow usually dropping me flat on my face because I couldn't think fast enough to roll into the fall and land on my butt instead. Eventually, we'd swapped me out with Avery, but Avery isn't here to be Brendon tonight.

I don't know how I had forgotten about our finale until now, seconds before we're meant to actually do it. Bow and I haven't rehearsed this in years, not since I was an entire foot shorter, but all I can do is hope to God that her morning trips to the gym with Enzo have paid off in our favor.

We lip-sync about spelling and how there's not an "I" in the word "team," but there is definitely a "me" in the word "awesome." Bow and I are stomping our feet, and we clap our hands together in double high fives like Brendon and Taylor do in the music video. Eventually, she spins me around, and I do a little dance that Bow refers to as "the bus stop." It was a move she'd picked from a '70s-themed homecoming dance in high school, and it hadn't been difficult for me to learn; the steps are all still ingrained into my muscle memory.

The end of the song is fast-approaching, our big finale hot on our heels as I glance at Bow through the sweat dripping into my eyes. It's gathering in little droplets against my upper lip, the stage lights as sweltering as six little suns hanging above us. The pleather sleeves I've sewn onto my flannel are sticky and clinging to my skin, so I don't even think before I do it—I rip off my flannel and toss it onto the stage behind me.

The Gallery's patrons go feral, as if this is something I've done for dramatic effect and not because I'm about to have a heatstroke. I don't think that I hate their enthusiasm, though, my confidence skyrocketing as wads of cash are thrown onto the stage at my feet. Tips—Bow's fans are *tipping* me, and this time it's unmistakable that the money is meant for me too.

She grins as she scurries up next to me, hooking her left arm around my waist and preparing to hoist me off the ground. Taylor and Brendon are promising each other that they'll never find another like themselves, and Bow braces her feet apart as I launch myself up into the air. She catches me on the way back down, snaking her right arm beneath my knees and cradling me like a baby against her chest. The crowd goes wild as I kick out my foot and pose, the very thing that usually knocks Bow off balance and sends us careening to the floor. But her arms are steady as she holds me, gripping me tight as she presses a kiss to my cheek.

I'm breathing hard as I look up at her, my heart beating like a raging drum inside my chest. Because holy shit… *I did it*!

Sure, my lip-syncing wasn't great, and sure, I'm not the best dancer, but Bow and I had performed the absolute fuck out of "ME!," and I'd only had a couple of small panic attacks.

Bow sets me down on my feet again, but faster than lightning, she swallows me up into a massive, bone-crushing hug. "I am so, *so* fucking proud of you!" she cries, rocking us back and forth as she teeters on the heels of her stilettos. "I *knew* you could do it, and look at you! You're a motherfucking *king*!"

Tears begin to well up in my eyes, thick and salty as they eventually roll down my cheeks, carving out a path through my contour. I wrap my arms around Bow Regard's corseted waist, hugging her tight as the crowd continues to cheer, catcalling us both as they toss more money onto the stage. Somewhere off in the distance, I hear a loud, ear-piercing whistle, and as I peek from around Bow's heavily rhinestoned shoulder, I find Achilles kneeling on a barstool, pumping their fists up into the air as they call my name from the bar.

"*Edgar Allan Foe! Edgar Allan Foe! Edgar Allan Foe!*"

It starts from the back of the dance floor, my closest friend and biggest ally proudly leading the charge, and soon the whole crowd has taken to mimicking their cries, chanting my name until the sound of it becomes a roar in my ears. It's deafening and terrifying and so freaking *exciting* I want to scream.

Gone in this moment is the girl who is anxious about everything. Who doesn't want to live. Who'd come to this city on the desperate whim of her brother.

How in the hell am I supposed to ever go back?

How in the hell can I be sad when my life could look like this every night?

I can't believe that everyone's chanting my name and not Bow's, especially when this was meant to be her show. And I'd feel guilty if she weren't chanting it now, too, gathering up cash from her fans near the stage only to stuff it into the palms of my hands. "That's all for you, baby brother! Fuck, I'm so proud of you I could *burst.*"

She presses a kiss to my blushing cheek before collecting her microphone from Jacklynn, who's standing beneath the threshold that leads back into the dressing room with a grin. Oh God, has she been standing there this whole time? Had she watched me perform with Bow? Maybe she'll have some tips for me on things that I can do to improve.

"Holy shit, y'all. Wasn't our little Edgar so *good?*" Bow holds her microphone out toward the crowd to amplify their cheers and the dying chant of my name. She winks at me from over her shoulder, and I take that as my cue to smile and wave at the crowd. "Look at him coming for my gig! But that's all right, y'know? Because Edgar is going to be the headliner one day, and I'm just gonna be proud to be his opener."

Bow reaches out to me and gently takes my hand, giving it a squeeze before nudging me across the stage to where Jacklynn is waiting with her arms open. Both the crowd and I laugh as she prepares to reclaim her show, and my drag mother bellows for me to come and hug her. "I think that's enough excitement for one night," she announces, playfully shooing me away. "I still have a big number to do, and I don't want to kick you in the face."

"Yeah, yeah," I say, smiling at her so that she knows I'm not upset. One song was enough for me tonight. "But can I tell everyone thank you and goodbye first?"

She immediately hands me her microphone, riding this bravery train right along with me while it lasts. "Of course! Take your time."

The pink rhinestones that Bow has bedazzled onto the handle of the microphone are sharp against my palm. I've never used one of these before, and I clear my throat to help shake away the nerves that are suddenly taking up root in my vocal chords. "Um...hi," I say, wincing at the way that my voice cracks. Why is this so much scarier than lip-syncing to Taylor Swift? "I just— um—wanted to tell everyone thank you. You know—um—for letting me perform with Bow tonight. It—It wasn't planned, or anything, and I've just never—uh—I've never really performed before, you know? So I'm sorry if I—um—ruined anyone's night or—or something. Um. Yeah. Thank you guys so much! I had fun!"

Desperate to flee from where I've word-vomited all over the stage, I shove the microphone back into Bow's hands before I can say something *really* stupid. That wasn't at all like the quick little "thank you!" I'd planned on telling the crowd, and now Bow has to clean up my mess.

She gives me a pat on the shoulder, and I know that we'll talk about this later. How if anything had ruined her set tonight, it was probably me addressing The Gallery. "Wipe that look off your face," Bow says fiercely. "You didn't ruin anything. I am so, *so* proud of you. But it looks like Jacklynn is, too, and she might kill us both if you don't go and skedaddle on over there."

"Who the fuck says 'skedaddle' anymore?"

She grins and kisses my cheek again. "Get off my stage, you little shit. I'll come find you when I'm done."

fifteen

Jacklynn and I are huddled near the vanity in the dressing room, Jacklynn's makeup spread across the top of it from where she's spent the evening getting ready. Earlier, when I'd asked her why she was getting into drag when she wasn't scheduled to perform tonight, all she'd said was that tonight was going to be special.

Little had I known that it was going to be special because of *me*, because Bow and Jacklynn had been planning this night for a week, painstakingly choosing a song that Bow knew I would perform to. "Welcome to the Black Parade" by My Chemical Romance had been a top contender, but Jacklynn had insisted I'd needed to be eased into performing, and whatever I did should be a duet with Bow.

"ME!" was a good second choice, but I could have performed the shit out of MCR.

"You were fabulous up there!" Jacklynn says, squeezing me

in a hug until my spine cracks and forcefully relieves the tension from my body. Who could be anxious when Jacklynn is smothering you with love? "Bow is a big personality and knows how to command a stage, but you held your own, and I'm proud of you. You did good, Edgar. Truly."

The tiniest bit of confidence floods back into me as she lets me go and smiles. "Are you *sure*?" I ask. "Because I know there's a lot I need to work on. I mean, I was singing the entire time. But how do you move your mouth and make it *look* like you're singing without actually making any sound?"

"Practice," Jacklynn says, like it's obvious. "Stand in front of a mirror while you're listening to music and move your mouth but don't speak. You'll get the hang of it."

She plops back down behind the vanity, and I rock onto the heels of my boots. My makeup feels like a sticky layer of grime from where I'd been sweating beneath the stage lights, but Jacklynn has forbidden me from washing it all off until we've taken photos for Instagram. My flannel is flung over my shoulder, damp and embarrassingly stinky, but if Jacklynn notices that I reek so bad I can smell myself, she's kind enough not to say anything.

"Oh," I say, and reach into the pockets of my jeans, where I'd stuffed all of my tip money before coming off stage. "Here. Um. I should count this. I owe you for helping me get fabric."

Jacklynn waves me away as I unceremoniously dump wads of cash onto the vanity. "Don't worry about it. You'll need more fabric for the contest. But here, let me help you. If you're any-thing like Bow, you can't count to save your life."

I should be offended, but considering that I nearly failed math this year, I watch as she gathers up the money. She straightens everything out, turning the bills so that they're fac-ing the same way before she separates each of the amounts. There's a considerable stack of ones, but there's a few fives, a ten, and even a twenty resting on top of her eyeshadow pallet. Once she's got it organized the way she likes it, Jacklynn starts counting out the ones.

"Fifty-two, fifty-three, fifty-four..." Jacklynn scoops up the pile and waves it at me with a grin, then starts to add up the rest. "Twenty-five in fives, a ten, and a twenty. Look at you walking out of here with over a hundred dollars tonight."

That's more money than I've ever had in my life.

No wonder Bow hustles for her tips.

"Everyone knows that performance was *not* worth a hundred dollars. Not with that busted-ass mug of yours."

My heart sinks down deep into my stomach, even though I know that I shouldn't be surprised Spencer has come and found me. I don't understand why he's so angry with me, why he'd left the crowd only to glare at me from back at the bar. It's not like I had planned for this to happen, but I guess maybe he doesn't know that.

"If you're only coming in here to be a bitch," Jacklynn snaps, meeting Spencer's bloodshot gaze in the mirror. "Turn your ass around and get out."

Spencer snorts as he saunters farther into the room, ignoring Jacklynn entirely. "Did you plan this?" he demands, and beneath all of the anger, there's something else there that I recognize. He's hurt. "Bow has been my drag mother for almost two years and I've never gotten to perform up on stage with her. She's never let me. Why the fuck are *you* so special?"

I blink at him, at the rage and the jealousy and the tears gathering in his eyes. Whatever had happened that made this day so hard for him, Bow bringing me on stage with her had set him off and reignited our feud. "I—I didn't mean to—no. It wasn't planned. I didn't know Bow was going to pull me onto the stage. I'm sorry if you—"

"Sorry?" Spencer crosses his arms, his bottom lip trembling like he's on the verge of hysterics. "Do you have any idea what I've been through? How hard I've had to work to do drag?" He laughs like someone has said something funny. "Of course not, because you're having this all handed to you. All of it, on a goddamn silver platter."

Jacklynn's makeup rattles on the vanity as I take a step back and knock into it. My hands are beginning to shake as Spencer raises his voice, taking something out on me that I don't necessarily know is my fault. But I don't dare tell him that. "Please stop yelling at me, I—"

"Yelling at you? This isn't me fucking *yelling* at you." His nostrils flare as he sets his jaw and glares at me, and if this isn't him yelling at me then I pray to God he never does. "My parents own this bar and wouldn't even give me a Tuesday night gig when I first started drag because both of them thought it was a handout. I had to *fight* to make a name for myself in a place that is literally my home."

"Spencer, hey, maybe don't blame this on Edgar——"

Spencer's head whips around to where Achilles is standing in the doorway, wide-eyed and holding two pink solo cups. "Stay the hell out of this, or I'll——"

"Or you'll *what?*" I finally snap, storming forward into Spencer's personal space. He immediately takes a step back, brow furrowed, but I follow him. "Belittle them, make fun of their drag? Because newsflash, you already do that. You think everybody is so fucking *beneath* you, and for what? If your fans all knew who you really are, I don't think they would call themselves your fans."

"What do *you* know?" Spencer demands through his teeth, and it's clear that I've struck another nerve; his cheeks have flushed scarlet beneath the dark brown stubble that he's painstakingly glued to his face tonight, either from outrage or embarrassment. It's hard to tell. "Your only exposure to drag culture has been Bow and *RuPaul's Drag Race.*"

I curl my fingers into fists. "I'm from ultra-conservative

Texas," I remind him. "The nearest gay bar is two hours away in a city I've never even been to, and there are brand-new drag bans being proposed every week. Sue me for having limited exposure. And how *dare* you talk about drag being a community when you're standing here trying to gatekeep who can do it."

"I'm not gatekeeping anything," Spencer says. "If you want to do drag, fucking go for it. But maybe you should learn how to lip-sync first because your performance tonight sucked balls—"

Jacklynn Hyde slams her hands onto the vanity, rattling both the mirror and her makeup. I nearly jump a foot out of my skin. "Enough!" she shouts at the two of us, loud enough that Achilles gets the hell out of dodge and immediately scuttles from the dressing room, terrified even though they're not a part of this. And I wish I could do the same, that I could bolt from this room and pretend this conversation never happened. But unfortunately, I'm one of the ones that Jacklynn is actually yelling at, and I don't have a choice but to turn myself around to look up at her.

Her orange-painted mouth is pressed into a thin, furious line as she glances back and forth between Spencer and me, her frustration practically palpable. "There is absolutely no reason that the two of you have to constantly be at each other's throats. Ain't y'all fuckin' tired? Because you—" she points her finger at Spencer, "need to sit down and check your privilege. Not everyone comes from where you do, and exposure to drag is exposure to drag, period. And you—" Jacklynn turns her gaze on me now, and I try not to cry beneath the heavy disappointment that I find there. "You need to stop letting him under your skin. Every time you argue with him, you're giving the little shit what he wants."

Spencer snorts and wipes a tear from his cheek. "And what, exactly, do I want?" he asks. "Other than for *Edgar* to not make The Gallery a laughing stock."

I twist around to look back at him, his expression pinched at every corner with a barely subdued resentment. I wonder if most people try to appease Spencer just because his moms own the bar, and if they're afraid that he might actually have some kind of sway over who does and doesn't get to perform here.

But if he *does* have any kind of influence, I guess that I just don't care—I am *done* trying to make nice with a king who only cares about himself.

"The only thing that will ever make The Gallery a laughing stock," I begin, watching as my words find their mark in the form of Spencer staggering back a step, "is you thinking you're God's gift to drag. Because you're *not*. I've seen better dancers than you in Texas."

"*Briar Vivienne!*"

The sound of Bow's voice is like a physical blow to the chest, and it takes me a moment to realize that the bar has grown quiet. Quiet-ish, anyway, now that Bow is no longer on the stage and screaming into a microphone for her fans.

Because of *course*, she had only heard my part in this. She has no idea that Spencer is the one who started it.

"Are you out of your goddamn mind?" Bow asks, storming into the dressing room where she flocks to Spencer's side. Bow wraps her arm around his shoulders, murmuring something that's too quiet for Jacklynn and I to hear. "You have absolutely *no* right to tell Spencer he's bad at drag when tonight was your first ever performance. If I'd known it would make you so cocky, I wouldn't have brought you onto the stage with me."

"Bow, you don't understand——"

"I don't understand *what*?" Bow asks, resting a hand on her opulently rhinestoned hip. "That you've had it out for Spencer since the moment I told you he existed? You're the one who has made this a pissing contest. Not him. No one said you had to do drag."

"But I *want* to do drag——"

"Then do it," Bow snaps. "But you don't have to be an asshole in the process."

I cannot *believe* Bow is actually taking Spencer's side in this. It isn't like her to not hear me out, to not sit me down in a quiet room and ask for my half of the story. She was always the mediator back home, a constant glutton for a misunderstanding simply so she could smooth it back out again, like our parents and I were a puzzle she enjoyed piecing back together.

I don't know what has happened between Texas and New York, but I *know* it has something to do with Spencer, my dragged-out replacement who has effectively stolen my brother from me.

Congratu-*fucking*-lations, I guess.

My heart clenches painfully in my chest, as if someone is squeezing it in the palm of their hand, trying to wring all of the blood out. "Fine," I say to Bow through my teeth, even though everything is very decidedly *not* fine. She has never once raised her voice at me, not even when we were kids and I had tried to steal her spotlight during our living room rendition of *High School Musical.* "I *will* do drag, but without you. Thanks a lot, big brother. I really appreciate the support."

Bow's expression softens as she frowns, and even Spencer has the nerve to look up at me from where he's been staring at his boots. "Fuck, B, hang on a minute—"

But I have already stormed past them both, angry and defeated and feeling more alone than I ever have in a building full of people. Fighting with Bow over something so stupid doesn't feel right, but I can't get away from her fast enough. Maybe Jacklynn will tell her what really happened, and maybe Spencer will come clean about having been the one to start screaming tonight, but the walls are beginning to close in on me, and I need to get out of this room before I'm flattened between them.

✦ ✦ ✦ ✦ ✦ ✦ ✦

"Briar, babe, *slow down*. I can't keep giving you free refills."

I wave my empty solo cup at Achilles anyway. "I'm trying to drown my sorrows."

They had found me crying in the bathroom, standing over the sink as I scrubbed at my face to wash away the contour and eyeliner. Achilles had grabbed a hold of my hands, coaxing me out of the bathroom and back to the bar where they had sat me down on a barstool. They'd finished wiping it all away for me, dabbing gently at my raw skin with a wet paper towel while grumbling about skin creams and breakouts.

I vaguely remember my brother giving me a lecture about proper skin care this morning.

But who cares about skin care when Bow is mad at me and Spencer is a raging dick?

Achilles grunts as they lift a box onto the counter, the contents inside rattling precariously, like it might break if they're not careful. "It's Dr. Pepper," they point out, reaching into the box to start pulling out bottles of alcohol. They place them down behind the bar, lining them all up on a hidden shelf for Enzo and the other bartenders. "If I thought you could actually drown your sorrows in it, I would have stopped giving you refills four cups ago."

I wriggle my cup at them like that's supposed to make it more enticing. "Another."

"All right, Thor." It's Enzo who snatches the cup from me, his dark brown eyes shining with concern as he fills it. "Last one, and then you have to tell me what happened. And pick your head up off the bar, please. Someone was just sitting there before you, and I haven't gotten the chance to wipe it down yet."

The countertop is cool against my skin, grounding in a way that the ice-cold water I had splashed against my face in the bathroom wasn't, and I wonder if the bar has been purposefully chilled to keep drinks cold. But on Enzo's orders, I peel my cheek away from the distressed wood and stare into the cup Enzo has placed down in front of me. "That's water."

"Yes," he says, raising an eyebrow. "Because you've had enough caffeine. What happened, and whose ass do I need to kick? I don't like seeing you this upset."

Bless him.

"Your stupid fucking boyfriend's," I say, giving Enzo pause as he scoops ice into a glass. "She yelled at me and took Spencer's side in an argument that I didn't even start."

Enzo heaves a suffering sigh as Achilles reaches around him and grabs a cocktail shaker. "He's not still mad about Bow bringing you up onto the stage with her, is he? Because we sat here and listened to him bitch the entire time you were performing." He watches Achilles fiddle with a bottle of vodka. "Please tell me you're not trying another Long Island."

Achilles balks and slowly sets down the bottle. "You don't like my Screwdrivers, either."

"Because you're way too heavy-handed on the liquor," Enzo explains, and I watch as the two of them launch into a conversation about alcohol. At nineteen, Achilles could technically be serving people alcohol so long as it was under Enzo's supervision, but it's Nathalie's rule that they can't, not until they're at least twenty-one. But that doesn't mean Keel isn't allowed to practice making drinks, and Enzo is usually their taste tester.

"Wait, wait, wait—that was too much," Enzo tells Achilles, who is flustered to have Enzo standing over them, their tattooed hands trembling as they pour vodka into the cocktail shaker. It probably wouldn't be so bad if Enzo wasn't touching their shoulder, his arm wrapped around them like he's ready to yank the bottle away if he needs to. Achilles' cheeks are on fire, blazing as red as my flannel, and in another life, the two of them would look so freaking cute together. "You don't have to eyeball it, if you don't want to. I can get you the measuring—"

"I can *do* it," Achilles insists. "Let me try."

Enzo takes the shaker and knocks back the vodka inside of it, wincing. "All right. Let's start over. Only pour it for two seconds, not five."

"You've got this, Keel," I say encouragingly, even though

I don't know the first thing about alcohol. They smile at me from over the end of the bottle, nodding as if to thank me for the support, and at least Achilles and I can have each other's backs in all this.

On the dance floor, the crowd has grown thin now that the night's performances are over; patrons are filing out of The Gallery by the dozen, stumbling into the lively streets of New York City at nearly two in the morning. A bouncer stops them at the front door, checking to see who's too drunk to walk home, then calls them a cab to make sure they get there safely. I wonder what time Bow and I will leave tonight, if she'll even come to get me or if Enzo will have to walk me home because I'm too scared to cross the street alone.

"Did you know," I begin, glaring at the ice cubes that are bobbing up and down in my solo cup. Enzo and Achilles turn to look at me. "That Bow said I was cocky and that *I'm* the one who's made this a pissing match between me and Spencer?"

Achilles uses a long, twisty spoon to stir whatever they've poured into the cocktail shaker. "Spencer literally went back there just to scream at you," they say, handing off the shaker to Enzo. He gingerly sips from the rim, like he didn't just stand there and instruct Achilles on how to make the drink. "I can talk to Bow, if you want. I heard everything."

"No one should even *have* to talk to her," I grumble, watching Enzo's face as he tries and fails to hide the pursing of his lips.

Achilles holds their breath and waits for a verdict. "She didn't even ask me for my side of it. Just walked in, yelled at me, and was like, 'No one said you *had* to do drag.'"

Enzo hands the shaker back to Achilles. "Still a little heavy on the tequila, but close. Pour that out and get to work on washing the dishes." He takes the dishrag that's slung over his shoulder and tosses it onto the bar in front of me. "Start wiping everything down if you're gonna sit there. And I wouldn't worry too much about Bow. She'll come around eventually. But in the meantime, we need to get you up on that stage."

I wipe down the countertop right in front of me, careful not to knock down any of the coasters, salt, or woven baskets full of napkins. "How?" I ask, sliding off my barstool to start cleaning off the rest of the bar, following Enzo back and forth as he works. "I was only on stage tonight because of Bow, and she's already said she regrets it."

"I have an idea!" Achilles says, shaking a lime loose from the bottom of a glass. "There's only a handful of us who perform during the week, so maybe we could talk to Nathalie and see if she'll let you join the roster? The crowds are small and they don't tip very well, but it's a great way to get some experience and build your confidence!"

Enzo grins at me from behind the tap, wiping it down from where beer has been spilled throughout the night. "That's actually pretty genius," he says, and Achilles beams brightly into a shot glass. "Bow and Spencer wouldn't be caught dead here on a weekday, and I wouldn't mind swinging by the apartment on my way home from the gym to walk you over."

Something like guilt starts to worm its way into my stomach, taking up a residence there that makes it twist into knots. "What about Bow, though? You guys are dating. I don't want her to be mad at you."

He shrugs and leans over the bar, taking my dishrag and plopping it down into the sink. "If we're dating, that makes you family, and you're important to me, too." Enzo tosses a bowl full of diced fruit into the garbage disposal. "You leave Bow to me, okay? I can handle her. But Nathalie is in the back, if you want to go talk to her."

I nervously bite at my lip. "Why is she here so late?"

"Nathalie doesn't leave until Spencer does," Achilles explains. "Just to make sure he stays safe. But I can go with you, if you want? Nathalie's not so scary if you have a friend."

She wasn't scary at all when I met her, but this time, it's going to be different. I'm literally asking for a job, one that will put me in direct competition with her daughter. Does she know that I'm trying to do drag, or that I've entered the contest that kicked off this rivalry between Spencer and me? Nathalie could say no and I'll be screwed, but it's a chance that I know I need to take. I refuse to get on stage again with Bow.

"Do you mind?" I ask, looking up at Enzo with uncertainty.

"Can I borrow Keel?"

Enzo jerks his head toward the doors that lead into the kitchen. "Her office is in the back, near the ovens. Keel can show you. Good luck, hermanita, and just remember to breathe. I promise Nathalie doesn't bite."

I *really* hope that he's right.

sixteen

Jacklynn Hyde is the goddamn tyrant of drag.

"*Stop!*" she calls out from the audience, which on a Monday is literally just a collection of four black folding chairs that Enzo had brought out from the dressing room. They're lined up in a row across the dance floor, with Achilles sitting on the edge of their seat on the left, Jacklynn and Enzo in the middle, and the one on the right empty for whenever I'm allowed to take a break. "You missed your cue—*again*. Let's run that again, from the top."

When Nathalie had said I could perform on Mondays and Wednesdays, I hadn't thought Jacklynn would come to every rehearsal. That she would stop me mid-performance if she didn't like what I was doing and make me start again *from the top*. And yet, here we are, the three of them watching me as I pant and sweat beneath the stage lights.

"What cue?" I complain, dragging my feet to the center of

the stage to start over. The Gallery is empty apart from the handful of people who are sitting at the bar, ignoring me. "The second verse? I came down onto the runway, like you told me to."

"You *walked* down onto the runway, and your shoulders are so stiff I could snap you in half like a glow stick." Jacklynn leans around Enzo to poke at Achilles'...armor? They're wearing a costume they've constructed entirely out of EVA foam, and whatever it is that Achilles is meant to be, it's badass. "Get up there and show him how to look like he's actually having fun. Because if you're not having fun, then *we're* not having fun, and the last thing I want is for you to get booed off the stage."

Great. I thought that only happened during bad auditions on competition shows.

Achilles bounds onto the stage like a human silver bullet, and I have no idea how Selene could ever shit-talk their drag, especially when it looks better than hers. The work Achilles has put into this garment is unparalleled, the hand-painted foam melding perfectly to their legs, chest, and shoulders. Layers upon layers of pleated foam make up the majority of the outfit, and every inch of it has been covered in sparkling rhinestones. They look like a knight who has managed to crawl out of a five-year-old's princess fantasy.

"All right, so!" Achilles' voice snaps me out of the hope that maybe someday they'll teach me how to make armor. "I don't really know this song, but I watched the music video this morning. The singer has a lot of mannerisms that you can incorporate into your performance."

I haven't watched the music video for Set It Off's "Lonely Dance" in years, but I guess this means it's time to revisit it. "He gestures with his hands a lot," I remember, and Achilles nods encouragingly. "So am I supposed to just...act like I'm the lead singer in a punk band?"

"Set It Off is *not* a punk band."

It's that stupid, antagonizing little rasp in the tone of her voice that heats my blood to a blistering boil beneath my skin, and I *shouldn't* be surprised that Selene is sauntering across the dance floor, especially given the fact that she lives upstairs above the bar. But that doesn't stop me from turning to Achilles for an answer that I know they don't have—what the *fuck* is she doing here, and why is she refusing to actually look at me?

Enzo had told me that she wouldn't be caught dead in here on a weekday, and yet here she is, plopping herself down into my folding chair. "They're pop rock at best," she says moodily, crossing her arms over the swell of her chest as she slouches in her seat to get comfortable. "It's also not a great song choice. Most people aren't going to know it, and you want the audience to be able to sing along with you."

I grit my teeth as Achilles goes rigid beside me, waiting for the blow of their own unnecessarily cruel critique. "No one asked for your opinion," I snap, reaching back so I can take Achilles' hand; they shouldn't have to be this afraid of her, and it makes me even angrier that their fingers are trembling against my palm. "What are you even doing here? I thought weekday performances were beneath you."

Selene rolls her eyes and says, "I'm not the one who is performing. I also don't want to be here. But Jacklynn insisted I come and be your drag inspiration."

Both Achilles and I whip around to look at Jacklynn, who appears unbothered as she motions for a sound tech to start the music over. "You need a fire under your ass. Selene's the match. I know it's a lot of pressure, given that the two of you 'hate' each other, but if you're going to perform in front of a panel of judges in the competition, you'll need to get used to it."

The opening notes of "Lonely Dance" flood into The Gallery, and I don't have the time to argue with Jacklynn and tell her how uncomfortable I feel with Selene being here. Achilles springs into motion behind me, dancing as if they already know the song, and I try to mimic their movements, thrashing around the stage like I'm a part of the band.

We make it to the second verse before Selene holds up her hand, stopping the music. "You're not feeling it," she says, and if I hadn't spent hours stoning this jacket and swapping out the hood for a cape that resembles a spider web, I would take it off and launch it at her face. "The song is literally about anxiety, and you're the most anxious person I've ever met. Channel that."

"I didn't *ask* for your advice——"

"No," Jacklynn says, cutting me off. "But you're going to take it anyway. Like it or not, Edgar, Selene is a performer with more experience than you, and her advice is invaluable to your success in the competition."

Achilles bites their lip and gently nudges me with their elbow. "She's...kind of right, too. I'm so sorry. It just feels like you don't have any energy. The song *is* about anxiety, so...maybe your movements could be a bit more manic? It's all about putting on a show."

"So have an anxiety attack, but not actually."

"Sort of." Achilles nods. "When he's talking about things being too loud? Maybe you could cover your ears, like the audience and the music are too loud, too."

Selene stands up and finally meets my gaze, her green eyes darker than usual, and she looks as if she hasn't slept in days. "Can I show you something without you flipping the fuck out on me?" she asks, and even her voice is lacking its usual bite. Maybe that's why I nod without complaint. "He talks about having social anxiety. You could hold up your hands, like this——" She turns her back to me and thrusts out both of her hands, shaking them. "And slowly back away from the crowd, like they're the root of your anxiety and you're trying to fend them all off."

I furrow my brow as I frown at her. "Isn't that...rude?"

She snorts, and I forget about how tired she looks. "It's all a show," she says. "The better of one you put on, the more tips you'll get, and if *anything* drives a performer to do their best, it's getting paid." Selene reaches into the pocket of the sunflower-covered overalls she's wearing, procuring a wrinkled dollar bill. "Try again, and maybe I'll come and give this to you."

Jacklynn sighs as I storm to the edge of the stage, snarling at Selene with my upper lip curled back over my teeth. "I don't need your money," I hiss, and Selene's mouth twists with an infuriating smirk as she crumples the bill in her hand.

She shoves it back into her pocket. "I only tip actual drag performers."

Achilles grabs me around the waist before I can leap off the stage. "I'll show you an actual drag performer!" I yell, clawing to try and get away from them. The absolute audacity of this *bitch*. "I'm coming for your spot on the weekend lineup!"

Selene blows me a stupid little kiss. "Bring it on, baby gay. I'm not worried." She turns to pat Jacklynn on the shoulder. "Mission accomplished, Mama Jac. There's his fire. Let me know if you need me to stop by again."

Jacklynn looks up at me and winces. "You really are a little shit."

She grins before strutting across the dance floor.

$$+\diamondsuit+{}_+{}^+\diamondsuit{}_+\diamondsuit{}_++\diamondsuit{}_+{}^+\diamondsuit{}_+\diamondsuit{}_++\diamondsuit{}_+{}^+\diamondsuit{}_+\diamondsuit$$

I've started a war with Spencer Read that I don't know how to win. "Boyfriend" by Dove Cameron is blaring over The Gallery's sound system, and Spencer is down on his knees, crawling across the runway like he's an animal. If his fans weren't eating it up, I'd say that he was being ridiculous, especially as he shoves their tip money down the front of his leather pants. "Your brother taught him that," Jacklynn shouts, shaking her head as we watch his stupid show.

Jacklynn and I are nowhere near the stage—it was bad enough that she had forced me onto the dance floor at all, claiming that I could learn something from watching Spencer perform—but unfortunately I can see him just fine. He'd be hard to miss anyway in the silver vest he's wearing, the sequins catching the stage lights like little disco balls.

"You don't have to act like a fuckboy," Jacklynn says, straining to speak over the music. "But do you see the way he engages with the crowd? All those smiles and the hand holding? He might be an ass, but he's charming. You need to learn how to do that."

"What," I grumble, "undress the entire audience with my eyes? No, thank you."

Jacklynn snorts and affectionately ruffles my hair. "We'll work on it," she says, then jerks her chin toward the stage. "But I would look alive, if I were you. We've got company, and he ain't coming to play."

The chorus of "Boyfriend" has kicked in, with Dove Cameron singing about clothes and being a gentleman, and I turn toward the stage only to find that Spencer isn't on it. Just as he'd done when I had first watched him perform, Spencer has come down into the crowd, dragging his feet in a torturously slow saunter that matches the speed of the song. His fans are all reaching out to touch him, skimming their fingers over the bare skin of his tattooed arms and shoulders, and a kernel of anger ignites in my chest because I know he doesn't like to be grabbed at.

But then I remember that when Spencer is performing, he's in control. Anyone who's touching him is doing so because he's allowing it. Because he's chosen to consent to their infatuation with him. He doesn't seem to notice anyone in particular who's grabbing at him, though, not when his eyes are fully fixated on my face.

Because of *course*, he's making his way toward me, lip-syncing the hell out of this song, and I really hate that he looks so attractive while doing it. It makes hating him that much harder.

Spencer is full of surprises, and I don't know why I had expected him to do what he'd done when we last found ourselves in this position—to indulge in me for just a moment before giving his attention to someone else. Honestly, it's what I'd prefer, especially since the crowd is beginning to close in around us, forming a tight circle that doesn't even include Jacklynn because she's taken a healthy step back. But what I absolutely. do *not* expect is for Spencer to grab me by the collar, hauling me closer to him as he makes me a part of his show.

I gasp in a breath as my heart leaps into the back of my throat, beating out a cadence that might burst through my skin if I can't get it under control. This is stupid, Spencer is stupid, but all I can hear is the sound of my pulse as it drowns out the sound of the music, of the crowd and their screams because Spencer is giving them a masterclass performance.

"What are you *doing*?" I hiss, stumbling as Spencer pulls me flush against his body, his fingers still twisted into the fabric of my thrifted T-shirt. With his fist pressed against the center of my chest, can he feel the way my heart is going haywire? God, like he needs another ego boost. "This isn't funny. What are we *doing*?"

Spencer smirks as he brushes his nose against mine. He's taller than me in his platforms, and his handsome—*infuriating*—face is angled down toward me in a way that feels both captivating and intimate, like I couldn't step away even if I wanted to. The second verse of "Boyfriend" has ended, and the crowd is going absolutely feral, cheering us on as Spencer keeps pretending to sing, and I can feel his breath against the curve of my cheek as he chuckles.

"It's a game," he whispers, touching his forehead to my temple, closing any gaps there are between us.

I swallow because I can feel myself blushing, because I can feel the warmth of his skin as it presses against mine, rough from the stubble of his beard. I have never, *ever* been this close to someone, least of all a drag king with a God complex, and I hate myself for not actually hating it. "Game?"

Spencer hums the melody in my ear. "The song's almost over, if you want to play," he says, loosening his grip on my shirt. "All you have to do is put on a good show, and you win."

"What is this," I ask. "A *lesson* in how to do drag?"

He places his fingers beneath my chin, tilting my head up so that I'm looking at him. "Maybe," Spencer answers, his mouth still quirked with an annoying little smirk I desperately want to wipe off his face. "Maybe not. The ball is in your court, angel face."

Maybe it's the fact that the audience is nearly tripping over themselves, screaming and tugging at the back of Spencer's vest to get his attention. *Maybe* it's the fact that Jacklynn has found her way back to me and is poking me in the spine, telling me that I had better give Spencer a taste of his own medicine. Or *maybe* it's the fact that I can't stop staring at his lips, at the silver barbells piercing through his bottom one, and wondering what it might be like to kiss him.

I thrust my palm against the center of Spencer's chest, pushing him back so that I can advance forward and lip-sync the last bit of "Boyfriend." His green eyes brighten with surprise, like he hadn't expected me to actually play this game with him, but he grins as he lets himself be pushed. Spencer and I circle each other into the center of the dance floor, moving our mouths as if "Boyfriend" were a duet and we were taking turns singing each line.

Eventually, he catches me around the waist, his fingers pressing firmly into the curve of my hip as he takes my hand like we're dancing. He's maddeningly good at it, too, leading me in a shuffle of feet and boots until I accidentally step on his shoes; Spencer snorts and graciously lets me go, probably so that I can't scuff the leather.

The song is nearly over, and Spencer and I are panting from the heat of the dance floor and all of the bodies pressing in on us. He's still grinning as he unzips his vest, beads of sweat collecting inside the dips of his collarbones, and he's wearing a binder underneath. I know what he's going to do before he does it, how Dove is going to sing about fitting clothes and Spencer is going to drape his vest over my shoulders.

It's the perfect way to win the game, and I can't let Spencer get away with it.

I grab him by the front of the vest before he can actually take it off and haul him against me so that I can plant my lips against his mouth. It catches us both by surprise—I'd only intended on using it to shove him away again, not drag him closer so I could *kiss* him, of all things—but Spencer doesn't really seem to mind, not as he gasps and tilts his head for a better angle.

Kissing Spencer isn't terrible, even if I hadn't meant to do it.

His fingers are gentle as he cradles the side of my face, his thumb brushing softly against my cheekbone. His other hand has found the small of my back, sending a torrent of butterflies loose in my stomach as he touches the skin beneath my T-shirt. It feels *nice* doing this instead of arguing, and I stand up onto my toes to kiss him deeper, to drown out the sound of my thundering heart by indulging in this moment alone with Spencer.

But then I remember that we're *not* alone, that he and I are standing in the middle of a room where people are watching us perform. Because that's *all* this was—a performance. Especially for Spencer Read.

"Fuck," I breathe, pushing Spencer away from me. He stumbles and opens his eyes, his blocked-out eyebrows drawn on with eyeliner creasing in the middle with concern. "Spencer, I'm— I'm so sorry, I—"

Spencer carefully reaches for my face again, tucking a strand of my tangled hair back behind my ear. "It's okay," he says softly, loud enough for only me to hear, and I can tell from his voice that he means it. He's not angry. But that doesn't mean that I haven't just messed everything up. "That was—that was nice, actually. I—"

"*No*," I say, shaking my head as I take a step back out of his reach. "No, no, no. I shouldn't have—I didn't even *ask*—"

"I promise, it's not a big deal—"

"I'm sorry," I tell him again, and it's getting harder to hear him over the crowd. They're closing in even tighter around us now, reaching for Spencer and poking at each of his tattoos, like he's an A-list celebrity trapped in a petting zoo. "Stop touching him!" I shout, because God, I shouldn't have kissed him. Not without Spencer's explicit consent when I know how much it means to him. "I need to go, I'm so sorry. You win."

Spencer frowns as he shrugs himself free from a girl who's admiring his vest. "Wait, hold on just a second. Briar—*Edgar*—come back!"

But I've already turned to make a run for it, scanning the bar for Jacklynn Hyde because I need to get out of this room. I need to flee back home to Beau's apartment. I need to put some distance between me and Spencer Read right this second because Jesus, I shouldn't have *kissed* him.

seventeen

"*I* still can't believe that you *kissed* him."

It's all Achilles can talk about on Monday night as we huddle around the vanity in the dressing room, surrounded by clothing racks that I've learned are from a burlesque show The Gallery had put on last fall. I'm already finished getting ready, forgoing most of my usual makeup because my face is suffering the consequences of poor skin care, so I'm watching as Achilles contours their cheeks with a mixture of blue and gray eyeshadow.

"I didn't *mean* to kiss him," I say. Achilles pauses to give me a look that is meant to call my bluff. "I didn't! It just happened, and I regret it, and I feel so freaking guilty that I want to fling myself from the top of a skyscraper."

Achilles pats my knee before beating themself in the face with a beauty blender. "I don't think you need to feel guilty," they say, patting the sponge against a particularly stubborn freckle that doesn't want to be covered by their eyeshadow. "Sometimes you *just* want to kiss someone, and when you've got the kind of chemistry that you and Spencer do, well…I've seen the videos on TikTok. Spencer wanted that kiss as bad as you did."

My parents and Avery had seen the videos, too, and Avery hasn't stopped pestering me ever since. "Who was that?" she'd demanded on the phone last night, dominating the call as my parents laughed quietly in the background. "What's his name? Is he a drag king? Ooooh I can't believe you kissed him!"

There was no point in reiterating that I didn't want to *actually* kiss Selene. Because sure, I'd wondered what it would feel like, if kissing someone with snake bites was any different than kissing someone without piercings (not that I would know any different), but that hadn't meant I'd wanted to shove my mouth against hers. I'd *just* wanted to win her stupid game, and that's what I am going to keep telling myself.

"What are you doing tonight, anyway?" I ask, trying to change the subject.

"I'm cosplaying as Ryuk from *Death Note*," Achilles says. "Have you seen it?"

I nod, grateful they've taken the bait, although I don't doubt that Achilles knows I don't want to talk about Selene anymore. "It's one of the first animes I ever watched," I tell them. "And it's still one of my favorites. Maybe the next time you do a cosplay from *Death Note*, we could both do L and Light? I think you'd make a cool L, to be honest."

Achilles' eyes brighten as they look at me, their mouth half-blue because they're working on mimicking Ryuk's terrifying grin. "You'd cosplay with me?"

"Sure," I say, not understanding exactly what I've just gotten myself into. "You'd have to teach me how, though. I've never done it before."

"It's just like dressing up for Halloween!" They're practically vibrating in their chair, the heels of their feet tapping with excitement against the floor. It makes me smile because Achilles is just *so* freaking pure, and if anything good has come out of my visit to New York, it's meeting Keel and being able to say I made a friend. "Sometimes you can buy a costume, but they're expensive, so I usually make them myself. Honestly, it's just like doing your makeup for drag!"

"Actually..."

Achilles yelps from the sudden sound of Selene's voice as she pops her head into the dressing room, her bottom lip caught between her teeth as she winces. Her eyes are teeming with an exhausted despair as I meet her gaze in the mirror, and she looks as if she hasn't been sleeping again; I duck my head so I don't have to see what I've done to her, staring at the makeup instead.

"I think cosplay is probably a lot harder," Selene says, taking me and Achilles by surprise, and I wonder if this is the first time that she's ever acknowledged their drag in a positive way.

"I spend most of my time trying to pass as a male-presenting performer, but...I couldn't do what you do, Keel."

Achilles squirms in their chair. "Um. Thanks. This is weird."

Selene has the decency to flinch. "I—yeah. You're right. I'm sorry." She rubs at the back her neck, sheepish and looking as uncomfortable as I feel right now, mostly because her being here can only mean one thing. "Briar, um...do you think we can talk, just for a minute? I know that you guys are still getting ready, so I promise not to keep you for too long." She bites at her lip again and hesitates before adding, "Please."

My heart beats itself into a frenzy, terrified and painfully out of rhythm, and I must be making some kind of face because Achilles takes my hand. "You don't have to talk to her," they say fiercely, rubbing their thumb across the back of my hand in small, soothing circles. "I can tell her to go away, if you want me to."

"I'll only be a minute," Selene repeats, her gravelly tone taking on a hint of desperation. One way or another, I know she's going to talk to me, whether it's alone or right here where Achilles can hear our conversation. "We need to—*I* need to talk about what happened, Briar. Please."

I let out a breath through my nose, one that's as shaky as the hand that Achilles is still holding. It's only fair that Selene and I talk about what happened, and after kissing her without her consent, I owe her an explanation and more than a rushed, "I'm sorry." My guilt and embarrassment don't outweigh what she needs right now.

"All right, then," I say stiffly, shaking Achilles loose. "So long as you promise not to yell at me again, we can talk."

Selene makes a show of using her finger to draw an *X* over her heart. "I won't."

The Gallery is nearly empty as I follow Selene into the hallway. She idly picks at her fingernails, chipping away a fresh layer of black and white polish, and I watch as she leans against the wall, her attempt at trying to make this feel casual. "So," she says, her green eyes dark beneath the cloudy, off-white fluorescents.

I can tell that she doesn't know how to start this, that she hadn't thought I would actually agree to have this conversation. But if talking about this is something she needs to move forward, well, I'm not in any position to deny her anything. Not when this was all my fault to begin with.

"Beau says the two of you aren't speaking right now."

Somehow, Selene continues to catch me off guard. "We're not," I say, and the ache of *that* particular wound threatens to double me over. Beau and I haven't spoken since last weekend. "He hasn't apologized for yelling at me."

Her shoulders cave in around her, and there are tears beginning to gather along her lashes, fat and round and threatening to spill down her cheeks. "Listen, Briar, I—" Selene's voice cracks as she looks at me, her mouth quivering as she sucks back a sniffle and sobs. "I am *so* fucking sorry, okay? I never, *ever* should have yelled at you." She wipes at her eyes with the back of her hand, and I don't understand what is happening right now. "I can tell you why I did it, and I can tell you why I thought it was justified, but—but it wasn't, and you don't deserve how I've been treating you."

This wasn't at all what I was expecting, not when she'd made it sound like she was wanting to talk about the kiss.

"It's not an excuse, but last Saturday was a really bad day for me. It doesn't matter why, so please don't ask, because I'm not going to bore you with the details. They'll only make you feel sorry for me." Selene drags a hand through her tangled hair and sighs. "I know it's not going to make sense to you, but right now...drag is the only thing in my entire life that feels right. And when Bow dragged you up onto the stage with her, I just—it felt like a snub that my drag mother was willing to perform with you, especially because she's never performed with me before." Everything about her deflates, like the air has been fully taken out of her. "I had no right to take everything that I was feeling out on you. The things I've been dealing with and my own insecurities about my drag...they're not your fault, and I'm sorry."

"Thanks," I hear myself murmur, because I don't know what I'm actually supposed to say. "For apologizing."

Selene nods as she continues, "I told Beau what happened and I asked him to be mad at me instead. And he is, sort of, but now he won't stop texting me because I think he's too afraid to talk to you. He feels really bad about having screamed at you."

I wrap my arms around my middle. "He should."

She nods again to show her agreement. "I don't expect you to forgive me——"

"I'm the one who should be apologizing," I blurt out, word-vomiting what we *should* be discussing right now. Selene appears taken aback, tilting her head as she frowns at me. She opens and closes her mouth, trying to work out a response, but I continue before she can speak, "I kissed you, and I shouldn't have, and I didn't even ask before I did it. If anyone around here should be angry, it's *you* who should be mad at *me*."

Selene looks as if she might start crying again. "You——is *that* what you think I'm upset about?" she asks, laughter beginning to bubble up and out of her. "Jesus, Briar. I'm upset because I know I hurt your feelings, not because I'm an antagonistic asshole and you kissed me in the middle of a show." Selene winces as she adds, "I'm upset about being antagonistic, too. I'm sorry."

"But——But I didn't even ask——"

She crosses over the space between us, taking my hands and holding them tightly in her own; her skin is warm against my clammy palms, but she doesn't seem to mind. "I appreciate that consent is so important to you——it's important to me, too, like

I've told you—and I appreciate that you understand how much I hate it when random strangers touch me. But you? You're not a stranger, Briar. And if you weren't going to kiss me after performing with me like *that*, then I sure as hell was going to kiss you."

All I can do is blink up at her, shocked by this new revelation. "Oh. *Oh.*"

Selene chuckles as she boops me on the end of my nose, as playful as a gesture as I'm used to with her. "I thought I've made it obvious that I like you," she muses. "But I feel like I just keep fucking everything up."

"You can be a bit of an asshole, sometimes."

"I know," Selene says, bowing her head until she's staring at the toes of her boots. "And I'm trying really hard to work on it. You have no idea how much it kills me that Achilles hates me, or that Jacklynn can't stand to be in the same room as me anymore."

I don't understand why she's having such a change of heart. Had Beau said something that might have resonated with her? He's always been good at bringing out the best in other people, so maybe that "work" had started with her complimenting Achilles tonight. But if she really has turned a new leaf and has decided that she wants to work on becoming a better version of herself... then maybe I can do that, too. And not just because I want to spite her, but because I think we both deserve better.

"I've been an asshole to you, too," I point out, and Selene hums her acknowledgement, still staring at the ground. "But maybe we can work on not being assholes...together? As friends, I mean. Not *together*, together."

A small smile curls at the corners of her mouth. "I don't know," she says, peeking at me through the ends of her ridiculously long lashes. "That kiss felt pretty *together* to me."

"Do you really have to ruin everything?"

Selene laughs as she squeezes the hand she's still holding, then brings it to her mouth where she presses a kiss against the back of it. My heart does a somersault in my chest. "That kiss can be whatever you want it to be," she says. "Just know that I thoroughly enjoyed it."

"Even though it was just a performance?" I ask, biting on the inside of my lip.

"*Especially* if it was just a performance." Selene winks, and it's infuriating, but it also makes my throat feel a little dry. Since when did I find her so attractive both in and out of drag? "If that's what you want to keep telling yourself, of course."

I groan and shove her away from me. "I'm going to get you back for that, you know."

"If I'd known that doing 'Boyfriend' was all it would take for you to kiss me—" She cuts herself off to consider my words, like it took her a moment to actually process them. "What do you mean, 'get back at me?' I thought that you and I were friends now!"

"We are," I say. "Just a couple of friends having a little... *friendly* competition."

Selene snorts and slings her arm around my shoulders, tugging me against her as she wheels us around toward the dressing room. The scent of her cinnamon perfume is overwhelming again, but in a good way, and I allow myself to be tucked into her side. "Prepare to be disappointed," she says, and for once, her tone isn't mocking. It's playful, and I can tell she's excited, hopefully as much as I am that this feud between us is over.

For now.

I guess we'll see where this goes, if the two of us can stay friends or if we'll be at each other's throats again by the weekend.

"I have more than just 'Boyfriend' in my arsenal," she continues. "And I'm not gonna take it easy on you because we're *friends* now."

I look up at Selene and smile, feeling more at ease as we share this moment than I've felt since first coming to New York. It'll be nice to call her my friend, and not my enemy. "I wouldn't expect anything less."

eighteen

There is a bowl of cereal sitting on the table in front of me.

It's Beau's third attempt at trying to get me to eat today.

Selene D'Angelo: please just let me know that you're okay...

I turn off my phone and stuff it beneath my pillow.

Eventually it dies because I don't bother plugging it in.

I'm jealous.

I wish I could find a way to unplug myself.

"Briar." Beau's voice is soft as he kneels down next to the futon. "Enzo and I are heading to The Gallery. Are you going to be okay here on your own?"

It doesn't matter if I'm going to be okay or not. Beau will never skip out on a show. Not again.

He sighs and grabs the blanket that I've kicked to the floor, covering me up so that he can make himself feel better about leaving. "Call me if you need anything, okay? Enzo and I are here for you, B. We don't like seeing you so sad."

Enzo sits down near my feet. "I don't need Achilles behind the bar tonight," he says, even though I know that's not true. It's Saturday night and there's a visiting queen on tour. "I'm sure they would be happy to come and sit with you."

A heartbeat of silence, then two.

Beau sighs again when I still don't answer.

"If we don't leave now, you'll be late again." He holds out his hand to Enzo, who takes it with a look of defeat. Enzo I don't doubt would stay behind if he didn't think he'd get fired. "I've got my phone turned all the way up if you need me. I'll try to come right home after the show."

He'd said that last night, too, and had come stumbling in at nearly four in the morning.

Priorities, I guess, because who would want to hang around the girl who's so depressed she wants to die?

I hate myself for not seeing it coming, because it always, *always* comes. Whether I'm doing well or not. Whether something triggered it or not. My depression rears its ugly head and I lose the will to crawl my way out of bed. To talk to my friends and have game nights with my brother and Enzo.

To eat.

To breathe.

To *live*.

This time, there was nothing that caused it.

There didn't need to be.

I'm depressed all on my own because my brain doesn't produce enough serotonin.

Or so people say when they don't want you to think that you're broken.

But a chemical imbalance of the brain? That seems like "broken" to me.

Selene and I had gone from having lip-sync battles during every show to her begging me not to cancel my performances. I'd told her that I was tired and my body hurt. That I'd thought I had pulled a muscle in the calf of my leg and didn't want to risk an actual injury. And it wasn't a lie, not exactly. My body aches like I've been tossed into traffic and run over.

I've thought about it.

Literally walking into traffic.

It sounds like a painful way to go, and it's not even necessarily guaranteed.

Earlier I'd watched a TikTok about a girl who'd been hit by a semi-truck and survived.

That would be my luck. That I couldn't even die right, if I tried.

"Do you think that you could maybe text Selene back?" Beau asks. I didn't realize that he and Enzo hadn't left yet. "She's really worried about you, B. I've literally caught her trying to steal my keys so that she could sneak over here and check on you. Twice. Achilles and Jac are worried, too. Maybe talking to them will help you feel better?"

I don't answer him. There's no point.

I am never going to feel better.

And I'm *not* going to text Selene.

Beau sighs again.

He turns on the same playlist he's had on repeat for days, the one with all of the "Born This Way" covers that we've come across over the years.

The front door opens and closes.

I'm alone.

As always.

Just me and my serotoninless brain.

There is a bowl of cereal sitting on the table in front of me.

I stare at it for the rest of the night.

nineteen

There is a plate full of pralines sitting on the table in front of me.

I can smell the vanilla and brown sugar. The toasted pecans.

They're one of my favorite snacks from back home.

I haven't had them in years.

"I asked Dominique to make these for you."

Beau is staring at me from the other side of the coffee table, slouched in a folding chair that he'd taken from The Gallery because I've barely left a space for him on the futon.

He could fit, if he wanted, but he chooses not to try.

Maybe he's afraid that my *I-want-to-die* mood is contagious.

He already looks like shit. Dark eyes. Hollow cheeks. Cracked lips.

He hasn't shaved since the weekend. That's not like him.

"I texted Mom and asked her for Grandma's recipe," Beau says. He runs his fingers through his short, messy pink hair, aggressively ripping apart the tangles. It's been so long since I've seen him without a wig that I'd forgotten he has his own hair at all. "They taste just like the ones that she used to make when we were kids."

Grandma's dead.

Nothing will ever taste like her pralines.

"Briar, *please*," Beau begs. His voice cracks. He sounds like he might be on the verge of tears. "I am trying really, *really* hard to be understanding and to support you. I've been giving you your space, and tracking down all your favorite foods, and—and I've been covering for you with Mom and Dad. They keep asking me why you won't reply to them, and Avery is worried that you're upset with her."

My phone is still dead beneath my pillow.

Off the grid and disconnected.

How it should be.

How *I* should be.

"Am I—am I doing something wrong?" Beau asks. I blink, and he's suddenly kneeling next to me on both knees. "If you'd just *talk* to me and tell me how to help you, I'd do anything. You have no idea how bad it hurts to see you like this." He roots around beneath the blanket that he keeps covering me up with, searching for my hand. It's tucked underneath me, just for this. "Are you still upset with *me*, is that it? Because I'm sorry, B. I never meant to yell at you, and I should have listened to you before I took Selene's side. Is that what did this? Did *I* do this?"

He doesn't deserve to blame himself.

I shake my head against my pillow.

Relief washes over him, and now maybe he can actually sleep tonight.

"What can I do, then?" he asks. "How can I help you?"

Nothing.

I'm beyond help.

I don't *deserve* help.

He drops his head when I don't answer. "Briar, *please*. I don't want to have to send you home early, but—but I don't know how to handle this. I don't know what to do." Beau places his hand on my shoulder. It's shaking. He's crying. "I *want* you here with me, okay? I need you to know that. I don't want you to go anywhere." Beau sucks back a sniffle and adds, *"Anywhere."*

Translation: He doesn't want me to off myself.

But I'm starting to think that I should.

At least then he would have space on the futon.

Beau lets out a quiet little sob, and I wonder if I've spoken out loud.

But no, he reaches for a praline.

"For me," he begs.

I don't take it.

twenty

Something inside of me has been telling me to do it for days now.

Grab a knife. Take some pills. Fill the bathtub.

I try to reason with myself, tell myself that it's because I want to *feel* something.

But truthfully, I *don't* want to feel anything at all.

Not tonight.

Not ever.

Not *anymore*.

So I am beating on Jacklynn Hyde's door.

Punching against the metal until my fingers bleed.

Until I'm sobbing and screaming her name.

Until her neighbors come outside to see what's happening.

Until the door disappears from beneath my fist and there's Jacklynn, standing in its place, dripping wet and wrapped in a fluffy purple bathrobe. She must have just come from the shower.

"Briar, baby, what's the matter?" she demands, dragging me into the safety of her apartment. I collapse once I've made it through the door, exhausted and aching and breathing so hard that I can't actually breathe at all. "Oh, God. Are you hurt? Where's all of this blood coming from, Miss Briar?"

I hold up my fist for her to inspect it, doubling over my knees as I sob into the carpet, "I'm sorry—so sorry—I *had* to! Please don't be mad at me. I'm so sorry."

Jacklynn grunts as she climbs down onto her knees. "You don't need to apologize. I'm not mad. But I need you to talk to me, Briar. Did you do something to hurt yourself?"

"No," I whimper. "But I was going to. I *want* to. But I feel so fucking scared."

Jacklynn immediately grabs a hold of me, gathering me into her arms so she can cradle me like a child against her chest. "You did the right thing by coming here," she says fiercely, petting my hair as I bury my face into her shoulder. "It's okay to be scared, but I've got you. You're safe now. So just take a minute to breathe, and keep crying. We can sit here for however long you need."

"Beau is going to be mad at me!" I sob.

She hushes me and holds me a little tighter, like she's afraid that I might break if she lets go. "No, he's not," Jacklynn soothes, rocking the two of us back and forth. "I don't think you can remember how loved you are, but that's okay, because I'm going to remind you."

"But I don't *deserve* to have anyone who loves me," I cry, because that's what the voice that is my fucking depression keeps on telling me.

That I'm terrible.

An inconvenience.

Pathetic.

"And it would be better for *everyone* if I was gone."

Jacklynn presses a lingering kiss to the top of my unwashed head. "I know you're not ready to listen to what I'm about to say," she begins, taking her fingers and running them through my hair, careful not to snag them on any tangles. I haven't brushed it in at least two weeks. "But it's something that you *deserve* to hear, so I'm going to say it anyway."

She draws in an exaggerated breath through her nose, her chest lifting my head as she holds the air in her lungs. I count the seconds in my brain, and right on cue, Jacklynn exhales through her mouth. In for five, out for seven, the same thing a therapist had taught me my freshman year of high school.

"You have more people who love you than you know what to do with, Miss Briar, and *all of us* would miss you if you were gone." She shifts uncomfortably from where we're sitting on the floor, and something somewhere on her cracks, maybe a hip or her knee. "And not only are you loved, but you're *wanted*."

In for five, out for seven again.

Jacklynn wants me to mimic her breathing.

I make it to three and five.

Choke on a sob.

She thumps her hand between my shoulders.

"You hardly even know me," I say, my voice coming out as a croak. Jacklynn whacks me on the back again. "All I am is Beau's little sister. Why do you care about what happens to me?"

"Because you're *not* just Beau's little sister," Jacklynn says. "You're my drag son."

I bury my face into her shoulder again.

Suck back a sniffle that would otherwise get snot all over her bathrobe.

"You're so much more than you think you are," Jacklynn continues, starting to pull her fingers through my hair again. They snag on a particularly large knot, and Jacklynn takes the time to gently ease it apart. "You're a daughter, a sister, and a friend. You're brave, and strong, and I know that you're going to make it through this."

I shake my head as a fresh round of tears spring to the corners of my eyes. "I'm not."

How could I?

Why *should* I?

"It might not seem like it right now," Jacklynn says. "But the fact that you came to me when you knew you needed help? Not everyone is able to do that, and I am *so* fucking proud of you for ignoring whatever voices are in your head, telling you that you don't deserve to be here."

A whimper cracks out of me from somewhere deep in my chest. "But what if I don't?"

"You *do*," Jacklynn insists. "And I'll say it as many times as I need to."

I don't know how long we've been sitting here.

If the sun has disappeared behind the skyscrapers.

What time it is, or if Beau has gone on stage yet.

Eventually Jacklynn groans, and I hear her hip snap.

"Do you think we can move this to the couch?" she asks, tentatively letting me go. A test to see if I'll fall apart. "These old bones of mine aren't what they used to be. Fuckin' arthritis and shit."

I wipe at my eyes with the back of my hand, still sniffling. "I'm sorry."

Jacklynn presses a kiss to my forehead, and it reminds me so much of the way that my mom takes care of me, the little ways she shows me she loves me, even if she doesn't know how to help take the depression away. "Don't be," Jacklynn says, but all I want to do now is call my mom and apologize to her instead. I'm *such* a piece of shit for not replying to her. For not taking her calls when she begs Beau to put me on the phone. "When was the last time you ate?"

All I can do is shrug. "I don't remember."

"Well," she says, grunting as she struggles to her feet. "That ain't the answer I was looking for. Sit down over there, baby. I'll make you something and call your brother so that he doesn't come home and call the police." Jacklynn offers me her hand to help me up. "Atta girl. Go get settled."

"Thank you," I tell her quietly, curling into the corner of the couch.

"Any time, Miss Briar. Any time." Jacklynn smiles before she disappears into the kitchen, rummaging through her fridge as she searches for something to make for me. "Do you like omelets? I make a *mean* cheese omelet."

"That sounds good, actually." My stomach rumbles as if to agree, and I think about all of the food that Beau has wasted trying to get me to eat something. Guilt replaces my hunger. "You really don't need to make me anything, though. I'm fine."

Jacklynn peeks at me through the small pass-through that overlooks the living room from the kitchen. "I *always* cook for my kids, especially when I know they're hungry. Now hush, so I can call your brother. I want to catch him before he goes on stage." She points with her phone at the small stand right next to me. "The remote is in there if you want to turn on the TV."

I find the remote buried beneath a magazine with Jacklynn Hyde on the cover. She looks beautiful in a maroon gown with gold accents, and she's wearing a wig that's longer than I am tall, dozens of braids hanging down around her and nearly touching the ground. It looks local, like she'd done a photoshoot with a small, queer media outlet here in New York and they'd given her a copy as a keepsake. I put it away before she can catch me admiring it.

I turn on Netflix and search for *She-Ra*. Achilles and I had planned on binge-watching it this summer, but with spending most of our time crafting costumes and performing, we'd never gotten around to it. My parents and I don't have Netflix, so I've never seen it before, but Keel had given me their login and offered to let me use it whenever I want, even after I go back home.

I miss them. Keel. The best friend I've ever had.

Adora has just met Glimmer and Bow—the character, not the drag queen—when Jacklynn starts murmuring in the kitchen, but her voice is so deep that it carries into the living room from the pass-through. "She's all right, honey. Calm down. I'm making her something to eat." The stovetop sizzles to life as Jacklynn cracks an egg into a frying pan, presumably with one hand. "No, I don't think she—well yes, but—Beau—*Beau.* Stop crying. The only thing that matters is she's okay. Just focus on that, and—" I hear her sigh as she cracks another egg into the pan. "Can you at least talk to Nathalie before—yes, I know she won't mind, but—of *course* she'll cover for you, but—no, absolutely not. Bringing them will just overwhelm her, and right now, all she needs is her big brother."

I pull the blanket tighter around me.

Who, other than Beau, would want to see me?

I haven't responded to Achilles or Selene in...

...However long it's been.

Selene, at the very least, is probably mad at me.

Achilles is probably worried sick.

I am *such* a terrible friend.

I don't deserve them or their worry.

"All right," Jacklynn sighs again from the kitchen. "We'll see you in just a minute."

She disconnects the call.

Pops her head into the pass-through.

"What do you like in your omelets?"

"Cheese," I answer. "Is Beau going to get in trouble for leaving?"

Jacklynn shakes her head. "Nathalie will understand, and Selene is going to cover for him on stage."

I slouch into the back of the couch, wishing that the cushions would swallow me up and take me somewhere far away from here. "Oh."

"Don't you worry about your brother," Jacklynn says. "I'll talk to Nathalie if she's upset. And don't be surprised when Beau comes bursting through that door. He's on his way over now and doesn't understand how to knock."

My mouth twitches with the smallest hint of a smile.

It's nice to know that some things never change.

twenty-one

Bow Regard slams open Jacklynn's front door without knocking. Only it's not *actually* Bow Regard, not really, just my brother in a sopping wet wig. It must be raining outside. His makeup is smeared in colorful streaks down the sides of his ashen face, and if not for the fact that his chest is heaving with a sob that shatters my heart, I would tell him that I think he looks cool like this. But instead, I brace myself for impact.

I am such a terrible sister. I don't think I've ever seen him so distraught before.

Beau dives around Jacklynn's coffee table, stumbling on his stilettos until he collapses onto his knees right in front of me. "Briar," he cries, taking my face between the palms of his trembling hands. Tears spring to the corners of my eyes. "Did you—did you *do* something? Are you hurt? Do Jac and I need to get you to a hospital?"

"No," I whisper, ashamed of myself for making him worry like this. "I'm so sorry."

"Don't you *dare* apologize," he says. "Because thank you. Thank you for coming here before you could do something to hurt yourself." Beau grabs a hold of me by the shoulders, and a soft whimper escapes from my lips as he drags me into the safety of his arms. His clothes are soaked from the rain, but that doesn't stop me from burying my face into his chest. It doesn't stop me from curling my fingers into the lacy fabric of his bodysuit. "I love you *so* fucking much, B. Do you know that? Literally more than anything in the world."

I sniffle and shake my head, because sure, I know that he loves me. But I guess, for a little while, it would be nice to hear him say it more often. "I don't understand what there is to love."

Beau squeezes me as tightly as he can without hurting me. "So much," he says, and I curl up against him as he thoughtfully provides me with a list. "You're hilarious, first of all. Like... you are *so* snarky and *so* quick-witted, and it's one of my favorite things about you. Second of all, you're super supportive and understanding, and even though *I'm* the older sibling, *you're* the one who would help me hide a body."

Leave it to Beau to make me laugh when I literally feel like dying. "Only because we would have to bury it, and I can't imagine you with a shovel."

"See? That's why I need you to stick around." Beau's voice breaks because as hard as he's trying to make me feel better, he's clearly devastated. What would have happened had I not come to Jacklynn for help? It's something he's going to ask himself for God only knows how long. "Did something happen, B? Something that—that maybe you're not telling me?"

I tuck myself further into his arms. "No. Nothing caused this."

He draws in a shaky breath, relief loosening the tension in his shoulders. "I guess I should consider myself lucky that I don't understand," he admits. I nod, because I'm glad that he doesn't. I never want Beau to have to feel like this. "I've—I've never really been depressed before, you know? I've been sad, but that's not the same thing." Beau's eyes flutter as he settles against the front of the couch to get comfortable. "When Connor died, I—God, I was so fucking angry. Not because I was still mad at him for breaking my heart, but because I was still in love with him when he passed." He blinks away the tears that are heavy on the ends of his lashes. "I ask myself all the time what we could have been, had Connor been able to love me without conditions."

Beau has never really talked about Connor before, not since he'd died and Beau's heart had been ripped from his chest. He's always said that he doesn't like to think about him, that mentioning his name is enough to reopen old wounds. But here he is now, being candid with me. Trying to relate to what I'm going through, and in the only way he knows how.

"I was so goddamn sad when Connor died," he says. "You saw me after his funeral and what a mess I was. But as angry as I was about the should haves, could haves, and would haves, that sadness and that anger wasn't completely all-consuming, not like whatever you feel when you get like this." Beau presses a kiss to my hair, wet from where I'm still laying against him. "When I came home, I channeled everything I was feeling into my drag. Did a lot of sad songs and drove Jacklynn up the wall with my crying. I did back-to-back shows every night just to keep myself busy as a distraction. But eventually, I had nothing left to give. I couldn't keep doing what I was doing, not without hurting myself." Beau looks ashamed of himself as he continues, "I was so fucking exhausted, and Jacklynn had to make me take a break. She canceled all of my shows at The Gallery, and no matter how hard I begged for Nathalie to put me back on the roster, she refused. It was a good thing, though, because it gave me the time to sit at home and actually grieve. I cried my eyes out until they were bloodshot, of course, but taking the week off to take care of myself is what I needed to feel better."

"You've never told me any of that," I whisper, gripping the fabric of his bodysuit. To know that he was hurting and that I hadn't been here to help him... "I thought you were okay, when you came back here."

He nods and glances at the pass-through, where Jacklynn is watching us carefully. "It took me a while, but I'm okay now. And don't get me wrong, because sometimes I still get sad, especially around the anniversary of his death, but it's nothing like what I know you go through just to make it through each day." He sighs and hooks his chin over my shoulder. "Can you explain it to me? Tell me what your depression feels like and how to help you? Because I thought that if I could just…get you to cope with it like I'd coped with my grief for Connor…if I could just get you up off the couch…that maybe you'd okay again, too."

No one has ever asked me what it feels like before.

"I don't know if that's a good idea."

Beau sits back so he can look at me. His eyes are red and puffy, and tears are still rolling down his cheeks. I wonder if he's stopped crying at all since Jacklynn called him. "I *want* to know what you're going through. I want to understand." He swipes at his cheek with the back of his hand and sniffles. "This is the first time you've spoken to me in weeks, B. You never even told me you were feeling this way."

I drop my gaze to the blanket that's pooling in my lap. The fabric is wet from Beau's clothes. "I'm—it feels like—" I swallow hard because the words are plastered to my tongue.

Beau smiles sadly in encouragement. "Take your time. Pretend like you're writing one of your fanfics. How would you describe a character who was depressed?"

That's…an easier way of thinking about it, I guess.

"All right. Um. It feels like…" I bite at the inside of my cheek, trying to peel syllables from the roof of my mouth because I've never had to describe my own depression before. "It feels like I'm trapped at the bottom of the ocean, and I—I can *feel* the weight of it pressing down on me. I don't know which way is up or down, and it's so dark that I can't see anything around me."

Beau swallows noisily and doesn't say anything. He wants me to keep going.

"It's like being in a constant state of drowning, because if I open my mouth to breathe, my lungs will fill up with water, but if I try holding my breath for too long, I'll suffocate." I wrap my arms around my middle, still staring down at the blanket. "Sometimes it's easier, just wanting to drown, than to try and claw my way to the surface. Especially when I can't see it."

My brother wipes a tear from his cheek. "Fuck, Briar, I'm—" His nostrils flare as he sniffles, and I bury my face into his chest again. I'm so tired of watching him cry, especially because it's always my fault. Beau's probably been miserable since the moment he picked me up at the airport. "I'm so sorry, I didn't know, I—*fuck*. I probably made it worse, didn't I?"

"No," I say, winding my arms around his torso to hug him. Beau wraps his arms around me, too. "This was never your fault, and all you've done is try to help me. You're the *best* big brother, Beau. I'm so fucking lucky to have you."

He shakes his head as Jacklynn joins us in the living room, utterly silent as she places a still-steaming omelet on the coffee table. "All those months ago," Beau begins, and I know exactly what he's going to say. "When Dad called me and—and said that you'd said you wanted to kill yourself—" A quiet sob cracks out of him, and I squeeze him as tightly as I can.

We've never talked about the night when our parents had called him, Dad hysterical as he begged Beau to talk me off the ledge. Avery had spent the night at a friend's house, and I'd locked myself in the bathroom with a knife and a bottle of Dad's pain pills. They'd pounded on the door for an hour, threatening to break it down as I screamed and cried and said that I wanted to die. That I was going to die and they just needed to leave me alone.

I hadn't dared to open the door until I'd heard Beau's voice through the phone, pleading for me to come out and talk to him. To tell him what was wrong and what he could do to make me feel better. There hadn't been much for me to tell him—I hadn't known why I felt that way, just that I did and that I'd needed to do something about it. But Beau had stayed up with me all that night, even as I slept with the phone still held to my ear.

If it weren't for my brother, I wouldn't be here, and he doesn't deserve to have to constantly keep coming to my rescue.

"I thought that if I brought you here," Beau continues, "and if you could see that there was something outside of Texas, that it would—it might—"

"Fix me?" I ask. Beau nods. "I don't think anything will ever fix me."

"I don't think that you need to be fixed," Jacklynn says, easing herself down onto the couch. "That implies that you're broken, and you're not. But what I do think is that you need to get help, the kind that Beau and I aren't equipped to give you."

Beau frowns as he wipes another tear from his cheek, his makeup nearly gone from the rain and how hard he's been crying. "What do you mean?"

Jacklynn gestures at something on the other side of the room. "Grab me that photo on the dining table," she says, waving at Beau as if to send him scurrying along. He grumbles and climbs to his feet, doing as he's been told because the lesson here is going to be an important one, perhaps one that he's received for himself already. "I think you need to consider seeing a therapist," Jacklynn tells me, watching as Beau retrieves the frame of a young Jacklynn Hyde. "And don't you go making that face, Miss Briar. Not every therapist is the right fit for every person who needs one, and it's going to take time for you to find someone you connect with and trust."

Sitting back down on the floor again, Beau hesitates before he nods his agreement, handing the picture frame to Jacklynn. "I know you've tried seeing a therapist before," he says. "And I know you hated having to talk to her. But she was a homophobic piece of shit with an office the size of a broom closet. There has to be someone out there who's better for you."

"You should talk to Rita Book, Achilles' drag mother." Jacklynn holds the picture to her chest, pressing it against the space above her heart. "She's a licensed psychiatrist who works with queer youth as her day job, and she might have some resources that'll work for you. She might have some recommendations, too. Her office does online appointments."

I stare down at my lap, unconvinced. What's the difference between talking to someone I know versus a therapist? Both can offer me advice, but only one of them actually cares about me. The other is being paid to pretend. "I really don't know how I feel about this."

"That's all right," Jacklynn says calmly, her dark eyes glassy as she turns the frame around and shows it to me. "The woman in this photo is my drag mother. Her name was DiDi Divine."

She hands me the photograph I'd been staring at all those weeks ago, back when Jacklynn had first taught me how to contour. I'd wondered who was in the photo with her, a young Jacklynn smiling bright as she squeezed DiDi Divine in a hug, an embrace that looks both celebratory and full of love. "She's beautiful," I say, studying the bejeweled crown that's sitting on DiDi's head. "Did she do pageants?"

Jacklynn nods in confirmation, and Beau reaches over me to place his hand on her knee. "That photo is from the year that she won Miss Continental," she says, her raspy voice thick with unusual emotion. "It's also from the same year that she died."

I snap my head up to look at her, and I have never seen Jacklynn cry before, not even when her bones snap during her pre-show warm-ups with Beau. It shatters what's left of my heart into a thousand tiny pieces, watching as she wipes a tear from her chin, and all I want is to crawl across the couch and go hug her. "Jac, I'm—I'm so sorry, I didn't—"

"It's all right, baby. I know." Jacklynn takes the frame from me and sets it down on the coffee table, right next to the still-steaming omelet. My stomach rumbles. "DiDi Divine took me in when I was eighteen-years-old and had no other place to go." She picks up the plate and sets it down in my lap, encouraging me to eat by stabbing the fork into the egg. Yellow cheese seeps out of it. "She put me in my first pair of heels, and she taught me what it meant to be a drag queen. To live my life as authentically as I damn well pleased." Jacklynn places her hand on top of Beau's, his palm still resting on her knee, and she squeezes his fingers like she somehow needs him in this moment. "She died from AIDS in the early nineties, and when I lost my mama, Miss Briar, as a young queen in a world that hated who I was..."

"I'm so sorry," I murmur. Beau parrots the sentiment, but I'm certain that he's heard this story before. Jacklynn knew to count on him for comfort.

"I'm all right, I'm all right." Jacklynn dismisses us with a brisk wave of her hand. "The reason that I'm telling you about my drag mother, Miss Briar, is because I want you to know you're not alone. Because I want you to know that for the longest time, I felt how you're feeling right now." She takes a deep breath before smiling at me, though it doesn't quite reach her eyes. "I am going to help you through this. Your brother, Enzo, and all of the other people who love you—we are going to help you through this. But we've got to start somewhere, and I think the best place for you is in therapy."

Beau presses the fork into my hand, a silent plea to start eating. "I think something online would be good for you. You won't even have to leave the house. Rita mostly does drag brunches on the weekends, but I bet you could get Achilles to ask her to come to one of your shows."

I shrug and pick at my food. There are too many emotions bursting through my brain, too many thoughts that are traveling at a thousand miles an hour. I still haven't fully processed Jacklynn's drag mother yet, that my own drag mother had shared such a personal piece of her heart with me.

"I doubt that I can still perform as Edgar," I point out. "But maybe I can talk to Rita at a brunch."

"Of course you can still perform!" Beau says, using his fingers to pinch off a piece of my food. He stuffs it into his mouth and groans, chomping noisily with his teeth. "Nathalie asks about you every night and says that you can come back whenever you feel better. She likes having another king at The Gallery, but she also just likes you in general."

I snap my head up to look at him, and something like excitement begins to flare back to life inside my chest. I figured that my drag career was over, especially after canceling all of my shows at

The Gallery, usually the day of or night before. "Are you serious?"

"Edgar Allan Foe ain't going anywhere," Beau says, smiling. "At least, not if you don't want him to."

Suddenly starving, I stab my fork into my omelet, ripping off a hunk of yellow egg and cheese. "I want him to stay until it's time for me to go back home, and I still really want to do the competition."

Beau leans forward and presses a kiss to my cheek. "We'll talk about it. But speaking of drag and the competition...you *really* need to text Selene. She's been worried sick about you, B. Achilles, too."

"My phone is dead," I tell him, retrieving it from my pocket and showing him that it won't turn on. "It's not broken, I just... haven't charged it. I haven't wanted to talk to anyone."

"There's a charger next to the couch," Jacklynn says. Beau reaches for the cord that's tucked behind the end table and gives it to me. My hands shake as I plug it into my phone, terrified to see the number of missed notifications that are waiting for me. It's so dead that it doesn't even come on right away. "I think there's something else we need to talk about."

Both my brother and I lift our heads to look up at her. "Like what?"

Jacklynn kicks her feet up onto the coffee table. "I'm glad that you want to keep doing drag," she says slowly. "And I'm glad that you're so excited to get back to it. But drag alone isn't enough to keep your mental health in check, and I'm concerned for when you go back home. How do you feel about medication?"

My phone vibrates to life between my fingers. "I've never tried it."

"I think it might be worth looking into," Jacklynn tells me. Beau takes my hand as I try to ball it up into a fist, like he agrees but doesn't want to say it out loud. "It doesn't mean there's something wrong with you, Miss Briar. That's not what I want you to take away from this. But there are a lot of people in our community who use these resources, with all we've been through, and you're lucky enough to have supportive parents who have insurance. It'd be a waste of your privilege to not explore your options."

"I know there's a stigma around being medicated," Beau murmurs, using his thumb to rub small, soothing circles against the inside of my wrist. "Stigma" is a frickin' understatement, especially where we're from. Most of the adults will tell you to just go outside whenever you're feeling sad, like warm air and the smell of nature is a cure. "But a lot of people take medicine for their depression, and if it could help you not to feel like this, B... don't you think it might be worth trying?"

I blink away the tears that are gathering in the corners of my eyes. Why can't therapy be enough for me? "What if the people at school find out? I'm enough of an outcast as it is."

Jacklynn leans over to rest her hand on my shoulder. "Don't give those little *fuckers* that kind of power over you," she says fiercely.

"No one would have to know unless you told them, and besides that, there is absolutely *nothing* to be ashamed of. You deserve to be happy, Miss Briar, and I think antidepressants could really help you." She gives my shoulder a squeeze. "I don't want to get a phone call after you go home because something happened to you."

My phone begins to vibrate in rapid succession as all of my notifications start coming through. "Can I think about it?"

"Of course," Beau says, his blue eyes wide with sincerity. "You don't have to decide right now. You don't even have to decide this week! I don't want you to feel like we're pressuring you into doing something you're not comfortable with."

I nod and wipe at my face, brushing away the tears that have started to roll down my cheeks. "I get it. Can we talk about something else now?"

"Sure!" Beau takes a peek at my phone. "How many texts do you think you have from Selene?"

Jacklynn snorts as she grabs the TV remote from the coffee table. "Fifty."

Beau narrows his eyes. "Fifty-two."

"It's really Achilles you should be betting on," I say, typing in my passcode to unlock my phone and unleash the mess that is my inbox.

Mom: Missed Call (17)

Dad: Missed Call (11)

Avery Vincent: Missed Call (6)

Selene D'Angelo: Missed Call (23)

Achilles Patrick: Missed Call (3)

"Jesus," I say. "She called me *twenty-three* times."

"Holy *shit*, go to your texts! I bet I guessed closer than Jac did."

Selene D'Angelo: Please just tell me you're okay...

Selene D'Angelo: Briar please...I'm really worried...

Selene D'Angelo: I'm so sorry if I'm who made you feel like this...

Selene D'Angelo: Do you think that maybe I could come see you?

Selene D'Angelo: Beau said you're not doing well, please call me...

Achilles Patrick: hi briar, i really really miss u. i hope ur doing ok

Selene D'Angelo: My mama made you these really weird cookies???

Selene D'Angelo: God I'm so worried... I think I might just come over...

Selene D'Angelo: Beau said you're not eating... please eat...

Avery Vincent: hi sissy i miss u pls text me back

Selene D'Angelo: I miss you so fucking much...

Selene D'Angelo: I need to see you... I need to know you're okay...

Selene D'Angelo: That was stupid, I know you're not okay

Achilles Patrick: im here if u need to talk ily bestie

Mom's Cell: Briar, baby, please answer your phone. Dad and I are really worried.

Avery Vincent: mom n dad tried calling u pls pick up

Selene D'Angelo: I'm losing my shit over here, Briar. I'm so fucking worried...

Achilles Patrick: did u know that earthquakes on the moon are called moonquakes???

Achilles Patrick: did u know that theres a species of shark that can live for 500 yrs?!!?!

Selene D'Angelo: I'm gonna come over there. I swear I'm gonna do it...

Achilles Patrick: did u know a group of jellyfish is called a smack???!?!!

Selene D'Angelo: FUCK PLEASE TELL ME YOU'RE OKAY????

Selene D'Angelo: Oh my god, Briar, please... ARE YOU OKAY?! Bow's on her way over...

Selene D'Angelo: Please tell Jacklynn to answer her phone... ARE YOU OKAY???

Enzo Santiago: I love you, hermanita. I'm coming by Jacklynn's after work.

Achilles Patrick: i need u to know how loved u are and that u got this <3

By the time that I've finished clearing out all of my notifications, I'm sobbing into my fist while Jacklynn and Beau argue over something on the television. Selene has texted seventy-three times, and neither of them were even *close*.

I have a lot of messages to send, but I start by typing out a message to Selene.

Briar Vincent: I am so sorry...

twenty-two

The Gallery is quiet as Beau and I come in through the front. We hadn't told anyone that I was coming tonight, not even Jacklynn, who checks in on me every morning—usually via video call so she can see for herself that I'm still breathing. The sentiment is always bittersweet—it's nice to know that she cares, but the calls haven't stopped me from wishing that I would die in my sleep.

Beau and I weren't sure if I could handle it, though, being trapped inside The Gallery and feeling smothered by the crowd that'll eventually come pouring through the doors. I'm still not even sure if I *can* handle it, despite being here, and since I don't want to disappoint my friends by telling them I would be here and then not coming, we hadn't told them anything at all.

Hopefully, it'll come as a nice surprise for them.

Especially since I had thought about walking into traffic on the way over.

It was Beau's idea to get here obnoxiously early, mostly so

I could have first dibs on whichever seat I want at the bar, but also because he's been dying to see Enzo. He's been keeping his distance while I "recover," insisting that he hasn't wanted to overwhelm me, and it's been driving Beau crazy because he misses him. That's probably why he squawks in a high-pitched outrage when Enzo notices me before him.

"Briar," he says, and I've never seen Enzo move so quickly before. He practically dives around the bar, closing the distance between us in record time so he can wrap his arms around me in a hug. "I'm so glad to see you, hermanita. Beau didn't tell me you were coming."

I breathe in the scent of his woodsy cologne and sink into the safety of his embrace. Enzo hasn't stopped by the apartment, but he's been texting me every single day, sharing the quieter parts of himself with me; the bits of him that understand what I've been going through. "I didn't want him to," I say, squeezing Enzo around the middle. "Just in case I couldn't make it out the door."

Enzo nods as he presses a kiss to the top of my freshly cut hair. Beau had spent hours trying to help me brush out the tangles, but after a while I decided that we should just cut it. A jolt of excitement had shot through my bones as Beau took the razor to my head, and I hadn't been sad to see the faded blue strands fall into the bathtub around me. Now, there's really nothing left, just a bit of blond he'd left on top, and I love it.

The haircut makes me feel...something. It's masculine, but

still kind of feminine, the perfect amount of in-between. I haven't been able to stop touching my head, and where I thought that I would hate having to see my scalp whenever I looked in a mirror...I don't. It's a great look for Edgar, too, and now I don't have to pull my hair back or wear a wig when I do drag. Win-win.

"Anything you need tonight, I've got you." Enzo lets me go so he can tend to my pouting older brother, who'd dragged us here so early that he's not even gotten into drag yet. "If you want to sit at the bar, make sure you grab the seat on the end, closest to the kitchen. No one except employees come through there, so you should have a fair bit of space."

"Sounds like a plan," I say, watching as Beau attaches himself to Enzo. He's got a garment bag slung over his shoulder, his makeup case strapped over the other, and Enzo winces as Beau accidentally whacks him with both. "Is Achilles working tonight?"

Enzo wraps his arm around my brother's waist and positions him in a way that he's not being attacked by his drag. "They're in the back getting some cups out of storage. Keel is gonna be *so* excited to see you."

I force myself to smile at him so that my guilt doesn't eat me alive. Achilles has been texting me with unusual fun facts for *weeks*, but I haven't been up for replying to them beyond my brief apology. And not because I don't want to, I just... I *know* that Achilles is both infinitely patient and understanding, and it's been nice having them as someone that I know I can slack on—at least until I'm ready to be social again—because I know they're not going to be upset with me.

They also weren't unhinged in their messages, not like Selene who I've had to keep responding to so she doesn't come beating down Beau's door.

"Is it okay if I go ahead and grab a chair?" I ask. "I can just wait for Keel while you two...do whatever it is you do."

Enzo coughs into his fist because the two of them *do* need their alone time, and Beau is trying to subtly pull him away from me. "Uh. Yeah. Of course. Here." Enzo reaches into his back pocket, procuring something shiny that he hands to me. It's his fidget spinner. "It's not a lot, but I've been bringing that to work with me in case you came back and might need it."

I press it tightly between my index finger and thumb and spin the blades. "Thanks. I really need to invest in my own fidget toys."

"You can keep that one," he says with a smile. "I have a few more of them at home."

Beau nudges him with an elbow. "You never give *me* gifts. That's rude."

Enzo rolls his eyes. "I give you *gifts* all the time. It's not my fault you're ungrateful."

"Those don't count." Beau smirks. "Not when I *always* return the favor."

I groan and cover my ears, wishing I were anywhere but here right now. "The two of you are fucking insufferable."

My brother plants a kiss on Enzo's cheek and smiles. "I guess this means we'll be going now. You know where to find me if you need us."

My chest tightens beneath the binder I'm wearing under my thrifted Metallica T-shirt, and all I can do is stand here and watch as the two of them turn around to leave. Enzo, at least, has the decency to crane his neck around and spare me an apologetic smile, like he's sorry they're abandoning me in the middle of an empty bar. I know he would stay with me if I asked, but Beau is desperate to get him alone, and since I already feel guilty for being the reason they haven't seen each other in the first place…I wave him away as if to tell him that I'm going to be fine, then immediately make a break for the bar, climbing onto the stool near the kitchen.

There's a couple of bartenders moving back and forth behind the counter, eyeing me suspiciously because the bar isn't open and no one is supposed to be sitting here yet. They're washing glasses and chatting quietly amongst themselves, and I can't help but to feel like I'm probably the topic of their conversations. I can only imagine what they're saying. "Who does this bitch think she is?" "I'm not going to ask her if she wants something." "Isn't she that suicidal sister of Bow's?"

I squeeze Enzo's fidget between my fingers, spinning the blades until they're a blur. Of course, the bartenders aren't talking about me. Why would they? I'm not that special, and I know that they've probably seen me around before, distracting Achilles and Enzo. Maybe *that's* why they're giving me the stink eye, avoiding me at all costs as they stick to the other end of the bar.

My knee bounces beneath the counter, and Enzo's fidget spinner isn't spinning fast enough. He'd said that Achilles is somewhere in the back digging cups out of storage... I wonder what would happen if I snuck back there? If I waited until the bartenders weren't looking at me, slid down off of my chair, and army-crawled through the double kitchen doors? Enzo would think it was hilarious, but I have a feeling if I got caught, Nathalie and his fellow bartenders would not.

But my bouncing knee is rattling the bar, Enzo's fidget spinner *still* isn't spinning fast enough, and my chest is still tight beneath my binder. Sitting here alone because my brother and Enzo had better things to do is beginning to wear thin on what little stability I have left right now, so I reach into my pocket with a shaky hand and pull out my phone to send a message.

Briar Vincent: Are you going to be at The Gallery tonight?

The recipient's response is immediate.

Selene D'Angelo: I'm finishing my beard right now...why? Are you coming tonight?

Briar Vincent: I'm already here.

Briar Vincent: Alone.

Briar Vincent: Beau and Enzo abandoned me for the bathroom.

Selene D'Angelo: Omg those assholes! I'll be there in 5!

A breath of air whooshes from my lungs in relief, and Spencer does not disappoint.

"Briar!" I hear him cry, and I check my phone to see that it's only been *three* minutes.

Spencer Read is panting as he bursts into the bar, the kitchen doors swinging shut behind him because that's where the stairs are that lead to his upstairs apartment. I don't know why I texted Spencer instead of Achilles, but seeing him now makes me want to cry, especially because he's already doing it, his tears smudging the thick black liner around his eyes.

"You're here," he says, towering over me in his tall, strappy black platforms. His pierced bottom lip is quivering as he balls up his hands, shaking them at his sides like he's struggling to find some restraint. "I'm—I'm so—*fuck*, can I just hug you, please?"

I blink at Spencer in surprise. "Um…sure?"

He launches himself forward and wraps his arms around my shoulders, holding me against him as he sobs into the curve of my neck. "I'm so sorry," Spencer cries, and all I can do is stiffly hold him back. Why on Earth is he so emotional? "I know I kept calling and texting you, and I know you needed your space, but—but I was *so* fucking worried, Briar. Beau was giving me updates and I know that he would never lie to me, but it's—it's not the same as hearing those updates from you, you know?"

He should have just slapped me across the face. Maybe it would have hurt less than the guilt that is eating me alive.

"I'm—I never meant to worry you," I say, gently patting him on the back. Spencer sniffles into the collar of my T-shirt and hugs me tighter against him. "My phone died, and I just...I never charged it. I didn't want to. But I *should* have. I knew you were texting me and I should have responded sooner."

"I understand why you didn't want to talk to anyone," Spencer says. He pries himself away from me and uses the sleeve of his bedazzled jacket to wipe at his nose. "It's just—I don't want to make this about *me*, but—but suicide is—it's really triggering for me, and—"

I frown and reach for his hand, floundering to ignore the depth of my guilt before it can drag me back under, trapping me at the bottom of my endless ocean of depression again. "Hey, it's okay. I'm still here. See?" I slide my fingers between his sweaty ones, and it's *weird*—I can feel his pulse as it jumps beneath the skin of his palm, racing to the beat of his heart. "You can't get rid of me that easily, Read. Someone has to kick your ass in the competition."

Spencer shakes his head, his nostrils flaring as he sucks back a disgusting sniffle. "I don't want to get rid of you, Briar. I want you to stay and to be happy. More than anything." He nods at the empty barstool next to mine. "Mind if I sit? There's something I want to tell you."

"Of course," I say, turning to pull out the chair for him. Spencer climbs up into it with a groan, muttering something about his *goddamn shapewear*, and I raise an eyebrow as he shamelessly unbuttons his leather pants. "Classy."

His smile is as sheepish as it is tired, and I wonder if he hasn't been sleeping again. It's hard to tell with all of the makeup smeared around his eyes. "How about *you* try and wear three pairs of tights so that you can squeeze your ass into some leather? These pants weren't made for sitting down in." Spencer raises his hand to flag down one of the bartenders, who must know what he wants because they don't even ask before pouring him a tall glass of Pepsi. "Do you want anything? Jeremy can just put it on my tab, so don't worry about it. You like Dr. Pepper, right?"

"I'm all right, I don't need anything. Why does it feel like you're stalling?" I ask, tilting my head at him as Spencer drops his gaze to the countertop, his green eyes narrowing like it's committed some atrocity against him. "You can tell me anything, you know. I'm really in no position to judge you, and I wouldn't, even if I was. Are you—are you *okay*? Has something happened? I know it's been a couple of weeks, but—"

Spencer wraps his fingers around his Pepsi, tucking the glass in close to his chest. "Has Beau ever told you about Piper?"

"No," I say, scooting closer because Spencer has dropped his voice. "Who are they?"

"Who *was* she," Spencer corrects me quietly, swallowing so hard that I'm terrified he might throw up on me. "Piper and I met at Pride when we were fourteen. I was walking in the parade with my parents and some of the queens, and I had a rainbow flag in my back pocket. It fell out, and Piper came running to give it back to me. We clicked right away, and she was just...my first *everything*."

He swipes at his nose with the back of his sleeve again, so I reach into the basket that's sitting across from us and hand him a stiff white napkin. "Thanks," he says tearfully, using it to dab beneath his eyes. "But Piper, she—she was the first girl who's hand I ever held, and the first girl I ever kissed. She was funny, and beautiful, and she had this fiery orange hair like Hayley Williams from Paramore."

The canvas hanging in his bedroom, the girl with the bright orange hair.

Spencer's voice cracks as he continues, "She *always* saw the glass half-full, until she didn't."

I shouldn't have to ask where Spencer's going with this, but I don't want to blindly make assumptions. Especially when this person is so important to him. "What happened to her?"

Tears are dripping from his chin now, and all I can do is wrap my arm around his shoulders, tugging him closer so that I can hold him. Spencer sinks into me without restraint. "She killed herself two years ago. Jumped right in front of a fucking *train*." I squeeze my eyes shut as he buries his face into my shoulder, his fingers curling into the black fabric of my T-shirt. "I was studying for a test, and she'd tried calling me. I didn't answer."

"Fuck," I breathe, because it's the only word that comes to mind. "Selene, I'm—I'm so sorry. I can't even imagine, and I'm—you *know* that it wasn't your fault, right? That you're not the one who made her do that?"

Spencer shrugs as he clings to me. "Maybe if I'd just answered my phone—"

"No." I lean back to tuck my fingers beneath his chin, forcing his head up so that Spencer has no choice but to look at me. His eyes are still watery as I gently cup his face, surprised when he leans into my palm. "Answering your phone would *not* have steered her away from that train, Spencer. She would have had to make that decision for herself, and there's nothing you could have done to change her mind. Are you listening to me? Do you *hear* me? You didn't kill her, Spencer."

"You don't know that—"

"I *do*," I insist, catching myself as I brush my thumb across his cheek, wiping away a tear that's blackened with mascara. "I've been there—I *am* there. I know what it feels like to not want to do this anymore, and if I hadn't made the choice to go to Jacklynn's that night, we wouldn't be having this conversation." I try to pull my hand away from his face, but Spencer immediately grabs my wrist to keep my palm against his cheek, and I don't dare try to move again. "What happened to Piper is tragic, and I can't even imagine the trauma you've been holding on to since she died. But I need you to hear me when I say that it wasn't your fault."

Spencer rests his head against my shoulder again, slumping into me with enough force that I nearly topple out of my chair. "I *want* to hear you," he says quietly. "But I just—when Beau told me you were struggling, I—I thought that if I kept texting you, and calling you, I could—" Spencer presses his face into my chest. "I'm really glad you're still here."

"I wish I actually *wanted* to be here," I admit to him, whispering like I'm terrified someone who's not Spencer will overhear me. Which is silly considering Beau knows I still feel this way, and it wouldn't matter if one of the bartenders tattled on me. "I don't want to trigger you, I just—I thought about walking into traffic on the way over here, and I don't know how to make intrusive thoughts like that go away." Spencer's fingers tighten around my wrist as he whimpers. "Beau was holding my hand so I couldn't, but..."

"But you still wanted to," Spencer finishes for me. "And that's the point."

I nod and slouch down against him, resting my chin on the top of his head from where he's still leaning into me. "Can I ask you something?"

"Anything."

"Your tattoo," I say, reaching around to poke at the spot on his arm. "It has a date."

Spencer chuckles before sitting himself up so that he can roll up the sleeve of his jacket. "Beau told me you were curious about it," he says, showing me his pumpkin tattoo. "June fifteenth is when she…" He bites his lip and glances up at me, and I can tell that he doesn't want to say it again, that this person who'd meant so much to him had died. But June fifteenth had also been the day that Bow had dragged me up onto the stage with her, and suddenly it makes sense why Spencer's eyes had been bloodshot. Why his face had been pale and he'd been so quick to anger. "The pumpkin is because that's what I always called her. Her hair was the same shade of orange."

"I like it," I say, ashamed of myself for thinking it was stupid. "I'm sorry you lost her."

"Me too." Spencer pulls his sleeve back down. "You'd have liked her, I think. She always had her nose in a book, and she did drag but was a bio queen on TikTok. Performing wasn't her thing."

"She probably didn't want to compete against you."

Spencer snorts as he retrieves his phone from his pocket, checking the time and then flipping it over to the mirror-like case on the back. "Shit. The doors are gonna open soon and I'm supposed to be on stage at nine. Look at what you did to me, Foe."

I hand him another napkin and watch as he starts wiping away the tear stains cutting through his contour. "Beau brought his makeup case if you need to touch anything up."

"I'll be fine," Spencer says, patting the napkin beneath his eyes. "But speaking of makeup, mind if I give you a friendly tip for your beard? Because you look cute and all, and I fucking *love* that haircut on you, but your chin, babe...stop using a whole stick of eyeliner."

I can't decide if I think Spencer is trying to insult me, or if I think that *he* thinks he's trying to help me; either way, I immediately cover my chin. "All I have is Beau's old makeup," I say, trying to remember exactly how thick I had drawn on the hairs of my beard tonight. "His pencil sharpener is dull and I can't get the stick into a point."

"Don't use a pencil at all," Spencer tells me. "You'll never get it to look like you've got little hairs on your face, if that's the kind of look you're going for. Use a mascara wand."

"Huh..." I've never even touched the tube of mascara that Beau had given me, assuming it was probably dried out. Guess that means that I need to buy a new one. "Thanks."

"Yep." Spencer uses his finger to fix his eyeliner, smudging it in a way that looks purposeful. "Hey, you're still gonna compete for Drag King of the Year, right?"

Ugh.

Why'd he have to ask?

I've been dreading this question since the moment I'd decided to come tonight, knowing Achilles was going to ask it, and assuming Spencer would, too. Because of course, I *want* to compete, and I want to go head-to-head with Spencer. But Beau and I have been talking for the last couple of days and wondering if the pressure might be too much for me; if competing is worth the toll it could take on my mental health.

He's tentatively advised me against it, insisting that I can always compete next year, but I don't want to back out of anything else I've committed to. It's bad enough that I'd canceled my performances at The Gallery, and I don't want to let Jacklynn down because she's spent so much time trying to mentor me.

"I want to," I say to Spencer. "But I'm really not sure if I can."

Spencer's eyes widen as he stares at me, looking more emo with his smudged eyeliner than I've ever seen him. "You *have* to!" he protests, jutting out his bottom lip in a pout. "I know I've been a dick about drag, but for someone so new to it...I've *seen* you on stage, Edgar, and I really think that's where you're meant to be."

I snort and nudge him with my foot. "You just want to be able to say that you beat me."

He rolls his eyes and playfully shoves his hand against my shoulder, careful not to knock me off of my barstool. "Are you nervous about getting back on stage again? Like, is that why you're not sure if you can do it?"

"Kind of," I admit, turning to look at the counter instead of Spencer. "Beau's really worried that the pressure of competing might *actually* send me over the edge, though, and right now I'm just barely toeing the line." I'll spare him the details of how Beau has pretty much begged me not to compete. "But, you know, I also haven't been on stage in a few weeks, and I feel like I'm completely unprepared."

Spencer drums his fingers against the bar, quiet for a moment, as if considering this. "There's still a couple of weeks before the competition," he points out. "So you've still got some time to work with Jac." Spencer bites on the backs of his lip rings, his fingers tapping faster against the counter. "Would you want to come up on stage with me tonight?"

"*What?*" I nearly topple off my barstool. "Don't you remember what happened the last time we 'performed' together?"

He nods, and his grin is so wolfish that I can feel myself blush beneath my contour. "I'm doing The All-American Rejects tonight, not Dove, but if you think that you can find an appropriate time to kiss me... You absolutely have my consent."

"You're unbearable," I groan, burying my face into the palms of my hands so that he can't see the warmth of my cheeks. Spencer laughs. "We've been over this—that was a *game*, remember? You asked me if I wanted to play, so I played."

Spencer hums an acknowledgement. "Yeah, but I'd be down to *play* again."

I kick him in the ankle with the heavy toe of my combat boot. "Why are you even offering to let me come up on stage with you? Isn't that what you would consider a handout?"

His expression immediately turns serious, his heavy brow furrowing deep with guilt. "No, and I never should have told you that Bow was giving you a handout by bringing you up onto the stage with her." He bites on the backs of his lip rings again. "I told you before that I think you belong on a stage, and if I can help you feel comfortable with performing again…"

"I…" My stomach twists as I wrap my arms around myself. It's a generous offer to be given the chance to perform on the weekend, especially coming from Spencer, and I almost don't even know what to do with it. But if this is my chance to return to the stage and not have to do it *alone*… "Maybe I could just do a song or two?"

Spencer's smile is brighter than the sun as he reaches for both of my hands. "I've got you. Now let's go and take care of that beard."

twenty-three

There is an omelet sitting on the table in front of me.

I stare at it for half-an-hour before I force myself to sit up.

Grab the plate.

Tear apart the egg with my fork.

Shove a piece of it into my mouth and try not to wince because it's disgusting.

Beau has never been a good cook—we've mostly eaten takeout all summer—but he's watching me closely from the other end of the couch, and it's mostly the thought *behind* the food that counts, not the actual taste. He could have used a little less salt, though.

It's the first thing I've eaten since yesterday morning, since I'd laid down on the couch after my last performance and refused to get back up again. My lip-sync with Spencer had done its job in getting me acquainted with the stage again, enough so that I'd resumed my weekday rehearsals with Jacklynn and Achilles. And it was actually going really well until it just…wasn't.

I don't know why this stupid futon has such a goddamn hold on me, or why my depression had loosened its leash around my throat before coming back in for the kill, trying its hardest to strangle me. Regardless, I am *tired* of feeling like this, of curling into a ball beneath an old, crocheted blanket that our grandma had given Beau and staring at whatever food he leaves for me on the coffee table.

I stuff another piece of omelet into my mouth.

Choke it down.

Try not to make Beau feel bad about it.

"I know it's not as good as Jacklynn's," he says, tucking his legs underneath himself. "But I've never actually made an omelet before, and Google wasn't clear on the instructions. If Enzo were awake, I'd have made him make it instead."

"You tried," I say, staring as an uncooked egg yolk seeps out of the omelet and floods into the center of my plate. Beau hangs his head with a groan, grumbling something about the man in his bed who's been trying to teach him how to cook, but even I know that it's safer to keep Beau out of the kitchen. I've seen him catch toast on fire. "Why don't we wait for Enzo to wake up and then order some donuts, or something?"

Beau snorts as he drops his chin into the palm of his hand and frowns at the *Jeopardy* rerun on the television. "Enzo's constantly on my ass about ordering out. He's not going to agree to get donuts."

"What's this about Enzo and donuts?"

Enzo yawns as he pads into my brother's messy living room, sidestepping fabric rolls and the misshapen mannequin I've been using to work on my costuming. Drag King of the Year is this weekend, and I'm not even *close* to finishing all the things I've been working on, each of them a necessity for the competition.

My goal has been to keep everything punk, masculine, and simple, and I hadn't thought that I had bitten off more than I could chew, especially because I kept in mind how limited my crafting skills are. But the competition consists of a stupid creative costuming segment, which isn't unlike the design challenges on *RuPaul's Drag Race*, and *nothing* that I've pinned onto Beau's old mannequin has been good enough to not scrap and start over.

And it's not that I *don't* have any ideas in mind, it's just...the idea I *do* have for the costuming segment is incredibly personal, and I haven't been able to execute it with any justice yet.

If I make it into the Top 10 for Drag King of the Year, my outfit for the final lip-sync battle is *mostly* finished. I'd spent hours cutting apart a gray flannel and a black leather jacket I'd found in the men's section of the thrift store, then a week sewing it all back together. The final product is a mash-up of leather and flannel patchwork, and I like it enough that it's currently hanging in Beau's closet, waiting to be rhinestoned with 'Edgar Allan Foe' on the back. But even that is going to take me a long time, and I just don't have enough of it left.

"If Briar wants donuts for breakfast," Enzo says, drawing my focus away from the empty mannequin. "Then I think we can make that happen."

"Breakfast?" Beau muses, scooting over to make room for him on the futon. "It's noon. And I...don't know that I've got the money to order donuts."

Enzo smiles and presses a kiss to his mouth. "I'll take care of it."

They're huddled together on Beau's end of the couch, scrolling through DoorDash in search of a good donut shop, when my phone vibrates on the coffee table. The cracked screen lights up with a new notification, and I stall by picking at my fingernails, tearing my cuticles into shreds. Is it even worth responding to whoever is trying to reach out to me? Because all I'll do is just make them upset by admitting that I'm fucking depressed again—that I've never *stopped* being depressed despite all of my efforts to try and feel better.

But then I remember sitting at the bar with Selene, holding her against me as she sobbed, trusting me with the parts of herself that still loved a girl who died of suicide.

Because I hadn't answered my phone, just like Selene hadn't.

I snatch it off the coffee table with a sigh.

But it's not Selene who texted me.

Achilles Patrick: how r u doing today bestie?

It's as loaded of a question as I would expect from a friend who's still worried about me, and I don't know whether to laugh or start crying; it's a toss-up these days as to which of my emotions my brain will latch on to and not let go of.

Briar Vincent: Not great.

My response isn't so great, either, but I don't want to unload on Achilles. I don't want to tell them I hadn't slept last night, or that I've been staring at the small, dusty kitchen window and contemplating how hard it would be to launch myself out of it without taking Beau's hanging plants with me.

Achilles Patrick: nooooo ilysm what can i do to help?

Briar Vincent: I'll be okay, don't worry about it.

Achilles Patrick: well im going to worry bc i love u

Achilles Patrick: tell me what i can do to make u feel better

I stare at my phone with a frown.

I don't deserve a friend like Achilles, not after I spent weeks trying to shut them out because I hadn't deserved them back then, either.

But Achilles…they *want* to be my friend, whether I think I deserve them or not, and if Keel is wanting to help make me feel better…then maybe it's time I let them try.

The window wasn't that appealing, anyway.

"Hey, Beau?" I ask, barely speaking above a whisper because admitting I might need someone is infinitely more difficult than I anticipated. He and Enzo hear me regardless, both turning around to look up at me. "Um. Would it be okay if—if I asked Achilles to come over?"

My brother blinks before smoothing out the crease in his worried, slightly alarmed brow. He grins so wide that my own cheeks hurt just from looking at him, and I can tell my question comes as some sort of a relief to him. "Of course!" he says brightly, bouncing against the rolled armrest of the futon. "The more the merrier. Actually, why don't you invite Selene over, too? We can make it an—*ouch*! Hey, what was *that* for?" Beau turns to Enzo with a pout, whose fingers are still clawed from where he pinched my brother's elbow. "She wants to be social, Lorenzo. Why am I not allowed to be happy about it?"

Enzo rolls his eyes, but his dark gaze softens as it lands on me. "You don't have to invite Selene over, if you don't want to. Your comfort matters more than you being social right now."

I nod and bite at my lip. "But if I *do* want to?"

He smiles and wriggles his phone, showing me that he's still on DoorDash. "Guess we'll need more than a dozen donuts, then. Ask what kind she likes when you text her."

As it turns out, where Selene is extra as fuck in life, she's plain as dirt when it comes to what she likes on her donuts: nothing. She likes *nothing* on her donuts but the donut itself, and she'll only eat them if they're chocolate and in their own separate box. *I don't like it when my food touches other food!* she'd texted me, sending along a flurry of angry emojis because I'd laugh-reacted to her message and called her weird, *and you probably like sprin-kles and icing…gross.*

Briar Vincent: Yep, you're DEFINITELY weird.

"And *you* are a judgy little asshole," she announces upon her arrival, carrying in the boxes of donuts that she'd taken from the delivery person in the elevator. Achilles trails inside behind her, taking in Beau's apartment with a grimace. "I was busy and dropped everything to come hang out with you."

"Busy doing *what*?" Beau asks knowingly. "Posting that thirst-trap on Instagram?"

Achilles and I ask together, "What thirst trap?"

Selene's cheeks redden with a blush. "Don't worry about it, Judgy McJudgerson. Now someone come and take these before I trip on a fabric roll. Jesus, Beau, why is your apartment so messy?"

"It's my fault," I say, jumping up to take the donuts from her as she teeters on the heels of her boots. Achilles steadies her with a gentle hand on her elbow. "I bought more fabric than I know what to do with, which is great, because I keep messing everything up."

"Don't be so hard on yourself," Achilles says, looking for all the world like Beau's apartment is a bed of nails and they're afraid to come in past the threshold. "Can someone…help me? I don't want to step on something shiny and expensive and ruin it."

Selene unceremoniously kicks a roll of sequined fabric out from in front of their feet. "You'll get used to the mess, unfortunately. It was a culture shock for me too when Beau first invited me over." She nudges them toward the couch so Achilles can take my spot on the futon, sacrificing me to sit on the floor somewhere with Selene. "I liked what you sent me for the outfit you'd wear during the final lip-sync. It looked like it was tedious to make, but well done, so what are you struggling with?"

I heave a sigh and plop myself down next to Beau's empty mannequin, the too-hard floor cushioned by the heap of sparkling black fabric at its base. "Both my outfit for the welcoming ceremony *and* what I want to do for the creative costuming challenge. There's no way I can get them both done in time."

Achilles frowns as they rifle through the donuts in search for one that they'll like. "If you need help finishing your costumes, I can help you. I'm already done with mine."

"So am I," Selene says, grabbing her own donut before sitting so close to me that her knee knocks gently against mine. She's mindful of the fabric I've left in a heap around the mannequin, studying it as she eats. "It's been a minute since I've made anything from scratch, but I still know my way around a sewing machine. Have you drawn anything up that I can take a look at?"

"No," I wince, feeling even more inadequate than I did when I first started drag. Am I supposed to sketch out my designs? Because Beau doesn't. He just sits behind his sewing machine and works. And is it really fair for me to ask for help from the people whom I'm meant to be competing against, even if they're done with their own costumes? "I'm not any good at drawing, so the design just kind of lives in my head."

Selene grins and points her half-eaten donut at Achilles, who steels themself like they're preparing for a verbal attack that never comes. "Fortunately for you, your best friend is in art school, specifically for fashion. If Keel can help you sketch out your designs, I can help you put them together." She sticks out her foot and kicks my brother in the ankle. "Not everyone can paint an image in their head and then transfer it perfectly onto fabric."

Beau sticks out his sprinkle-covered tongue at her. "It's not my fault that drag, fashion, and lip-syncing are the only things I'm good at. And besides, not all of us have a bestie who makes our garments for us at a discount. I *wouldn't* make my own stuff if I didn't have to."

"You didn't make *any* of your own stuff for the competition?" I ask, trying not to sound so accusatory. But Selene takes offense to it anyway as she stuffs the rest of her donut into her mouth, glaring at me as she nearly chokes on the chocolate.

"Of course I did," she grumbles, slapping her knee against mine. "Cora doesn't make *everything* I wear. Just the expensive stuff. And *only* because xe has access to the fabrics that I like but can't afford." Selene turns to look at me and deflects the conversations into something else. "So, Edgar, what do you say? Can Keel and I help you finish your drag?"

I bite at my lip and stare at the holes in my leggings, where the fabric has torn across my knees. "It doesn't feel fair," I say.

"And if I can't get it all done in time on my own, then I don't think I should be competing anyway."

"Bullshit," Selene says at the same time Achilles shouts, "You *have* to compete!"

I flinch and look up at Beau, who's busied himself with taking a selfie with Enzo, likely so that his input can't affect any decision I might make here. "I really don't know that I have what it takes," I tell my friends, one of whom is currently trying to scramble over fabric rolls to get to me, while the other places her hand on my knee. "I've only been on stage a handful of times, and hardly ever on my own. I don't deserve—"

"Yes, you do," Selene says, her tone more fierce than I've ever heard it, and it's enough to give me pause. "I want to compete against the best, and that includes you. So what if you've only been doing this for a few months? Everyone has to start somewhere, and I've known people who've done it for less and still compete."

"You *have* to compete with us," Achilles adds, sweeping a hand through their dirty blond hair that still looks sticky from the spirit gum they use to keep their wigs on. "You've worked too hard to just give up now, especially when Selene and I can help you."

Selene takes my hand and gives it a tight squeeze. "Keel was right when they said that this is what kings do. We help each other." I wonder if it pains her to admit that Achilles was right about something. "I know that it's your guilt talking when you say that it doesn't feel fair, but it *is*. Keel and I wouldn't be offering to help if it wasn't."

"Exactly!" Keel says. "You have no idea how helpful it's been for me to have you around this whole summer. No one has ever really appreciated my kind of drag before, but you didn't even question it when I told you that I did a lot of cosplay, and that felt *so* freaking validating. It's also been nice to have someone to hang out with and go fabric shopping with." Their smile is one of secret understanding, like they know what it feels like to think that they don't deserve to be here. "Besides Enzo, you're really one of the only friends I have, so let me help you in the same way that you've helped me."

"Jesus, Keel. Quit it. You're making Briar cry."

"Shit," Achilles says, their eyes wide with alarm. "I'm so sorry, Briar. I—"

"Don't be," I tell them, wiping at my eyes with the back of my hand. I hadn't expected to start crying from an emotion that finally wasn't depression, but it's nice to know that there's still something else beneath the surface. That being sad isn't the be-all, end-all of my existence. "I love your drag. I think it's cool. And one of the best things about this summer was getting to meet the both of you."

Selene blinks. "The *both* of us?"

I nod and smile through my tears. "The both of you."

"Does this mean you'll let us help you with your costumes?" Achilles asks, bouncing against the roll of fabric tucked beneath them. It's black with little antique books on it, something that I've been wanting to use for my look for the opening ceremony.

I turn to Achilles and nod again. "I'm sorry I don't have a sketch pad."

Achilles' grin is blinding as they dig into their pocket, retrieving an expensive-looking pencil. "All I need is something to draw on."

Enzo tosses them the lid for the donut box, and Achilles and I spend the next several hours working on what Selene considers to be a drag masterpiece.

twenty-four

My costumes are finished and hanging in the back of Beau's closet, ready for tomorrow morning. As it turns out, Selene is quick with a sewing needle and extremely familiar with Beau's sewing machine, but I hadn't let her sew the majority of my garments. Only enough for her to teach me how to work with the design patterns that Achilles and I had come up with. And sure, the seams aren't perfectly straight and I wasted most of my fabric through lots of trial and error, but even Jacklynn had been impressed when she stopped by the apartment this afternoon, eager to see what Selene, Achilles, and I had been working on.

The pride in her eyes as she studied each of my costumes had made me so giddy that I'd nearly forgotten how terrified I am for the competition. But at least I've got my friends to keep me company tonight; Selene and Achilles had offered to sleep over just in case I needed them. In case my anxiety gets the better of me and I try to tap out of the competition before it even begins.

The welcoming ceremony for Drag King of the Year is supposed to start in eight hours, but Selene and I are *both* too anxious to sleep. We huddle together on the floor between the coffee table and couch, wrapped in the blanket Achilles has shoved off the futon. They're snoring softly because apparently they're more tired than scared, but we're wide awake and scrolling through TikTok on Selene's phone to watch other drag kings for inspiration.

"I fucking *love* Landon Cider," Selene says, tapping her thumb against one of Landon's videos and liking it a dozen times over. "I wish my costuming was on his level. Did you see when he competed on Dragula? *Ugh.* I wish I could do that, too."

I rest my temple against her shoulder, watching as she scrolls through Landon's punkish feed. "Why can't you?" I ask, stifling a yawn against the back of my hand because my body is physically exhausted. It's my brain that won't actually let me close my eyes and sleep. "I bet the Boulet Brothers would love you."

Selene shrugs. "I'm a good king, angel face. But not a great one. I'm nowhere *near* the level it would take to compete on something of that scale."

"But you could be," I tell her. "You're nineteen. You've still got time to get better."

She shrugs again, reaching for the bottle of Pepsi that's sitting on the coffee table; Selene takes a swig that lasts so long, I'm worried she's going to drown in the soda. "Maybe," she says, turning her head to burp. "Or I could just stay here and eventually headline at The Gallery every weekend. Beau isn't going to be there forever, you know. He's too good."

I tilt my head back to look up at her. Selene's lips are pressed together in a thin line as she stares intently at her phone, refusing to look back down at me. Her nose is crinkled with disgust, and I can't decide if I think she might be upset with me, though I can't actually figure out *why*. I hadn't thought that I'd said anything wrong by trying to be encouraging.

"What is it with you and drag, anyway?" I ask curiously. Selene quirks an eyebrow but doesn't look away from her phone. "I've never seen anyone so determined before. Even Beau wasn't as persistent in the beginning, when he thought that he'd never get the chance to move to New York."

Selene chews on the backs of her lip rings, scrolling rapidly through TikTok without actually stopping to watch any videos. "The drag community is the only place where I've ever felt like I fit in, and doing drag is really the only thing that I'm good at." Her voice is softer than I've ever heard her speak, and it's not because Achilles is curled up asleep against our backs. "I've spent *years* trying to carve out a space for myself, mostly because kings are still so new to the mainstream scene, and we've all had to prove ourselves. It sucks when we don't get the same credit or validation that queens do."

We've all had to prove ourselves.

Something I haven't actually done yet.

"Is that why you hate that I'm doing drag?" I ask, expecting her answer to be a harsh one.

But Selene only offers me a half-hearted shrug as she likes another of Landon's videos. "I don't *hate* that you're doing drag," she tells me. "I think you're good at it, and you have a lot of potential. But what I do *hate* is that you had people to help you, and you didn't get any pushback from anyone."

"But I *did* get pushback," I say carefully. "You."

Selene winces. "I never should have treated you the way I did, especially in the beginning when all I did was tell you that you weren't cut out for this." She finally sets her phone down. "I can try to explain where all of my anger was coming from, but only if you want me to. I'm sure it'll sound like I'm just making excuses for myself, and I wouldn't blame you if—"

I cut her off and say, "Tell me."

She turns herself around so that she's facing me, and I've never seen her look so *small* before, like she's completely shrunken in on herself with her shoulders hunched around her ears. "Drag is…" Selene swallows noisily as she tugs her knees into her chest. "I can express myself however I want to. I can fuck with gender roles and be someone else because sometimes being *me* just…sucks." She wraps her arms around her legs as if she's physically holding herself together. "Spencer didn't lose Piper. Spencer didn't have to be homeschooled because he wasn't able to keep up in a normal classroom. Spencer didn't *not* get into art school."

Had she tried to go to art school for her photography?

I want to ask, but it's clear she needs to talk.

"My parents *hate* that I do drag, even though they literally raised me above a gay bar." Selene rests her head against the futon, staring at the empty space between us. "When I first started out, Mom refused to put me on the lineup, even for a spot during the week. She thought it would discourage me from doing drag entirely, but it didn't, and I practically *begged* for Jacklynn to help convince her that I could do this."

"Did she?"

Selene scoffs and shakes her head. "No. She said she was done with having drag kids, and that she didn't want to be responsible for me. Didn't want to teach me the ropes."

Fuck.

No wonder she got so hostile after Jacklynn offered to be my drag mother.

"I thought, okay, maybe she just doesn't want to piss off my parents since she works here. But then Beau came in from Texas, and Jacklynn *jumped* to be his drag mother. She found him a place to stay, got him his first couple of gigs, introduced him to my parents and helped get him put on our roster...I didn't understand why she couldn't have done that for me. Why Beau was good enough, but I wasn't." Selene wipes her nose on the blanket, like she's sniffling, but it's hard to see her face without the light from her phone. "Not that I don't think Beau deserves all the good things, I just...I wish I had deserved them, too."

"You do," I say, loudly enough that Achilles stirs in their sleep. We both sit still until they settle again. "I don't know why Jacklynn chose my brother over you, but I...I *kind of* know how it feels."

Selene frowns at me and asks, "How?"

"All summer long, it's felt like Beau has been choosing you over me." Selene winces. "He wouldn't help me do drag, either, and he's *always* taken your side. He's *always* been the first one to defend you. It's just kind of felt like ever since he came to New York, he hasn't needed me, and it feels like you've been my replacement."

"What? No way." Selene shuffles closer to me and rests a hand on my knee, giving me a quick little shake. "I am *not* your replacement, and I don't want to be. I quite like being an only child." She gives me a smile that doesn't reach her eyes. "All he does is talk about you, you know. How funny you are, how big of a nerd you are...I've literally seen every single picture you've ever sent him on Snapchat because, '*awww look how cute my sister is!*' Believe me, Briar. Beau is still your brother no matter where he is, and I'm sorry if he's ever taken my side in something he shouldn't have."

"Thanks for saying that," I tell her, smiling. It's nice to know that Beau has never forgotten about me. "While we're apologizing,

I—I *never* meant to upset you by doing drag. I mean, at first, I really just wanted to spite you. You were so mean to Achilles and for literally no reason, I just...I *wanted* to knock you down a peg. I entered the competition just so I'd win and you would lose."

"Oh, I know," Selene says, her own smile brightening, too. "I couldn't fucking *believe* that this little bitch from Texas was going to challenge me at my own game, especially not after everything Beau had told me about you. But I'm glad you decided to do drag, and I'm glad you coming here gave me a reality check. I've been *such* an asshole since Piper died, and it took meeting you for me to acknowledge it."

"Oh, I know," I say, and Selene nudges me with her foot. "For what it's worth, I really do enjoy drag. I don't feel so nervous whenever I'm in drag and on stage, and that's—it's a new feeling for me. I've never *not* been anxious, and coming here feels like I've turned a new leaf with my mental health, even if I did want to..."

Selene nods in understanding. "You don't have to say it." She sighs and looks up at Achilles, whose lips are parted around snores that are increasing in volume. "I guess I owe Keel an apology, too."

"They definitely don't deserve the way you've treated them."

"I know," she says. "And I hate that I've let myself do it. That I knew it was wrong and did it anyway. Has Keel ever told you how we know each other?"

I frown and shake my head. "I assumed you two knew each other from The Gallery?"

"No," she tells me. "Keel and I have known each other since we were kids. They were one of my best friends growing up. But I ruined that."

Keel had once told me that they used to have a best friend, but that they hadn't been friends in a long time. That they hadn't been real friends at all.

She drops her gaze to the empty space still between us again. "People *always* used to pick on Keel, first because they're autistic but then because they came out as nonbinary, and I hated it, especially because Achilles takes whatever you say to them to heart. They'd call them stupid, and worthless, and annoying, and Keel would just stand there and take it, so I—I *always* stood up for them, and eventually we got really close."

"So...what happened?"

Selene glances up at Achilles again. "Keel got into art school after we graduated, and I didn't."

"Did you guys just stop talking?" I ask.

Her tanned cheeks redden with what I think might be shame. "No, I—I yelled at them. I treated them like shit just like everyone else, and I told them it wasn't fair that they'd gotten into art school and not me. That I was just as good as them, if not better."

"I mean, you could have just apologized," I tell her, blinking through my confusion because Keel is a fashion student and

Selene would have likely gone for photography. Comparing the two is like comparing apples and watermelon: you can't. "They didn't deserve to be treated like that, but Keel is pretty forgiving."

"I don't deserve their forgiveness, just like I don't deserve yours." Selene tucks her chin against her chest, and I wonder if it's because she's trying to hide the tears that are gathering along her lashes. "I miss Keel every single day, but when they first came to The Gallery and said they wanted to do drag, I was afraid they might take it away from me, and yeah, I know how stupid that sounds. But I had found something that I was good at, and I was afraid that Keel would come along and be better, and it would be just like art school all over again. And then when Piper died and I didn't know how to handle it…"

We sit together in silence as Selene stares at the floor. Achilles is still asleep on the futon, their arm flopped over the edge and draped across the front of my chest, but I don't dare move and risk waking them. Eventually, though, Selene whispers a quiet, "I'm terrible."

"No, you're not," I say. "You just owe a couple of apologies, and maybe you should stop shit-talking Keel's drag." I carefully scoot a little closer to her and rest a hand on her shoulder; Selene nuzzles her face against the top of it. "Obviously it's not my apology to accept, but I don't see why the two of you can't be friends again. Who cares if you both do drag? Think of all the things you could do together, especially once I'm gone and out of your hair."

Selene snaps her head up to look at me. "Fuck, that's right. You're leaving next week."

I try not to look so sad about it. "My parents want me home before school starts."

"Do you *have* to go back?" she asks. "Because you just said New York has been a turning point for you. Maybe it'd be best if you...stayed."

The thought of staying has never occurred to me before. I always just thought I would go home to Texas and maybe come visit Beau again next summer. "I don't know if I can. I still have a year left of school."

"I was homeschooled," Selene reminds me. "Sort of. My parents enrolled me in an online program where teachers could still grade my assignments, but I did all the studying and stuff from home at my own pace. Maybe it's something you could look into? If you wanted. Sorry. I didn't mean to jump the gun. I just don't want to see you go home next week."

I bite at the inside of my cheek. "Does it cost anything?"

Selene nods. "It isn't super expensive though, and they have payment plans."

It's something my parents and I would have to talk about. Extensively. Money is tight as it is, and who knows if Beau would even be okay with me living here. Staying for the summer is one thing, but moving across the country to come and *live* with him... It probably doesn't matter how exciting the idea might sound, how nice it would be to actually stay in New York where I finally feel like I belong. Beau won't want me, not permanently.

"I'll talk to them and see what they say, but it'll probably be a no."

Selene sinks back against the futon. "Oh."

"I want to, though," I say quickly. Selene's eyes dart up to my face. "To stay, I mean."

Her green eyes brighten with something that resembles hope. "Oh!"

I raise an eyebrow. "I didn't think you'd want me to stay. You know. Because I'm your competition, and all that."

Selene's expression turns serious. "I want you to stay. More than anything."

"Even more than you want to win tomorrow?"

She rolls her eyes and presses her forehead against mine. "Don't you ever shut up?"

Before I can answer, Selene leans in, and she kisses me.

I forget all about tomorrow morning.

twenty-five

"*W*here the hell are my cuff links?"

Selene is half-dressed in drag, half-dressed in pajamas as she bolts around the apartment in search of the cuff links that she *swears* she left on the kitchen counter. But *I* swear that she never took them out of her duffle bag, which is sitting untouched on the edge of Beau's bed, still zipped. Now I understand why her room is so meticulously organized—outside of it, she's a mess.

We've been hearing about these stupid cuff links all morning, how she'd commissioned them from an artist on Etsy who had attached small, black amethyst geodes to a pair of cuff link fasteners. From the pictures that she'd shown us to aid in her search for the stones, they perfectly match the glittering tuxedo that she's wearing for today's opening ceremony, the jacket of which is currently slung over her shoulders.

"I'm serious," Selene announces, her tone a warning for whoever she thinks might have moved the cuff links. "They were expensive, and my whole look will be *ruined* without them, so whichever one of you accidentally moved them, kindly put them back and you might survive the morning unscathed."

Huffing a sigh into the smudged mirror of Beau's vanity, Achilles sets down their eyebrow pencil, an odd shade of blue that they're using to make their brows look like...bubbles? Keel's drag will never not fascinate me. "I have *never* met anyone more dramatic in my whole entire life," they complain, turning sideways in their chair. "Briar, hand me her bag. I'll bet you I know right where she put them."

Selene's duffle is absurdly heavy as I plop it into Achilles' waiting lap. "I'm pretty sure it was her frickin' gauges that she put on the counter before actually sticking them in her ears." I watch as Achilles has absolutely no qualms about rifling through Selene's belongings, taking special care not to look too long at anything she might not want them to see. "Check the—"

"Ah-ha!" Achilles retrieves a small plastic baggie with the cuff links still inside. "I found them!"

"Where were they?" Selene demands, storming into the bedroom and snatching the bag from Achilles. She studies the cuff links to ensure that the amethyst hasn't broken, then nods and deems them acceptable. "I looked everywhere!"

"Clearly not," I say, taking her duffle and setting it down on the floor. Selene drags it toward herself and carefully begins to go through it, muttering something about a bracelet. "I told you twice to check your bag, but—" I pitch my voice as low as I can to mimic Selene's deeper intonation. "'—*I know where I fucking put them, Briar.*'"

She flicks me in the ankle from where she's kneeling on the ground now. "Thanks, Keel."

They smile down at her with a wink. "Any time. I still remember where you hide shit."

Selene takes a moment to smile back at them, and the shift in their relationship ever since Selene had apologized to Achilles a few hours ago has been…both beautifully glorious and incredibly annoying. After a long talk and quite a few tears, Keel's not afraid to bicker back at her anymore, or take her side in any of our friendly disagreements. But at least they've both agreed to work toward putting the past behind them, whatever that might look like, and Achilles has been giddy all morning, happy to have their real best friend back.

Guess that means they won't be needing me anymore.

Maybe it's a good thing I'm going home next week.

"Hey, Briar?"

I nearly jump a foot out of my skin, lost in thought about the people I'm leaving behind.

Beau is standing in the doorway, half in drag and leaning against the threshold as he watches the three of us get ready, though I haven't actually done anything except style my hair because Achilles takes forever to do their makeup. "Can we talk?"

My breath catches in the back of my throat because "can," "we," and "talk" all strung together in that exact order is never a good thing. "Yeah. Sure. Is everything all right?"

He nods and gestures toward the living room, indicating I should follow him there. "Can you guys give us just a minute?" he asks. Achilles and Selene both look up at him. "We won't be long, I promise. I'm just gonna close this door."

Selene heaves a sigh as she faceplants onto Beau's unmade bed. "Sure," she says. "Of *course*. It's not like all of my makeup is out there in the bathroom or anything, and it's not like I need to get ready for this *really big* competition that starts in just a few hours."

Beau rolls his eyes and tosses something shiny onto the bed. "I got that for you, son. Hopefully it'll tide you over until I'm done talking to my sister."

I follow him from the room as Selene squeals. "What'd you give her?"

"A pocket watch," he says, closing the bedroom door behind us. "She's been wanting one to wear with her suits, and I thought it might match something she's wearing today. But forget about that, and come and talk with me."

"About what?" I ask carefully, sitting on the edge of Beau's futon.

"About how fucking *proud* I am," he answers, plopping down next to me after setting aside a few pillows and a blanket. "I cannot believe that you're here, B."

My cheeks grow warm with an unwelcome blush, and I force myself to look down at the coffee table, where Selene has set out the things that she needs to glue her beard on. "I haven't done anything worth being proud of."

Beau takes both of my hands, his lavender acrylics flashing beneath the lamplight. "Yes, you have, B. And so many people are so, *so* proud of you. But no one more so than me." He squeezes my hands until his fingers shake with emotion. "I feel like such a shit brother, you know? Because I—I *doubted* you, Briar. I fucking doubted you and didn't think that you could do this. I thought the pressure would get to you or you'd lose interest. I thought that Selene would scare you off and you'd quit. But you're *here*."

I'm not sure where I think he's going with this, but he's not exactly helping with my confidence right now. "Um. Thanks?"

"Don't thank me," Beau says. "Because I should have believed in you from the beginning. I should have helped you." He looks like he's on the verge of tears, but the last thing I want is for Beau to ruin his makeup, especially when his smokey eye is on point today. "Who gives a shit if Spencer Read is my drag son? You're my sister, and I love you more than anything."

"You'd already made a commitment to Spencer," I remind him gently. Beau crinkles his nose so that he doesn't sniffle. "I shouldn't have expected you to go back on your word, and I'm sorry if I've made you feel guilty." I slide a little closer to my brother, and I'm careful as I wrap my arms around him in a hug, mindful of his long, curly blond wig. He returns the gesture with a tight squeeze around my torso; I try not to wince because the opalescent rhinestones on his corset are digging into my skin. "I love you more than anything, too."

Beau lets go of me and quickly wipes at his eyes, cursing when he pulls his hand away and notices that his fingers are smudged black with eyeliner. "I'm going to miss you so fucking much," he laments. "The apartment is going to be so quiet without you typing up your fanfics at all hours of the night."

I chip away at the black polish that Keel had painted my fingernails with last night. "I wish I didn't have to go home," I admit quietly. Beau looks up at me in surprise. "I have to go back next week, I know. I can't just invade your life for an entire summer and then *stay*. But I wish—"

"Why can't you?" Beau asks. "You didn't *invade my life*, B. You came here and made it better because you're the little piece of home that I've been missing." He grins despite the tears still in his eyes. "I just *knew* that you were gonna like it here. I knew you were going to make friends. And there's so much here you haven't seen yet! I don't see why you have to go back."

All I can do is blink at him.

"You're serious."

It's not a question.

Beau tilts his head at me like he's wondering how I can be confused. "Of course I'm serious. Why *wouldn't* I be serious?"

"Because I'm a depressed piece of shit, and a burden, and not your responsibility, and—"

Beau puts his hand over my mouth, promptly shutting me up. "Have I ever said any of those things to you?" he asks. I shake my head and contemplate licking his palm, if only so he'll let me go. "Then what makes you think that *I* think any of those things about you? Because yeah, all right. You have depression. But we've talked about different things we can do to help you, and I think I understand what you need now: a couch, reassurance that you're loved, and that therapist you're supposed to meet with next Tuesday. Rita says they're super nice." He smiles and flicks my nose. I gnash my teeth at his fingers.. "But you are *not* a burden, and as long as I'm breathing and you're still my baby sister, you will *always* be my responsibility. That's how this 'family' thing works."

One minute, I'm staring at the coffee table.

The next, I'm sobbing into Beau's shoulder, bare from where he hasn't finished getting dressed yet.

"I don't want to go home," I say, curling my fingers into the stiff blue fabric of his corset. Beau pets the back of my hair, hushing me. "People at school ignore me, and I don't have any friends there, and I—I want to keep doing drag, but—but I can't do it without you, and I would miss you and Enzo and Keel and Selene *so* frickin' much if I went home. If I could stay, I promise that I would FaceTime with Mom and Dad every single day, and—"

"We'll talk to them," Beau says, pressing a kiss to the top of my head. "There's a lot that we would need to work out, and we'd need to find a bigger apartment so that you could have your own room and I don't know what we'd do about school, but..."

"Selene was homeschooled," I offer.

Beau snorts. "If you think I'm good enough at math to be your math teacher, you've given me way too much credit. I used to cheat off of Connor." He pats me on the back to let me know that he's joking. Sort of. He probably did cheat in calculus. "We can talk to her parents about the program she was in, and maybe Nathalie can help us find a bigger place."

"I could get a real job, too," I suggest. Beau tilts his head at me. "Keel and I saw a hiring sign at the craft store. Maybe I can apply when I come back? It'd probably be a fun place to work, anyway, and just think of all the discounts we'd get on fabric!"

He nods, smiling at my enthusiasm. "Sure, if that's what you want. But none of that is what you should be focusing on right now. You've got a crown to win."

I force myself to sit back and look up at him. "You really think that I can win?"

Beau's smile is brighter than the UV light that he's invested in to help keep his succulents alive. "I *know* you can. We've just got to get you ready first."

For a moment, however brief, I believe him.

✦ ✧ ✦ ✧ ✦ ✦ ✧ ✦ ✧ ✦ ✦ ✧ ✦ ✧ ✦

"Oh, God. I'm going to throw up." Beneath his contour, Spencer's skin has taken on a sickly shade of green. He purses his lips and slaps his hand across his mouth, his fingers trembling like leaves on a vine as he makes a dramatic show of swallowing. "Why did I let you two talk me into eating breakfast?"

"Because I don't think that the judges would take too kindly to you passing out on stage." I shuffle past Achilles to stand behind him, and Spencer is so nervous that he doesn't even realize I've moved. "You're going to be fine, Spence. You've got this. But *please* don't puke on these boots." I rub my hand between his shoulder blades, trying to loosen some of the tension there. "Haven't you done this before?"

"Yes," Spencer groans. "And I *lost.*"

The Gallery's dressing room is bursting at the seams with at *least* two dozen drag kings from all over New York, most of whom have already lined up in the order they're meant to strut onto the stage in. Achilles, Spencer, and I, however, are still huddled together in the far corner of the room, away from everyone else because Spencer doesn't want anyone to see how anxious he is.

"You came in second place," Achilles reminds him, flapping their hands as they bounce on the heels of their boots. Keel had had their own panic attack this morning, sobbing into their cereal about how winning Drag King of the Year would mean so much to them. I'd needed to rub their back, too, but Achilles had calmed down relatively quickly, unlike Spencer who's been pacing and throwing up since he first finished putting on his cuff-links. "And you're the front-runner for this year. You're going to be okay."

"Think we should stick him in the freezer?" I ask. Keel snorts and adjusts the bright blue tulle around their neck, a loofa-looking collar that Beau had fallen in love with and asked to borrow after the competition. "Sure as shit calmed *me* down."

Spencer whips around to look at me; beads of sweat are beginning to gather around his temples, and his skin still looks green beneath his glittering obsidian makeup. "Freezer? When the hell were you in the *freezer*?"

"The night you found Achilles and I in the kitchen," I say. "I was having an anxiety attack, so they shoved me into the freezer to calm me down."

Achilles, dressed as a dragged-up Vaporeon from Pokémon, turns around to whack me with the giant tail that's strapped around their waist with a fish net. "I did not 'shove you into the freezer!' I went in there to get you some ice, and I just *happened* to bring you inside with me. That's not the same thing."

"No one is shoving *me* into any freezers—"

Jacklynn Hyde appears in the doorway that leads onto The Gallery's main stage. "Five minutes!" she calls out, her booming voice effectively silencing the room except for Spencer dry heaving into the garbage can. "There's a lot of you this year, so do us all a favor and limit your stage time to *about* forty-five seconds." Jacklynn's eyes scan the crowd for anyone who might have something to say, then continues. "If we want to stay on schedule, we need to get through Nathalie's welcome speech and introduce all of you before *noon*."

A king near the front of the line raises their hand. "When do we get to talk to the judges?"

Jacklynn launches into a detailed timeline of today's events for whoever might be listening and didn't read the itinerary she'd passed out to each of us this morning, all the while Achilles and I busy ourselves with tending to Spencer. His hands are still shaking as we guide him away from the garbage can, which reeks something horrendous because Spencer has already puked in it.

"We've got to get ready to go," Achilles says, eyeing the gap near the front of the line where they're meant to be standing, almost like they're terrified that someone else is going to take their place. Spencer groans like he might vomit again. "You could literally do this in your sleep, Spence. You've just got to pretend like it's a Friday night and you're here to lip-sync for tips."

"Fridays are different," Spencer grumbles. "My mom never watches me perform, and I *actually* get paid in tips. We're not making shit today and everyone's getting free entertainment."

It's weird seeing Spencer so unsure of himself. Where is his usual cocky attitude? His confidence? It makes my heart ache in a way that it probably shouldn't, especially when we're about to start competing against each other.

"Two minutes!" Jacklynn calls out again, staring intently at a ticking timer on her phone.

I grab a hold of Spencer by his sparkling shoulders and give him a gentle shake. "Forget about your mom today, Spence. Don't even look at her." My own hands are trembling as I smooth out the lapels of his black, pinstripe tuxedo, the glittery fabric scratching against my palms. As uncomfortable as the outfit looks, it's perfectly tailored to cling to all of his curves, and I would be lying if I didn't admit that I find him *ridiculously* attractive right now. "Nathalie doesn't get to decide how good of a king you are, and drag isn't something she can take away from you. Who cares if she's one of the judges? Today, it's all about *you*."

I poke him in the chest with my index finger, hammering in my point so he'll believe it, though I'm selfishly grateful to have something to focus on that'll keep my own anxiety at bay.

Spencer and I can't *both* panic.

"You don't have to prove yourself to her," I add softly, standing up onto my toes and pressing a kiss to Spencer's cheek. His face flushes scarlet instead of green, and I can feel Achilles staring at us, wide-eyed. "You've already proved yourself to an entire community that loves you, and that's what matters. Not your mom. So you're gonna go out there, you're gonna blow everyone away, and you're *probably* going to come in second place again, but only to me or Keel."

All Spencer can offer me is a half-hearted smile before throwing his arms around my neck, holding me against him as tightly as he can without hurting me. "I don't deserve you," he murmurs, quietly enough that Achilles can't hear him over the excitement building in the room. "Whatever this is—whatever *we* are—I don't deserve it. You really are the best, Briar."

I wrap my arms around his torso, trying not to think about the way he had kissed me last night. The way he had taken my face between his hands and planted his lips against mine. We haven't said a word about it since it happened, the competition taking priority, but if we had shared a few more kisses in the early hours of the morning, well…that's our business. "You deserve everything."

"Am I missing something here?" Achilles asks, trying to wedge themself between us. Spencer snorts and lets me go, wiping at his eyes because apparently they'd started watering at some point during my speech. "Are you guys a thing? Do *non*-thing people just kiss each other on the cheek at random? Because I ship you two so frickin' hard—"

"Gallery kings, get your asses in line or I will start this show without you!" Jacklynn is staring at us from the stage wall, hands on her hips because we're the only ones not lined up yet.

Achilles scrambles into place, whacking a few kings with their Vaporeon tail on their way, but I hang back just a minute to look up at Spencer and smile. "We'll figure out whatever *this* is later," I say, gesturing between the two of us. Spencer nods. "But right now, I've got a crown to win because goddamn it, you're going *down*."

Spencer laughs and playfully shoves me toward my place in line. "Bring it on, angel face, and I might let you try the crown on when *I* win."

I take my place behind a king who's dressed in beads from head-to-toe, each of them shaped like colorful skulls and hanging from their clothes like fringe. Their smile is friendly as they look back at me, introducing themself as Drew Bauchery and confiding in me that this is only their fourth time in drag; it makes me feel a little better about competing.

One by one, Jacklynn calls our names, introducing us to both the crowd and the judges from the wings, telling them where we're from and who our sponsors are. Achilles is the second king to take the stage, and even from the dressing room I can hear their mentor, Rita Book, screaming from somewhere in the bar. It makes the rest of us chuckle, easing the bit of tension that's visible in all of our shoulders.

Drew Bauchery takes their turn, sauntering onto the stage with their teeth barred, and I lean against the threshold as Jacklynn nudges me with her elbow. "Good luck, baby," she whispers. "I'll be impartially rooting for you from here. You know, since I'm the host and all that jazz." She bends her knees to duck down and press an almost-kiss to my forehead, her lips hovering in the air above my skin to avoid leaving any marks from her lipstick. "I'm proud of you, Edgar. You've come so far just to make it here, and I hope you can see that for yourself."

I'm still smiling tearfully when Jacklynn announces my name because she's right—I am *finally* starting to see it for myself.

twenty-six

I knew Selene's outfit for the creative costuming challenge was going to be good, but *damn*.

Keel and I can't stop staring at her as she dips the flattened bottom of a long, curling horn into an open bottle of liquid latex. She's bedazzled it with sparkling black rhinestones, and as she presses the silicone to her red-painted temple, holding it there until the latex begins to dry, she meets our gaze in Beau's vanity mirror. We hadn't planned on getting ready back at the apartment, but when I saw how many kings were gathered in the dressing room at The Gallery, my anxiety went into overdrive.

"Could the two of you please stop watching me?" Selene says, glancing back and forth between Achilles and me. "What did you think I was doing when I picked up a paintbrush and literally started painting myself red?"

"I thought you were doing HIM from the Powerpuff Girls. Not a devil with horns and a pitchfork," I say, busying myself

318

with gluing down the wig that Achilles has let me borrow for my outfit. It's firetruck red and already styled in a similar fashion to Selene's natural hair, shorter on the sides and swept off to the side on top, but I'm ready to rip the damn thing off my head. "Why can't I get this to stay on?"

Selene turns around in her chair, still holding the horn to her temple. "Beau didn't give you his wig glue, did he? I hate that shit. It takes forever to get tacky, which is fine when you've got hours to get ready, but we're on crunch time. Here." She tosses me a bottle of spirit gum. "Don't overdo it or you'll rip half your skin off later. And don't forget, angel face, that you're not in small town Texas anymore. A devil in drag isn't controversial when you'll see worse things walking in Times Square."

"Drag shouldn't be controversial at all, though," Keel says, using an art sponge to paint a swirling galaxy down the length of their exposed left arm. "We're not doing anything wrong by expressing ourselves, and yet they're still trying to ban drag left and right. It's so stupid." They huff into the mirror that they've propped on the edge of Beau's bed. "Do you know how scary it is to be a drag king and nonbinary? It's terrifying. And goddamn it, I don't care about your children. Literally no one is grooming them."

"You aren't wrong," Selene agrees, working on her second demon horn. "And that's what you should have told Sara Tonin instead of 'it sucks' when she asked you about your opinion on the current drag climate."

Achilles groans and drops their chin against their chest. "I still can't believe that was my answer."

During the quick Q&A segment of the competition, where the judges had asked each of us a drag-related question, Achilles' was probably the most political, and it was clear that they hadn't been prepared for it. Mine had been simple and they'd asked me about my drag inspiration—I'd gushed about my brother for a solid sixty seconds—and even Selene's question had been a relatively uncomplicated, "Where do you see your drag career five years from now?" Of course, she'd been ready with an answer, but Keel and I have been kicking ourselves ever since.

"At least you didn't trip during the opening ceremony," I point out, ripping off my wig so that I can clean off the remnants of Beau's wig glue.

"That was *not* your fault," Selene says, staring at me intently in the mirror. "You wouldn't have tripped at all if the asshole in front of you hadn't spilled those beads all over the place."

I've been trying not to think about the look on Drew Bauchery's face when a strand of their beaded fringe had burst all over the stage. The crowd had gone silent as Drew stood there, frozen like a deer trapped in the thrall of a car's headlights, staring at the little skulls as they scattered. A custodian for The Gallery had spent five minutes trying to sweep them up, but of course, not *all* of them had made it into a garbage can; my leather boot had found the one she'd missed, and I'd tumbled to both knees in front of the judges.

"How many points are they going to knock off my score because I didn't fall more gracefully?" I ask, patting down the edges of Achilles' wig. Selene winces in the mirror but doesn't answer. "Your mom looked embarrassed on my behalf before writing something down on my score sheet. I don't suppose she's the kind of person who'd feel sorry for me?"

She turns around to look at me with both of her horns attached, a sticky layer of still-wet latex gathered around her temples that, once it's dry, will make the horns appear as though they're protruding from her skin. It's a nice testament to her makeup skills. "No, but...it really wasn't your fault, and if your score suffers enough that you don't make it into the Top Ten, I swear to God I will kick Drew's ass all the way back to Rochester."

"Go easy on them," Achilles says, finishing up the galaxy that they're painting on their arm by flicking white stars across their skin. "They were sobbing backstage and felt awful that Briar tripped. It was an accident, and sometimes things just happen. We can't control those things, just how we react in the aftermath, and Drew has already apologized to Briar."

Selene stares at Achilles through the solid black contacts she's wearing. "Just because you look like an alien doesn't mean you have to sound all wise and shit."

Achilles snorts and blows on their arm to dry the paint there. "All I'm saying is to leave them alone because they've already suffered enough. I can't imagine having a wardrobe malfunction in front of *everyone*."

The two of them are still bickering about Drew and their beads as I disappear into the back of Beau's closet. It's surprisingly large in comparison to his small bedroom, and it's a colorful mess of glitter, sequins, and rhinestones, his drag for Bow Regard intermixed with his everyday wardrobe. I trace my fingers over the metallic fabrics and material, wondering what it might be like to step into Bow's shoes and if I think it might be similar to stepping into Edgar's.

Safely in a garment bag in the very back of the closet is my outfit for Drag King of the Year's creative costuming segment. Selene and I spent days putting it together, and although it's not *quite* as elaborate as Selene's demon or Achilles' alien from another universe, it's something I feel proud to have created.

Sort of.

I *had* felt proud until I saw what my friends were wearing.

Achilles' iridescent bodysuit is literally out of this world, decorated with foreign flora that glows in the dark. LED lights bring the oozing mushrooms and damp-looking moss to life, and they sway in sync with Keel's movements, an extension of their body and the character they've created for this challenge. The exposed skin of their left arm and face is painted to resemble small galaxies, and of all the things I have seen Keel wear, they've never looked more beautiful. Ethereal. Like a goddamn *king* deserving of a frickin' crown.

I hope it's Keel who wins tonight.

Selene, for her part, has painted herself red and bedazzled a beard onto her chin, but more impressive than the dozens of black rhinestones she'd glued to her face is the silicone chestplate she's wearing beneath her open, crushed-velvet suit jacket. It's hyperrealistic (apart from the red bodypaint, of course), complete with pecs, abs, and chest hair, and I don't know why she has waited until now to dig it out of her closet, but even Achilles can't stop gawking at her.

"I can't do it," I whisper once I'm dressed, studying my outfit in the mirror that's attached to the closet door. It's perfectly tailored to my body, hugging my smaller frame in all of the right places, but in comparison to my friends and the other kings that I've seen today, it doesn't feel like anything to write home about. "Why did I think that I could do this?" I say, bursting into the bedroom where Achilles and Selene are putting the finishing touches on their makeup.

"What are you talking about?" Selene asks, and it's hard to take her seriously as a knockoff devil with a chin that glows beneath Beau's ring light. "Of course you can do this—look at you! You look great. Give us a twirl because God do I love that jacket."

I spin on the heels of the knee-high boots that I'd borrowed from Selene for this costume. "I feel so stupid," I tell her, blinking my eyes to rid them of the tears that are quickly gathering in the corners. Selene jumps up from the vanity. "You guys look so good, and imaginative, and like you actually understood the assignment, and I—"

Selene reaches out for me and cradles my face between her hands; she's wearing red satin gloves that are tufted with black fur around her wrists. "What you have on is something that those judges have never seen before, and believe me, I would know. I've been watching this competition since I was a kid." She tucks the hair from Achilles' wig back behind my ear. "This is raw, angel face. You're making a statement that's never been made on that stage, and I think I can speak for all of us when I say I am *so* fucking proud of you."

I bury my face into Selene's silicone shoulder, surprised to find that her muscular chestplate actually feels like skin, though it lacks her usual warmth. "I'm not going to win with this, am I?"

"You never know," Selene says, wrapping her arms around my shoulders. She tucks my head beneath her chin, and I can smell the cologne that she's doused herself with. "Something this personal might just tug at their heartstrings, and maybe it'll earn you a few extra points to make up for where you fell."

"You're also a really good lip-syncer," Achilles adds from the floor, using a stick of white eyeliner to draw a constellation on their cheek. "I think between that and your outfit—which, you look great, by the way!—you have as good of a chance of winning as we do! But speaking of lip-syncs, what songs are you guys performing to, anyway? I don't think we've ever actually talked about it, and like, I am *so* excited for mine."

Keel's enthusiasm will never *not* be a welcomed light in the dark.

Selene presses a kiss to the top of my head before carefully prying herself away from me. She smiles reassuringly and plops back down behind Beau's vanity. "Mine's a secret," she says, grabbing a paintbrush so she can paint the latex around her horns. "You'll both think it's stupid and I need to feel confident in my life choices, otherwise the risk won't be worth it."

Achilles and I look at each other, their eyebrows raised and mine furrowed, and I think we've both forgotten how dramatic she is. "Well...I'm doing 'DEADNAME!' by FLASCH," Keel says, fanning their cheek with their hand. "It feels fitting, you know? Since my family still deadnames me every time I talk to them."

"Ugh. *Still?*" Selene asks, shaking her head. "What's it been, five years now? Six? I've never liked your family, for the record."

"Get in line," Keel snorts. "What about you, Edgar? What are you lip-syncing to?"

All I can offer them is an insecure shrug, because just like Selene, I *don't* want to tell them about my song choice. Not because I think they'll think it's stupid, and not because I'm afraid that they'll think that it's not worth the risk, but because it's as personal as my costume is, and Beau and I had spent hours discussing whether or not I should even do it.

We'd ultimately decided that I should—that telling a story and crafting a narrative was something that was really important for me, and the song I've chosen is a perfect reflection of my summer here. All the highs and lows and in-betweens, because life and mental health aren't linear. Which is why I allow the music to speak for itself, and later, when I step onto the stage at The Gallery, dressed in a crisp white tuxedo with the suicide hotline painted all over the fabric in red paint and glitter, I lose myself to the lyrics of "1-800-273-8255" by Logic.

twenty-seven

" *I* cannot *believe* that you lip-synced to a cover of 'Anti-Hero' dressed as the goddamn devil. You don't even like Taylor Swift!"

Spencer is still panting as we huddle together in the dressing room, smiling from ear-to-ear because he's just come flouncing off the stage. Achilles and I had watched him from the wings, cheering so loud that he'd turned to us in the middle of his performance, offering up a wink before he'd done a fucking *cartwheel* and skillfully landed in the splits.

"Well, shit," Achilles had said, staring at Spencer as he crawled down onto the runway. "He'll definitely make the top ten now. Why does he have to be so *bendy*?"

And why does he have to look so good while doing it?

I kept that thought to myself, though it definitely still stands as he slings his arm around my shoulders, pressing me against him despite the fact that he's still trying to catch his breath.

Keel's performance and mine had been fine. Simple, and

definitely without any tricks up our sleeves, but fine. Achilles had crept across the stage, moving about like an ethereal being from a planet consumed by nature. Spencer and I had cheered for them, too, and them for me when it was my turn. My own performance had earned me a standing ovation, but my confidence has been dwindling since watching Spencer kill his lip-sync.

"Hey," says Spencer, his voice just barely above a whisper, and I know that it's me he's speaking to, not Achilles, when he taps his hand against my shoulder. "Don't stare at the ground with that face. You did great out there, baby gay. Be proud of yourself."

I scrunch up my nose to erase whatever expression he's talking about—*and* to deflect the conversation. Sure, I might have done well, but Spencer and Achilles had done better. "What face?"

Spencer uses a gloved finger to gently lift my chin, forcing my head up to meet his gaze. His pitch-black contacts are unnerving, but beneath all of the red paint and contour, his own expression is strikingly soft and sincere. "You know *exactly* what face I'm talking about," he says. "It's the one that you make when you're stuck in your head and think you're not good enough to be here."

"Oh," I grumble, hating that he can read me like an open book and that he's learned how to decipher my pages. "*That* one. Great. Don't look at me."

Spencer chuckles quietly and presses a soft, comforting kiss to my temple, one that lingers for a moment too long to be casual. My heart threatens to burst through my rib cage, quickening its pace beneath the weight of Spencer's lips. The hugs, the hand-holding, the secret kisses shared in the darkness of Beau's living room...

Ugh.

We definitely have some things that we need to figure out, but it can wait until after the competition. For now, though, Spencer can comfort me however he deems fit.

"Aren't you nervous?" I ask, resting my head against the center of his silicone chest. Achilles huffs and mentions something about "sickening lovebirds." "This is mostly all you've talked about since I met you. What if you're not the one who wins?"

Spencer pauses to consider my question before answering, and I wonder if it's his ego that'll respond to me, insisting that there's no way he *won't* win, especially after doing a stunt like that on stage. "Then I'll try again next year and do better. This isn't the be-all, end-all of my drag career. I just really want to prove a point to my parents."

"But there's nothing left for you to prove," I say. "You've already made it as a king."

"A truer statement has never been spoken in this club."

Our heads snap up to find Jacklynn watching us with a smile.

She glides across the dressing room to come and stand with us, her mauve-colored gown shimmering beautifully even under the harsh fluorescent lighting. "All *three* of you have nothing left to prove, but especially you, Miss Briar." Jacklynn takes my hand

and pries me away from Spencer, pulling me into a hug so tight that I can't decide if my chest feels constricted from the emotion welling up in me or her death grip. "You would never know that it was your very first competition. And this outfit?" She plucks at one of the studs on my shoulders. "*Perfection.* Win or lose today, all of you have done The Gallery proud."

"All of us?"

I crane my neck around to look at him. Spencer's voice is shockingly small as he stares up at Jacklynn with uncertainty. "You said all of us, but—but that *does* include me, right? I've done The Gallery proud?"

Jacklynn loosens her grip and lets go of me. "You've come a long way since you first stepped out onto that stage, Mr. Read." She playfully ruffles Spencer's hair, mindful not to actually knock his wig off. "I know that you and I don't always see eye-to-eye, but I'm proud of you, too, nonetheless."

Spencer's face twists into something sour. "Is that why you made me do this all on my own? Because you didn't see eye-to-eye with me?"

The hurt in his tone is as clear as the sky is blue, and Jacklynn's expression softens into something I don't recognize. "When you first came to me and said that you wanted to do drag, you weren't ready for me to mentor you." She places her hand on his shoulder. "You were a cocky little shit and thought you had it all figured out, but you weren't ready to *learn*. Not yet." Jacklynn snorts and gives him a gentle shake. "I figured the scene would eat you alive, no matter how talented you thought you were. How talented I *knew* you were. And as it turns out, I was wrong."

Spencer's jaw drops open. "Did you just say you were *wrong*?"

"You're still a cocky son-of-a-bitch," Jacklynn continues. "But now you have the goods to back it up. Bow coming along and offering to be your drag mother was the best thing that ever could have happened for you. It wasn't my kind of mentoring that you needed, all of the constructive criticism and tough-love that you would have fought tooth-and-nail against."

"You think that Bow has never criticized me?" Spencer asks, wiping a tear from the corner of his eye with the satin fabric of his glove.

"Sure," Jacklynn snorts. "Your cuticles, maybe. But that's the kind of guidance that you needed, and she gave you the space to figure out who you were without pressuring you to be someone you're not. Me? I would have stuck your ass in more pageants."

Spencer raises an eyebrow. "You didn't put Edgar in any pageants."

Jacklynn gives me a wink. "Edgar is a bit more fragile."

My expression deadpans as Achilles pats my hand. "Thanks, Jac. I appreciate it."

"Any time, my love." Jacklynn frowns and reaches down the front of her dress, shifting aside her breastplate to procure her phone from wherever she'd stashed it underneath. "Well, all right, then. It looks like we have ourselves a Top Ten."

The entire room goes silent.

Spencer sucks in a breath.

"What I'll have y'all do now is line up against the back of the stage, and wait for your names to be called." Jacklynn makes a show of trying to shoo us all from the dressing room. "As soon as the Top Ten are announced, I'm sorry, but the rest of you won't be moving forward, and you'll be free to come back here and get out of drag."

The process of everyone lining up on stage is a blur, but at least we don't have to stand in any particular order. I'm sand-wiched between Achilles and Spencer, holding their hands as Jacklynn speaks with the judges, waiting for them to give her a piece of paper with the names of the top ten kings on it.

Achilles is bouncing with excitement, as good of a sport as one can be at the turning point of any competition. Spencer is a little more reserved, but his hands are shaking as I squeeze his fingers in reassurance. "Your name will get called, I'm sure of it."

He tries to smile at me and fails, grimacing instead. "But what if it doesn't?"

I lift his hand and press my lips against the back of it. "It will."

And it does, indeed.

Spencer's name is the first to be called, and I have never seen him so happy before. He throws his fist into the air, jumping up and down as the crowd cheers his name, my brother the loudest one of all. "Fuck yeah!" Bow screams, leaping out of her chair from where she's sitting at a small, round table just to the left of Nathalie. "That's my drag baby! That's my son!"

Even Nathalie spares Spencer a smile, though she doesn't clap because she can't show him any partiality. Behind her, though, Dominique is up on her feet, shaking her hands to sign applause so that Spencer knows she's proud of him.

I kiss him on the cheek and nudge him forward. "Congratulations, Spence."

A few names later and Achilles gets to join him at the front of the stage because their name has been called, too. Rita Book, Keel's drag mother, climbs up onto a barstool and cheers at the top of her lungs, though it's short-lived because Enzo yanks her back down. He glares at her from across the bar, warning her not to do that again, and then hands her a celebratory shot.

Time begins to fly, and soon there are a total of nine drag kings standing at the front of the stage. I draw in a breath to make peace with the fact that I know I won't be the tenth, and I meet Bow's gaze in the crowd. She smiles and gives me a thumbs-up, not a hint of disappointment on her contoured face because she knows that I did my best. And *I* know that I did my best, too, that Selene, Achilles, and the other kings who are moving on have been doing this longer than I have.

It'd still be nice to be standing up there with them, though.

Jacklynn clears her throat, her dark eyes scanning the piece of paper she's holding, and as she brings the microphone up to her mouth, I hold up my hands to start clapping. As soon as she reads the final name on the list, I can head backstage and get out of drag, and I can support my friends from the crowd. Achilles and Spencer deserve this.

"The final person rounding out our top ten kings is..."

I don't even listen to the name, but it's likely Drew Bauchery because they've turned to me with a blindingly white smile, clapping their hands. They're excited to move on to the final category, and I don't blame them—I wish that I could be moving on, too. The stage lights are blinding as I look up at them, returning Drew's smile because at the very least, I can congratulate them. Spencer might hold a grudge because they're the reason I'd fallen during the welcoming ceremony, but I'm clumsy enough to know that accidents happen.

A pair of tattooed arms wrap around my waist from behind me, and suddenly my feet are off the ground. It's Achilles holding me in the air, spinning us around until I feel like I'm going to be sick, my stomach lurching as my vision blurs. "Put me down!" I complain. There's no cause for celebrating and taking this moment away from Drew.

The second that my boots are firmly planted on the stage again, Spencer crashes into me with all the energy of an exploding sun.

"You did it!" he screams, scrabbling to grab a hold of me and hug me close to his chest. "Edgar, babe, you did it! You made the Top Ten—I'm so proud of you!"

I take a step back to look up at him, my brows pinching with confusion. "What are you talking about? Drew—"

"Was congratulating you!" Spencer takes my face between his hands, his fingers gripping my cheeks so tight that it purses my lips into a pout. "Briar, babe, it's *you*! Jacklynn called your name, and you're in the Top Ten with me and Keel!"

An ocean's worth of tears flood into the corners of my eyes, matching the ones that are glistening in Spencer's black ones. "I really made the Top Ten?"

He nods and wipes mine away, smiling like he can't believe it either. "Hell yeah, you did. Edgar Allan Foe is coming for the crown, and I'm so fucking stoked that I could kiss you right here in front of everyone."

"Do it," I say, staring up at Spencer beneath the stage lights. "Kiss me in front of everyone. I *dare* you."

I don't have to tell him twice, and kissing Spencer feels *almost* as good as making it into the Top Ten with him.

twenty-eight

Briar Vincent does not exist on this stage tonight.

I've buried her somewhere deep inside of myself, tucked away from the blinding lights and The Gallery's restless crowd; they stare at me expectantly from the dance floor, their faces blurring into a sea of color and scrutiny.

Briar would be terrified if she were here.

But the place where I've hidden her is unreachable. She doesn't have to worry about embarrassing either herself or her drag family, nor is there any fear of her being booed off the stage because people don't like her performance.

No, Briar Vincent has officially vacated the building, and in her place is *me*.

Becoming Edgar Allan Foe and stepping into his shoes is like taking that desperate first breath after you nearly drown. The air fills your lungs in a way that you've never known you needed before, and it consumes you. Relieves you.

Saves you.

You *never* forget that first breath.

That feeling of finally *wanting* to breathe, and not drown.

I close my eyes as the opening notes of Adam Lambert's "Whataya Want from Me" comes flooding through The Gallery's sound system. The hushed, drunken chatter from the bar's patrons falls away beneath the music, and the lights have dimmed from a vibrant pink to a soft, moody blue that's perfect for a lip-sync about begging people not to give up on me.

I'm standing center stage behind a microphone stand, one that Enzo had dug out of storage for me this morning. He hadn't asked why I needed it, and not even Spencer had inquired about what it was doing in the dressing room, though he *had* raised an eyebrow when I'd carried it out onto the stage with me, perplexed as to what I could do with it. What tricks I might have up my sleeves that maybe he hadn't thought of.

In front of the mirror in Beau's bathroom, I'd rehearsed "Whataya Want from Me" so many times that muscle memory has started to kick in.

Adam Lambert's voice has become my own as I croon his lyrics into the microphone. I sway back and forth with the mic stand, drag it across the stage as I plead with the audience to keep coming around and tell me what it is that they want from me.

Embodying Adam isn't hard. He's confident, and melancholy, and has his own kind of drag-like flare; I'd based my entire look for tonight off his outfit from the "If I Had You" music video, just with a bit more flannel and a little less leather. He moves about the stage in a way that's unhurried but still purposeful, and I'm trying my hardest to mimic some of his mannerisms by using the microphone stand in my performance, swinging it around like an extension of myself.

But mimicking Adam for this entire performance isn't going to help me win tonight, which is why, midway through the song and when the chorus breaks into the bridge, I remove the microphone from its stand and step down off of the stage. The long, narrow runway that juts out from the front of it is rickety beneath my boots, and I have always *hated* using it during my performances. But in this moment, despite how scared I am that the metal will collapse underneath me, the runway leads to exactly where I want to go: out into the crowd and to where my brother and Enzo are sitting at a table next to the judges.

Bow shakes her head as I approach them, tears in her eyes as she leans into the arm that Enzo has wrapped around her shoulders. "What are you doing, Ed?" she calls out over the music, and so what if this entire bar is watching me? I reach for Bow's hand so I can hold it, squeezing her fingers as I beg her to please not give up on me—as I promise that I will never let her down. "I love you so fucking much," she sobs. "More than anything."

My gaze meets Enzo's as I lip-sync, making him the same promises, too.

He smiles at me and takes both of our hands, sandwiching mine and Bow's between his palms. "I love you, too, hermanita. Bow and I will *never* give up on you."

I lean over the table and hug them both against my chest, lip-sync be damned because even if I don't win Drag King of the Year when this is over, I've won my life back.

Sort of.

Now I just have to hold onto it.

And just like that, "Whataya Want from Me" is over, the final guitar riffs fading into the silence of the bar. All three of tonight's judges are spun around in their seats, staring up at me, Nathalie's mouth quirked with a gentle grin as she offers me a subtle thumbs-up. It's nice to feel like I have her support in this, but it's even better to have Spencer Read's, who's leading the charge in my applause.

"GO, EDGAR!" he screams from the wings of the stage, jumping up and down with his arm looped through Achilles' elbow.

Keel is screaming their head off, too, but their movement is limited by the bulky, renaissance-era ball gown they've changed into for their final performance, the fuchsia fabric pooling out around them like a bubble. "YOU DID IT, BESTIE! YOU DID IT!"

Jacklynn is huddled up behind them, grinning as if I've actually made her proud; she claps her hands with as much enthusiasm as she's deemed appropriate for being the host of the competition, but that doesn't stop her from beaming at me.

"Edgar Allan Foe! Edgar Allan Foe!" Spencer turns to Achilles with a frown, shaking their arm with enough force to rattle their shoulder loose from its socket. "You gotta help me cheer for him, Keel. He did it!"

Spencer pumps his ring-clad fist into the air, yanking Keel's up with him, and together they lead the singsong chant of my name.

Edgar Allan Foe!

Edgar Allan Foe!

Edgar Allan Foe!

The sound of it follows me off the stage, and for once in my life, I think I might actually feel confident—like I've *actually* done something worth cheering for.

The moment I'm safely in the wings, Spencer and Achilles sweep me up into a crushing embrace where I'm caught in a death grip between them. Spencer presses a kiss to my cheek, his black-painted lips smacking against my skin with a *mwah*, and Achilles' dress has swallowed me up into the flower-patterned fabric that looks like it cost a small fortune.

"All right, all right!" I laugh, wriggling to free myself from their hold on me. Achilles steps back with a grin, their thick, unruly faux beard flashing with what looks to be a thin strand of fairy lights that offsets the color of their gown. I don't know what they've got planned for their final number, but Achilles has made us promise to watch their *entire* performance—to not look away for even a second. "I think my aesthetic is Adam Lambert."

Spencer stands behind me and wraps his arms around my waist. "You were amazing out there," he says, resting his chin on my shoulder. "I'm glad that you picked that song. And Bow? Jesus. She's probably *still* out there crying."

Keel peeks out into the audience. "Yep! She is! That's how you *know* you did good. I think some other people are still sniffling, too."

"In case y'all didn't know," Jacklynn suddenly says into her microphone. Keel, Spencer, and I turn to look at her, watching as she addresses the crowd with a confident ease. "Edgar Allan Foe is my drag son, and this was his first competition." The audience cheers and raises up their shot glasses in my honor. "Thank you all for being so kind to him. He's worked so hard just to be here, and he's made me such a proud mama tonight. I love you, baby. Go celebrate!"

My bottom lip quivers with emotion, and the strangled sound of a tearful whimper cracks its way out of my chest. But it's a *good* whimper, even if Keel looks at me in alarm, and these are happy tears that I wipe away with the patchwork sleeve of my jacket. "I can't believe that I actually *made* it here."

Spencer squeezes me tightly around the middle. "I'm so fucking happy you did."

We stand near the stage wall as two more drag kings take the stage before it's finally Achilles' turn. They're the last of the Top Ten to perform tonight, and after taking a breath to steady their nerves, Achilles glides out into center-stage with an unexpected air of confidence. Their chin is raised as they stare down their nose at the judges, hands on their hips as they smooth out the fabric of their ball gown.

"You've got this, Keel!" I call out, and from beneath the dizzying pink stage lights, Achilles looks back at me with a grin.

Spencer takes my hand as the opening notes of "This Is Me" from *The Greatest Showman* trickle through The Gallery's speakers. I'm not super familiar with the song, but Spencer is excited as Achilles moves across the stage, connecting with the audience in the same way I had tried to do with Bow. They touch everyone's hand who reaches out to them, declining tips from the patrons who'd come late and not heard the rules about no tipping tonight, and I watch in surprise as Keel bends down onto one knee.

Drew Bauchery is seated in front of the stage, staring up at Keel like they're mesmerized; Spencer gasps as Achilles caresses their face, murmuring something that I know doesn't match up with the lip-sync. "Oh my God, I think Keel might *like* them. No wonder they were so quick to defend Drew!"

I snort and squeeze his hand. "Hush and watch the show. I have a feeling that Keel has something big planned."

"Something big" is understatement, because Achilles Patrick came to win and show the rest of us how it's really done.

Halfway through "This Is Me", Keel rips their wig off. Their natural hair flies free around their shoulders, and as the music swells to a set of lyrics that talk about the sun and becoming warriors, Achilles does a twirl. They're a blur of fuchsia as they work to untie their corset, and it's as their skirt falls away and the corset comes off that the audience leaps to their feet.

No *wonder* their dress was so bulky—underneath all of the pleated satin is the same set of armor that Achilles had worn the first time we'd ever performed together, only *better*. The silver EVA foam has been carved to look like dragon scales, and Keel has taken the time to meticulously distress their greaves, shin guards, and chestpiece, splattering them with red glitter paint like they've just endured battle at a craft store.

"Ho-ly *shit*," Spencer gasps, hopping up and down as Achilles dances across the stage, their armor gleaming beneath the stage lights. "I can't believe Keel planned a reveal and didn't tell us!"

The reveal pays off because the crowd is still on their feet when Achilles comes prancing off the stage, giddy that their performance has gone over so well. "What'd you guys think?" they ask Selene and me, panting for breath as we guide them down into the nearest chair in the dressing room. Spencer thrusts a bottle of water into their hands. "I *almost* couldn't get the dress off."

"You were awesome!" I say, wrapping my arms around their neck in a hug because I'm terrified of crushing their armor. Keel leans into me with a laugh. "I couldn't figure out why your dress was so huge, but I thought it was rude to ask."

Spencer, apparently confident in how well Achilles' armor is held together, wriggles into their space and plops himself down on their knee. "I'm offended you didn't tell me about the reveal. *Ugh.* I wish I'd thought to do one, too. The crowd was eating you up. And *Drew*!"

Achilles cheeks flush scarlet. "We're friends."

"Oh, sure," I say, poking Keel in the side. They yelp and swat me away. "Friends *totally* caress each other's faces. Come here, Spence. Let me lovingly touch your cheek because we're *friends*."

Achilles sticks their tongue out. "I sent them a message on Instagram after the welcoming ceremony. I wanted to make sure they were okay," Keel admits. "And we...kinda-sorta haven't stopped texting ever since. They're super sweet, and we really like each other's aesthetic."

"You mean *ass*-thetic," Spencer hoots. Achilles covers their face. "What? I'm being serious! Drew is cute when they're not tripping Edgar with little skull beads."

Spencer and Achilles bicker about Drew Bauchery for another half hour before the top ten kings are called to return to the stage, Jacklynn announcing from the curtained wings that Drag King of the Year has a winner.

"Fuck," Spencer breathes, and my heart does a backflip in my chest. "This is it."

Crammed into the stairwell in a single-file line, Jacklynn marches us back onto the stage in alphabetical order. She reintroduces us to the crowd, and I'm fortunate enough that there's no one to stand between Keel and I, no other kings whose name comes before mine. Spencer, on the other hand, is at the end of the line with four other people between us, and if I lean forward far enough, I can see him shaking out his hands.

"He's freaking out," I whisper to Keel, who bends a bit backward to frown at Spencer down the line. "I wish we could just go and stand with him."

Achilles, from the look of concern that's etched into the lines of their face, is about to suggest that we just *do* it, rules be damned, when Jacklynn steps out onto the stage. She's holding both her microphone and an envelope, and any thoughts of standing with Spencer have flown out the window for the both of us. We're too rooted in place with anticipation.

"Before we begin, I would just like to say that *all* of our kings are winners tonight." Jacklynn's smile is absolutely dazzling as she looks at us all. "For the king who takes home the crown, there is a cash prize of five-thousand dollars and a chance to headline here on the weekend."

Achilles grabs ahold of my hand, squeezing it so tight that his fingers are trembling against my palm. Five grand and the chance to headline The Gallery is something that I know would mean a lot to them.

But it would mean a lot to the rest of us, too.

Jacklynn doesn't pull any punches, opening up the envelope with the names of the top three drag kings. She's a saint not to drag this out for us—no pun intended. "In third place," she begins, and I know that it won't be my name that gets called. I won't get that lucky twice. "Is Syn Onymous from Buffalo!"

Keel and I clap our hands, and Syn Onymous looks as shocked as some of the rest of us as he steps away from our lineup. My brother, who's responsible for handing out the awards tonight, offers Syn a small bouquet of red roses, congratulating him on a job well done.

"In second place…" Jacklynn says into her microphone.

Achilles squeezes my hand, almost as tightly as they squeeze their eyes shut with anticipation. Their fingers are still trembling against the curve of my sweaty palm, and although I know that Keel would still be grateful for coming in second place, losing again this year would be devastating, the kind of thing that might make them choose art school as their backup plan.

"…Spencer Read!"

I whip my head down the line.

Because maybe Achilles would be grateful for coming in second, but Spencer…

Everything about him has deflated, as if someone has steamrolled right over him. His heavily padded shoulders are sulkily caved in around him, and he's clenching his jaw so terribly tight that I'm worried he might shatter his teeth.

Ugh. I just want to hug him.

Tell him that it's going to be okay.

Spencer walks stiffly across the stage, accepting a slightly larger bouquet of red roses from my brother. Bow offers him a few words of quiet encouragement, but Spencer doesn't listen to her and drops his gaze to the ground, sniffing back tears as he returns to his place in line. I try to reach out to him as he slumps past me and Keel, but he purposefully makes a wide arch around us, like he doesn't want us to help make him feel better.

"In first place, the *winner* of Drag King of the Year..."

Achilles turns to me with a frown. "I really thought Spencer would take the crown this year. God, did you see his face? He's *devastated...*" Keel leans around me to get a better look at our friend, but Spencer is standing with his head down, the bouquet of roses clutched tightly against his chest like he's afraid they'll wither away already. "Maybe after this over, we can——"

"Achilles Patrick!"

The deafening scream that cracks out my chest is a testament to how much I love Keel, especially because they're staring at Jacklynn, eyes wide, and shaking their head in disbelief. "Keel!" I cry, grabbing them around the middle and trying to lift them off the ground, but their armor makes them too heavy for me to pick up. "Keel, you fucking did it! You won!"

And because I can't pick them up, it's Spencer who comes barreling across the stage. He hoists Achilles off their feet, spinning them around until Keel is swaying in his arms. "You're a winner, baby!" Spencer says, grinning despite the fact that it's not his name that's been called. Because at least if he had to lose to someone, it was one of his closest friends.

Achilles lets out a sob, catching me off guard as they throw their arms around my neck, specifically choosing *me* to celebrate with. "Edgar, I *did* it!" Keel cries, squeezing me so hard that it hurts to breathe, but I won't take Keel's win away from them. I'll hug them all night if this is what they need. "I won the whole freaking *thing*!"

"Yeah, you did!" I yell, hoping that they can hear me over the roaring crowd because *everyone* is excited that they won. "Get over there and get your crown, Keel! You earned it, and you frickin' *deserve* it."

My best friend smiles through big, salty tears, and I don't have to tell them twice.

Achilles struts across the stage, confident and still sobbing like a baby as Bow places the crown on their head.

twenty-nine

I don't think anyone's noticed that I'm missing yet.

There is a party taking place inside The Gallery, one that's meant to celebrate Achilles' win and the kings who had competed alongside them. Even from out back in the alleyway, where I've left the door that leads into the kitchen propped open with a rock, I can still feel the beat of the music, the pulsing bass as it thuds into the soles of my feet.

I'd snuck outside after Bow tried handing me a microphone, trying to convince me to help her start an impromptu karaoke session, like the ones we used to have with Avery back home. She's had *way* too many celebratory Fireball shots. Even sober she can't sing a lick in tune, her voice pitching too high or too deep, and Enzo had confessed to me that he was afraid that Bow might scare away the kings who'd come to compete from out of town.

My muscles all spasm as I lower myself down onto the curb, stretching out my legs because my body is positively *aching*. Drag should be considered a contact sport with how hard performers work to put on a show, always dancing and stomping and throwing themselves around on stage. I dig the heel of my hand into my thigh, massaging the knot there from where I've been mostly on my feet all day.

A cool breeze tousles my hair as I breathe in the stillness of the alley. It reeks of rotting food and gasoline, but this moment is so significant that I don't really care what it smells like.

Not too long ago, I'd have been too terrified to come out here and sit on my own. I would have rather found a corner to go cry in, to let the walls of The Gallery close in on me and swallow me whole. It wouldn't have mattered if I needed space to breathe, to escape from the drama and the thunderous beat of the music— out here alone was never an option for me.

Until now.

A smile tugs at the corners of my mouth as I hear Bow's voice belting along to "Girls Just Want To Have Fun." Through the small crack from where I'd propped the door open, it sounds like Enzo might be trying to wrestle the microphone away from her, begging her to slow down on the Fireball. It's her drink of choice, but Enzo is in control of the bar, and it won't be long now before he starts pumping her full of ice water.

I can't believe I'm sitting out here *smiling* about it.

All summer long, I've been terrified of what would happen if I didn't win Drag King of the Year. Would I crack beneath the pressure and fall apart on stage? Vomit all over Achilles and be banned from The Gallery forever? But my biggest fear had always been Selene, that she would win and not me, and that she'd use her new crown to tear me down beyond repair.

But instead of all that fear, that quiet jealousy that Selene might be a better king than me, all I feel now is content.

Because I'm proud of the part of myself I'd left inside on the stage tonight, that I'd made the Top Ten for Drag King of the Year as the least experienced drag king in the bar. That alone was a win for me, and I didn't need the crown that was rightfully bestowed upon Achilles.

When I'd first arrived in New York, I'd assumed that this place was meant for people like Beau, who are so charismatic and so determined to fight for what they want that I would never be able to carve out a place for myself here. But after spending my summer in Manhattan and making the closest friends I've ever had, maybe—maybe—this city was meant for people like me, too.

"Briar!" comes a familiar rasp, and I nearly jump out of my skin as the back door of The Gallery flies open. Selene comes stumbling into the alley, a look of concern darkening her eyes. "I've been looking all over for you. Are you all right?"

I pat the curb next to me and smile. "I'm fine," I say. "Come sit down with me."

She doesn't hesitate.

She's wearing her oversized denim jacket, the one covered in colorful patches I'd worn on my first night in town, offered by Selene after she'd spilled her drink down the front of my T-shirt. It's slung over her shoulders as she plops herself down onto the ground, swallowing up the checkered jumpsuit that was a part of her Freddy Mercury tribute. She'd lip-synced to Queen's "The Show Must Go On" during her final number, and Achilles and I had been certain she'd win with it, especially after she'd ripped off a leather jacket to reveal the cape underneath made with red AIDS awareness ribbons.

"How are you doing?" I ask, bumping her with my shoulder because I know she's still upset about losing tonight, even if she's happy for Achilles. "For what it's worth, we both thought you'd win."

Selene snorts and leans back to rest on her elbows. "I knew they were going to win the second they tore off the dress."

We fall into an easy silence, Selene taking the moment to close her eyes as I stare up at the jagged skyline above. There's a surprising lack of stars, and between the smog and towering buildings taking up most of my view, I can't see the moon either, just its reflection in the glass pane of a window. "I'm going to miss that," I say eventually, breaking the quiet. Selene cracks an eye open to look at me. "Seeing the stars, I mean. We can see *tons* of them from my backyard."

"You'll see them when you go home," Selene says. "Aren't you leaving on Wednesday?"

I shrug, because I haven't told Selene this. "Yeah, but I'm probably coming back."

Selene practically bolts off the curb, twisting herself around so that she's facing me. "What do you mean, you're probably coming back? Doesn't school start for you in the fall? Or is Texas really as backward as they say it is?"

"It is." I try my hardest not to smile. "But like you said a few weeks ago, I don't need to be in Texas to finish high school, and Beau's already said I can come live with him." My mouth twitches, and I fail, smiling so big that my face hurts. "We just have to talk with our parents first and explain that this is something I really want, and that it'll be best for my mental health."

She holds her hand over her mouth, as if she's physically trying to keep in whatever she wants to say. Selene shakes from the effort, like it's a struggle. "Really?" she squeaks through her fingers, her mossy eyes wide open. "Because I—I would *really* like it if you came and lived here. There's so much of the city you haven't seen yet! And right out of the gate, you're so good at drag, and you're only going to get better." Selene inches closer to me and knocks her knee against mine. "Please tell me you're not joking."

I smile and bump her knee back. "I'm not."

Selene flings her arms around my neck, holding me against her as she rocks us back and forth. I bury my face into her shoulder, breathing in the scent of her woodsy cologne as we sit together in the shadows. "Can I ask you a question?"

I snort, because I can't believe she's even asking. "Sure."

Selene sits back so she can look at me, her eyes roving over every inch of my face, from my own eyes down to my lips, where her gaze lingers for a moment too long to be casual. I try to fight the blush that creeps into my cheeks beneath her stare. "I know we've kissed and that we haven't put a label on what this *is* yet, but—but I have to know if you even actually like me." Selene drops her gaze to the checkered pattern of her jumpsuit. "Because I really, *really* like you, and I'm afraid that I might have screwed up my chances for something real."

"You didn't screw up anything," I say immediately, and Selene lifts her chin to look up at me again, her head tilting curiously to one side. She has no idea what I am going to say to her, no idea where either of us might be going with this. "I really like you, too, Selene, and maybe someday, we can actually put a label on this." I bite the inside of my cheek at the spark of hope that ignites like a flame in her eyes, and I absolutely hate myself for knowing that I need to snuff it out. "I really don't think now is a good time for us, though, because I like you, and I want to do this right. I *need* to do this right."

Selene surprises me by nodding, her expression gentle as she scoots closer to me. "Me too," she says, slipping out of her jacket and holding it tightly in her lap. She picks at a loose thread on a patch. "Whatever you need, I'm willing to do. I'd be stupid to walk away from whatever this is just because I'm too impatient."

Her smile is genuine as she playfully bumps my knee with her own again. "I think you could be good for me, Foe. I think we could be good for each other."

Her willingness to wait before jumping headfirst into this *thing* that might easily crash and burn gives me hope that what I'm doing here is right. "I need to work on myself before I can be good for *anyone*," I say, hoping Selene understands. Because maybe she thinks we're a good fit, that our jagged edges and sharp corners somehow line up perfectly, but we both deserve a better version of me. "There are a lot of things I need to work through—my anxiety, my depression, probably some unresolved trauma." I swallow so noisily that she frowns, and I don't know why I'm getting emotional. Why my eyes are welling up with tears. "I've thought a lot about this—about *us*—and I think I need to figure out how to stand on my own before I can stand with someone else, even if that someone is you."

"I get that," Selene murmurs, and she means it. "And maybe I should take a page out of your book, because the way I've been acting and how I've been treating both you and Achilles...My coping skills are literal horseshit, and I don't want to keep being this version of myself. I want to be someone better."

I sniffle and wipe my nose on my sleeve, drag be damned. "You deserve that," I say. "But your coping skills really are horse-shit." A startled laugh bursts out of Selene that echoes through the alley around us, reverberating off steel and concrete. I drag my fingers through my hair as she settles herself, the strands slick with a cool sweat from being outside behind The Gallery. "Beau and Jacklynn think I need therapy and medication, and those things scare me but, I...I think they're probably right."

"They're not so scary if they're what helps you," Selene says, and hearing the affirmation from someone who isn't one of the adults in my life makes me feel a little more validated. "I was in therapy after Piper died, and honestly, I should have kept going. I wish that I would have kept going. But I quit when I thought I was feeling better, which is probably when I needed help the most."

I hold out my pinky to Selene, who raises an eyebrow and stares at it. "We work on ourselves first," I say. "And then we can work on being together, if that's something we still want."

Selene wraps her finger around mine. "You're *always* going to be what I want. I have a thing for blond Texans who try to put me in my place."

"You are *literally* ridiculous," I laugh, leaning my head against Selene's shoulder.

She presses a kiss to the top of my hair and loops her arm through my elbow. "I think that's what made you fall for me," she says. "Me and my ridiculous ways."

"Ever the humble drag king. Maybe I'll have to take a page out of *your* book."

Selene and I sit together in the warm, end-of-summer air, enjoying each other's company until Achilles tracks us down around midnight, right as Selene is finishing up a story about her very first time in drag. She's taken her jacket and wrapped it around my shoulders, burying me in the denim. The patches are familiar and heavy, the threads messy on the inside of the fabric, but I've curled myself into it anyways, soaking in the warmth of my favorite king and the smell of his woodsy cologne.

"You guys are totally missing the party!" Keel complains, eyeing the jacket with a grin. They're holding their new crown on top of their head because it's slightly too big to stay on straight, the gold metal and emerald jewels gleaming beneath the floodlight perched above the back door. "Rita and Jacklynn are playing some weird drinking game, and Bow keeps trying to dance to Pony. *Pony*, you guys, of all the things. She's probably gonna end up going viral on TikTok."

"Guess we'd better go save her the embarrassment, then." Selene does a stretch before rising to her feet, then offers me a hand to help me up. "The crown looks good on you, Keel. But I think you should be nice and let me borrow it sometime."

"What?" I turn to look at her with a pout. "If Selene gets to wear the crown, then *I* get to wear the crown, and there's no way she's trying it on before me."

Achilles tilts their head. "Who do I look like, Cady Heron? The Gallery isn't the high school in *Mean Girls*, and we're *not* splitting my crown three different ways." We think they might be serious until Achilles takes off their crown, handing it to me with a wink. "You both get five minutes with it, and then it's mine for the rest of the night. We can talk about sharing it tomorrow."

I take Selene's hand and pass the crown to her. She immediately places it on her head. "I don't need to borrow your crown," I tell Keel. "Because I'm coming for my own next year."

Selene grins as she holds open the door for me and Achilles, ushering us back inside and into the lively chaos of my brand-new home away from home.

I think I'm going to like it here.

the end

acknowledgements

I never know what to say here, because there aren't enough words in any known language to describe the gratitude I feel for my support system. This book was by far the hardest thing I've ever written, and without the people who made it all possible, *Don't Be a Drag* would simply not exist.

To Jen, my beautiful love. You are the shining light that led me through the darkness of this book. You held me as I cried, promised that it was going to be okay, and read so many variations of *Don't Be a Drag* that you probably know this book better than I do. Thank you for everything that you do for me, and thank you for loving me a little extra on the days when life gets hard. I will always love you more.

To my fabulous editor, Tamara. When Moe and I sat down and decided that I was going to write *Drag*, neither of us were sure that she could sell it. But I wrote it anyway, and I am so beyond grateful that this book found its home at Page Street.

You're a gem in this industry, and *Drag* wouldn't be half of what it is without your endless insight and hard work. Thank you for taking a chance on our kings.

To Moe, my badass agent. Thank you for never giving up on me. I send you a million emails, always need your clarification on things, and am the actual worst at picking a project and sticking with it. But somehow, you take it all in stride, and you've guided my career into something that I'm so, so proud of. I couldn't do any of this without you. Thanks for being the best agent an anxious enby could ever ask for.

To my Page Street family, the best in the business. Thank you for everything you do for not just me, but for all of your authors! Page Street is a dream and I'm forever grateful that both *Forward March* and *Don't Be a Drag* found their homes with you.

To my brilliant bestie, Ginny. You are, without a doubt, the greatest friend I've ever had. I'm so thankful that you jumped into my DMs all those months ago, asking if we could be friends and talking to me about marching band because you were excited for *Forward March*. Thanks for always being around to listen to my woes about publishing, to help me work through plot holes, and for just being a good friend. Jen and I love you so much.

To my favorite king, Benn D Books. From the second I told you about this book, when you jumped out of your chair to show me your crown, you've been one of *Drag*'s biggest supporters.

Thank you for letting me pick your brain about the drag community and what it means to be a king. You're the best.

To my author friends, who've shown me nothing but kindness since I first set out on this journey: Melissa See, Anna Meriano, Debbie Rigaud, Claire Winn, Mindy McGinnis, Amanda Quain, Crystal Maldanado, Brieanna Wilkoff, and so many others.

To The Book Loft, Prologue Bookshop, and Kicks Mix Bookstore: Thank you for everything you do for authors, and for welcoming me with open arms.

To Shannon, Denise, and Melissa at the Northwest Ohio Teen Book Festival: Thank you for inviting me to my first ever festival as an author, and for being so accommodating to my needs as a wheelchair user. TNWOTBF will always hold such a special place in my heart.

To my wonderfully supportive family: Mom and Nannie, thank you for always encouraging me to follow my dreams. Mom and Dad, thank you for your endless support and for always being down for a good road trip. Nancy, Jesse, and Rain, thank you for supporting me since the very beginning and for being the best sibs and niece we could ever ask for.

Amy VanBlarcum, thank you for coming back into my life when I needed you the most and for being the best big sister in the world.

To Mariah. We love you. Always.

To Moo and Shiro, my faithful writing buddies. Thanks for keeping my feet warm.

To our beloved Pumpkin: We love you, and you will always be our favorite "what if."

To every reader who picks up this book, especially those who might be struggling: Thank you. Please know that you are not alone, that it's okay to ask for help, and that you are worthy of all the love in the world.

author bio

Skye Quinlan (they/them) is a queer, autistic author of YA fiction. They're an avid reader, have an absurd amount of crystals and gemstones, and if they're not tending to their garden, you can usually find them playing *Animal Crossing*. Skye lives in Ohio with their wife, two dogs, a snake, and two lizards.